SKELMERSDALE

AUTHOR		CLASS	
	BIDISHA		F
TITLE	Too fast to live		

TOO FAST TO LIVE

TOO FAST TO LIVE

Bidisha

Duck Editions

First published in 2000 by
Duckworth Literary Entertainments, Ltd.
61 Frith Street, London W1V 5TA
Tel: 020 7434 4242
Fax: 020 7434 4420
email:DuckEd@duckworth-publishers.co.uk
www.ducknet.co.uk

© 2000 by Bidisha Bandyopadhyay

A CIP catalogue record for this book is available
from the British Library

ISBN 0 7156 3008 3

Typeset by Derek Doyle & Associates, Liverpool
Printed in Great Britain by
Redwood Books Ltd, Trowbridge

PROLOGUE

Every night, Alun lies awake in the dark and thinks about how he can get her. He knows he is better, stronger, cleverer than her lover Jon Duke; that he can show her a nicer life, give her a warmer bed and tie her to him. He will handle her with just the tips of his fingers, and instead of slang she'll hear from him a kind of street poetry which will make her nerves vibrate like harp strings. She is never out of his mind. Isobel Aurora Paine, the name of a queen.

He thinks of Jon Duke, with his pockets full of old receipts, with his liar's face and twitching hands. Softly spoken, with a small rosebud mouth. Friend of the friendless. Provider of hope to those who've almost given up. Fit for nothing. When she is with him, Isobel Aurora Paine wears a sapphire ring and a sad smile. She is superior to him, by birth, by breeding. A rich, clever girl whose life fell apart when she looked into Jon Duke's hollow eyes. It's a far cry from the white houses and wide streets of Chelsea.

Duke bought her a dog whom she called Sleaze, a Great Dane, a skull on stilts that follows her around like a witch's familiar. He lives in their flat and sleeps at the foot of their bed, and so much time has gone by that she has forgotten whether she loves Duke or not. Each morning in the bathroom mirror Isobel sees a face which could have achieved so much. A narrow oval with a sharp, straight nose and a thin mouth. Grey eyes which slant upwards, with gold lashes. High cheekbones, gleaming white, the face of a queen. The kind of beauty that seems to have been engraved in stone: all-conquering, all-governing.

It is the early 1980s and people are beginning to have money. They weigh it in their palms and imagine all the things they can purchase with it. London awakens and unfolds and its disciples strut like peacocks. As a teenager, Isobel had always planned to live right in the centre, that electric space where the glamour would come to her a little soiled, and she'd go to parties where the men would cast dirty, dangerous looks at her. She would drink coffee at midnight, her feet red from dancing, and take a series of dark-haired, rich Italians as lovers.

She finds herself now in Warren Street, fifteen minutes' walk from Soho, in the centre just as she wished, but it is not quite what she'd expected. Instead of hanging white muslin, the windows are graced with an iron grille. Since the intercom was disabled by an iron bar, people knock until their bare knuckles are bloody. Men and women with jaundiced skin and a menial, snivelly demeanour come round at midnight and are still there the next morning, lying half on the couch, half on the floor. An old blanket scarred with cigarette burns keeps the draught from the door.

Upstairs in the King of England pub, Alun does press-ups and thinks of Isobel Aurora Paine. His name – and that *is* how he spells it – is bland enough, but the tattoo covering his entire back and left shoulder tells you just what kind of person he thinks he is: a Chinese winged reptile with rolling eyeballs and a tongue of flame, the permanent domestic pet of Alun the Dragon, proprietor of the aforementioned pub, which (the sign says) serves the finest ales in London. And it is a wonderful

2

thing to be Alun, owner of a thriving business, close confidant of many, host with the most. He throws himself up off the floor and claps, once, before he falls again. It is difficult to imagine a barrel-chested man in his early fifties doing this, but all that flesh is rock hard and packed with strength. His head is shaven, grey hair curling down his back. It is three in the afternoon and the hostelry's enjoying a little break before opening up. All July the sun has beaten down on the pavements from ten each morning. Teenaged girls in wedge sandals are out with their friends, the young men of the town are hanging around conducting their own particular business, regular workers push through the holiday crowds with red, resentful expressions. Alun likes to think he can rise above all of this. He knows the men at the top, and they like and respect him. He has buddies in the police, and little chums in the dirtiest gangs on the streets. Young gents bearing leather jackets, stereos, drugs, all pass through Alun's public house, and he gives each a nod and a wink to indicate his approval. Respect is the name of the game in his particular vocation.

He's breathing hard but he has to reach one hundred before he finishes. The floorboards creak and he grunts with each lift. The muscles lining his back stand up, sweat-mottled and hard, because this is all he does in his spare time, when he's not doing 'business'. He lifts and lowers, lifts and lowers. Alun doesn't stop for anyone. He knows that by nine tonight The King will be packed with punters looking to make a deal, hustle a buck, flog and buy. They'll be selling harmless pipedreams and under-cover services. He knows Jon Duke will wait with Isobel by his side, like a Pope greeting his suppliants, as one by one people edge up to him and whisper their requests in his ear: give me salvation, give me absolution, give me annihilation. Promise me a better life. Isobel will stand there silently, that cold, damaged look on her face, a woman who can make a pair of stolen jeans and a market T-shirt look like Armani – which, incidentally, Alun has a stock of in a back room. When Alun has Isobel he'll take her out dancing and buy her a different dress for each night of the week. He'll put a platter of oysters before her at breakfast, and fasten a silver Tiffany's chain with a heart-shaped locket around her neck.

Jon Duke is in the front room, chatting to his 'mates'. Everyone is his mate, but he doesn't know anyone's name. Recently he's been getting lazy. People shout through the letterbox – 'The Duke in? David sent me … Mark sent me … I'm a friend of Paul's.' And Jon will spring up from the sofa, sunshine in his face, his gold tooth glinting, fling open the door with an 'Alright, mate, come on in. We'll get you sorted out. Nice and easy.' He'll usher them through to the kitchen, capering and joking, put the kettle on before doling out the cellophane wrap or the neat, miniature paper envelope. One day she knows he'll open the door and a policeman with narrow eyes and a slavering Alsatian will be standing there.

Isobel lies on the bed next to Sleaze. She remembers what she was like when she was younger: full of optimism. She never believed that some people were simply not decent. She thought villainy couldn't help but reveal itself immediately: the stash of stolen jewels, the midnight attack, the knife to the throat. But Jon Duke came at her in his insinuating, weak way, belly low to the ground. He took her out for meals and paraded her on his arm as though he'd memorised a magazine article on how to woo women. He sent letters and notes and, once, flowers. He didn't really listen to anything she said, although she didn't notice at the time. He boxed her off in some small, separate area of his life, and before she knew it she was hanging around the flat, staring into space while he performed and produced for the junkies of WC2. Men would come over and, nodding towards her, say to Jon, 'That the girlfriend, is it?' Jon would shrug and say, with a grin, 'I suppose it is, pal.' He never hit her, just wore her down.

Recently she's been thinking of getting out of there. She doesn't do smack or coke any more; whatever Jon gives her she takes down to the wine bars she frequented in her early twenties and palms it off on girls called Amelia and Carrie. Isobel picks up the mirrored tile from the bedside table and looks at her face. Thin, high, arched eyebrows. So blonde they're nearly white. The sliver of mouth with its intelligent smile. She turns her face to the side, still looking in the mirror. It took a while for the old survival instinct to kick in, but she got there in the end. As soon as she realised Jon Duke wasn't the visionary his 'clients' took him for. Once she realised he wasn't on his way up in this world. When she realised there was nothing to fear. He would never do anything; he wasn't the kind of person to hunt her down once she'd gone. He'd just shrug and say, 'Life is such a mystery, innit? Can't predict what's going to happen next.'

And tonight's the night. She hears laughter from the front room, confident male laughter shaking the walls. Next to her, Sleaze yawns. Earlier on in the relationship, when Isobel could feel herself going under, when she could feel the Duke's blackened fingertips reaching down into her brain, even while she slept, a certain thought kept occurring to her. If I ever get out of this, what's the first thing I'll do? Why, I'll find an obliging young squire to track down Mr Duke, then I'll slip the barrel of a gun down his gullet, posting a bullet straight into his neck. I'll blow him apart so hard they'll be finding his toes in Albuquerque.

The front door slams and Jon comes into the room. He

5

doesn't look at her but opens a drawer and puts a twenty-pound note into a box. He picks up his keys and the dog lead. Before he takes Sleaze off for a walk he winks at Isobel and says, 'Tonight's the night, yeah?'

Yes indeed, she thinks.

Isobel knew who to speak to: Alun the Dragon's best friend, the man who makes things possible, the one who could coax the stars from the sky. His name is Marlon, because his old mum loved Marlon Brando. He is only twenty-six with the taut face of someone who'll never show their real age.

He sits in Soho Square at dusk now, killing time before going down to The King of England. He was the original street-boy, a rat from the gutter. He discovered the city from the bottom up. Thieving, lying, cheating, he did it all. He never went to school. Marlon looks at the buildings around the Square and can remember when that design consultancy was a shabby restaurant, when it was a deserted shack, a squat, when rioters and chancers threw flaming newspapers through its empty windows. Every day in Soho a new place to go and gorge yourself springs up; every hour, a new selection of things to stuff down your gullet – it's sickening, he thinks. People's greed, people's hunger, people's thirst.

He lives in a small flat above Old Compton Street so the noise of the city is always in his ears. Laughter in the daytime, arguments at night. As soon as darkness falls, the gossip and greetings become tears and recriminations. At first, Marlon was fascinated by the activity around him. It seemed as though his life just went on, from breakfast to lunch until dinner, while everyone else's existence was a waltz of social engagements and love affairs. But that was years ago, before he fell in with Alun. Now he can't get away from the city. London makes him the boss, the man, the top cat, and without it he's nothing. The voices he hears floating up from the street feel like wires poking into his brain and he wishes some tidal wave would occasionally thunder down the streets of Soho and wipe these people out of their tiny, petty lives so he could get some rest.

The apartments above Old Compton Street are minuscule, more like hutches and kennels than flats, but Marlon has stripped his down to the plaster and floorboards and painted everything dazzling white. Art books are piled on the floor, next to the long window– the flat's only redeeming feature. Last month Isobel knocked on his door. She loitered in his room, the futon still open and the sheets twisted, while he stood awkwardly by the cooker in white karate-kit trousers. She cast her eyes over his hard, tight, golden body and jagged contours. No piercings, no tattoos. When he is with Alun he's 'on duty'. He wears a broad smile and a narrow suit, wide shoulders and lapels, crisp midnight-blue silk with a crimson lining. He wears four signet rings on each hand, heavy gold. But Isobel caught him off guard. She wore an expression that Marlon has seen many times before: the elusive gaze of people desperate enough to beg for help or haggle for favours. For a few moments, he was tempted to tell her there was no need to go to Alun, that he himself would do what-ever was necessary, no charge. But business is business. At the end of the day, Alun has given him a lot more than Isobel ever could. Alun saved him from the streets. He saved him from a life spent strictly in the small-time. Isobel would shower him with – what? – gratitude and eternal thanks. But gratitude doesn't pay the rent. You can't wear it, drive it, smoke it or drink it. Marlon had grinned and handed Isobel a mug of coffee. 'I've got to tell you, Isobel love, Alun doesn't need no more money. Alun's got money comin' out his ears. You're

7

gonna have to pay him back with something else, you know, something sweeter.'

Marlon shivers and gets up from the bench. Sometimes he thinks about what it would be like to wake up with his arm curled around a warm, sleeping body. At night he imagines a lover kissing his forehead, or walking with her fingers wound around his. He imagines someone's lips pressed against his eyelids for a moment, and a hand touching the back of his neck. He would like to know that a woman is thinking about him, but whenever he tries to picture her he can't. It is sheer, physical closeness he wants; not companionship, not a marriage of minds, just a hand to hold. He didn't use to care. For years, he would sneer at the lovers he saw, entwined on benches or meandering down the street with bovine, contented smiles on their faces. Their love seemed fake and tinselly, their conversations the product of boredom and indifference. He was never intrigued by what really went on between those couples. Now he would like to find out, but it feels as if it's too late. He's lost the habit of talking to people about things that don't involve getaway cars and late-night heists. In his mind, he runs through nightmare scenarios where he takes someone out to dinner, and all he can think of to say is, 'You know, there are several ways to kill a man with just a length of wire and a steel pipe. More wine?' or, 'I'm terribly sorry, I'd love to come in for coffee but I've got to mastermind a drugs coup south of the river, and you know what taxi drivers are like.'

Soho Square is full of old men talking to themselves. The summer evenings bring out all the nuts in the locality: the harmless ones, grinning and staggering, trailing beer-can ringpulls; the thin-faced, untrustworthy ones, with eyes like pellets. People with little black books full of names and numbers, making connections all over the city and drawing them tight

8

together to instigate a little mayhem. Marlon, with his dancer's torso, is one of these. Alun the Dragon will be opening up now, and it's time to help him greet the punters. There's some talks to be had, and a rack of Lacroix to be disposed of. Tonight Marlon will dress to impress, and make sure everything goes swimmingly.

Isobel plays 'Respect' on the turntable and gets ready for tonight's business. As she sits at her dresser – the only decent piece of furniture she and the Duke have – she smoothes foundation across her cheek bones. Next is a faint slick of pale silver eyeshadow called 'Angel' and two coats of mascara. Then sticky red lipgloss. She slips on a white cotton shift dress and calls Duke in from the kitchen to zip it up. He does so without really looking at her. On her feet she has black leather ballet pumps.

Jon Duke shrugs on his greasy long coat. Even in the blazing summer he is always cold, and the coat is his trademark. Bottle green with a narrow black velvet collar and deep square pockets, a paisley-print lining and a label saying 'Collins-Hunter Gentlemen's Outfitters, of Westminster'. The King of England is his main office, the best place possible for direct customer care. Of course, like all the men in London at his level, Jon has outside interests and remote operators. It's the only way to move forward in this age of cut-throat market opposition. He has what he calls a 'portfolio career': a little bit of legal, a little bit of not-so-kosher. Men working for him on one side of the line, and a few flirting with the alternatives. But drugs, hard drugs, that's what gives Jon Duke a real thrill. 'A mega, one-hundred-and-ten per cent message of love to the synapses,' as he would say. 'The best present you can give yourself,' he might add, 'a birthday gift for your brain.'

The King of England is where the best customers are.

Students with their grant money, regulars with their habits, City boys and sleek girls dropping by on their way to somewhere better. Everyone looking for something a little special, something to push depression back into its box. Jon Duke reads the papers each Sunday and knows they've got it all wrong. The boys at the top, they don't know what makes us tick, he thinks. People come to him for a hundred different reasons. Some do it out of boredom, some to impress their friends, some because they just have too much money. Well, the Duke's always willing to unburden your wallet. Alun-mate, which is what he calls the Dragon, only asks for ten per cent. Ten per cent is the Duke's weekly business tax, his rent, his front-desk duty. Nothing in comparison to the other ninety per cent filling his money box at home. Enough to keep up his modest habit and buy new stock for his customers who are just going crazy over the bargains he offers – 'Know what I mean, sweet?'

Alun's looking magic tonight – not at all bad for fifty-something. Over his black rocker's jeans with the narrow turn-ups and key chain he's got a billowing red Hawaiian shirt. Beneath his bald pate the grey eyes are dancing. He grins, all the teeth showing, as the King of England hosts another successful evening. Moody boys in the corner, girls with glossy skin drinking G&Ts on the banquettes. Marlon is in his suit and Billie Holiday's playing on the jukebox. Jon Duke has just walked in with Isobel by his side, and now the place is really jumping.

'You awright there?' asks Duke without turning.

'Fine, Jon,' says Isobel, her hand pressed to her brow. 'Just a headache. I might go home after an hour or so.'

Alun is sweeping towards them both with his arms outstretched. 'How you doing my lovelies?' he asks in one breath.

'Not so bad, Alun-mate,' says Duke.

Dragon doesn't really look Isobel in the eye but she can feel his attention slowly gluing itself to every inch of her skin. Isobel is glad of her dense, bitter-smelling mask of makeup like those market-stall porcelain dolls. The red gloss forces her to keep her lips motionless. Otherwise they'd curl deep with disdain as Dragon gets an eyeful. 'Little lady feelin' a bit out of sorts?' he asks. Duke just shrugs. 'Little word in yer ear, Jon-mate, if I may,' adds Dragon, his grin never wavering. Palm trees bedeck his shirt. He beckons Duke over to the side of the bar and ushers him through the door to the back rooms.

Isobel thought she might experience a twinge of remorse as she watched Duke follow gamely after Dragon. But instead, she feels a rising elation. She wants to follow them and give Duke a little shove, hurry him along. The mythical headache no longer seems to be troubling her, as she looks through the pub windows to the streets outside, where rain is falling through the twilight.

'My favourite time, this, when it's all blue,' says Marlon as he approaches her. 'When I was a kiddie, about nine or ten, I used to take myself for a little walk around town at dusk every night. I never had money, so I used to hang around outside all the cake shops licking my chops like a stray dog.' He nods at the barman, who slides a glass of champagne down to them. 'You're very brave,' Marlon tells Isobel. 'And you've done the right thing. There are people in this world who'll just go on taking. They need to be stopped or else they'll just go on. They're only out for what they can get, and they don't care who they fuck over on the way. Some people, you have to hurt them, so they remember not to do it again. You have to put yourself into their nightmares, so they see you every time they close their eyes. You eventually have to

11

pay for everything you do in this life, and Jon Duke's just got his bill.'

Jon Duke, his delicate face bisected by a length of chain, is a beautiful sight to behold. Alun knows just how little ten per cent is, and isn't really that sorry to let it go. Losing ten per cent of a dealer's profits is nothing compared to the thrill of having a man kneeling in front of you with his eyeballs rolling and a tenner's worth of metal links wrapped around his neck. Evidently, Alun-mate is not one of Jon Duke's chums any more. He watches as his 'best boy' Bald Kevin grips the ends of the chain in his wide, fat hands and pulls just that little bit harder. Duke's tongue has swollen up and his eyes are bulging out of his head, though their expression is as bland as usual.

Down there on the floor, Duke ponders this strange turn of events. The green coat is torn and in two pieces under his knees. This isn't what he expected tonight. He thought he'd be whiling the hours away at his usual post, handing out salvation in plastic wraps and giving chemical alms to the spiritually needy. Not swallowing his own blood in a back room with a rack of genuine designer jeans on one side and a box of dirty videos on the other. Bald Kevin's crotch stinks, even through his black trousers. Isobel said she might go home. And there's nobody else to notice his absence. But it doesn't hurt much. His brain is flooded with dopamine anyway. The edges of his vision go dark green then black, and the room starts to diminish. It's just like falling asleep.

Alun feels adrenaline run from the crown of his head to his soles. One of his businesses is the export of authentic English memorabilia – the usual pictures of London's architectural and historical successes on china plates, mugs, badges, T-shirts; pens, keyrings, erasers; caps, patches, tea-cosies, just the essentials.

Sold to America, mostly, where 'they eat it all up like ice-cream sundae', as he says. On the bottom of each plate is a little sticker with the Union Jack on it, and some gold lettering: 'Lovingly hand-crafted in the East End of London'. Apparently the Yanks go crazy for that sort of thing. Authenticity sells. So you can be sure the Dragon's going to employ all his sincerity when Duke's body gets packed up and shipped off with all the other mugs. At some point in the next twelve hours there's going to be a little accident, then a certain brown packing box with a distinct odour might find itself sinking slowly to the bottom of the sea. That evening Duke had walked into the King of England and told his first client that he had 'a big fucking Valentine's box of surprises' up for grabs. Well, trust Duke to always know the score.

In the main bar, Bald Kevin comes and whispers into Marlon's ear. Isobel looks down and sees, with a pang of horror, welts and bruises on Kevin's palms. Marlon is grinning at her. 'All done, Isobel. You can leave as soon as you want to. Just pack the essentials and you're laughing. I'll walk you home.' He takes a firm hold of her elbow and steers her through the crowd. People call out and greet them both and he keeps a broad smile on his face as he nods to them, but they keep moving. Once they're out on the street, she keels over with nausea. Marlon holds onto her shoulder as she tries to get some blood to her head.

She laughs weakly. 'My first dead body, eh? You'd think I'd handle the whole thing with a bit more panache.'

'Yeah, you're one of us now,' replies Marlon. They are tainted in the same way. She has crossed that invisible line which divides normal people from those who sleep in the day and 'work' at night. Isobel has unwittingly bonded herself with Marlon. They are now kin – at one with the fury and ferocity which underlie the conventions and polite rituals of other people's lives. It is as though the language with which she had previously defined her world has been augmented by an entirely new vocabulary written in blood. Vengeance and punishment have become her currency. She has bought into the criminal market. Any fondness she may have felt for Marlon evaporates in that instant as she sees him for what he is: an agent, a doom-carrier, taking and giving death according to orders. He doesn't actually care. All that stuff about Jon Duke finally having to pay his bill, Marlon failed to mention the cut Alun was getting.

Marlon says nothing. He can feel Isobel's horrified stiffness as she walks beside him, her arm subtly squirming for him to loosen his grip. He was like that, the first time. He was fifteen and it started out as a simple mugging. It was midnight in December on the Embankment – a young businessman-type who thought he could fight his way out of it, with his soft-knuckled fists and lumbering body. Marlon didn't even kill him properly, just fastened his hands around his neck until he lost consciousness, then heaved the body over the low white railing until it dropped gracelessly into the Thames. As he watched it sink in the dense, numbing water, he'd had a feeling, partly of victory, partly that he was now somehow married inextricably to his fate. That because he'd done it once, conquered another human being entirely, he could never go back to what he'd been like before.

'Now I have to keep my end of the bargain –' Isobel begins.

'You do indeed,' he cuts her off with a curt laugh. Nothing is going to come and 'save' Isobel now. The flat is already in sight. 'Got your keys? Right, in we go.' He practically throws her inside. Sleaze is fast asleep in the lounge, head down between his paws. 'Let's make you a lovely cup of tea,' Marlon says. She stands in her own kitchen as he looks round. Her phone rings and he answers it. When he comes back his eyes are flinty and dark. 'Actually, I'd better fuck off,' he says. 'I'll give you a month to clear your stuff out and formulate a plan. And don't worry. Nobody's going to come sniffing around.' She walks him to the door and at the last moment he turns. He was never good at being tender. He would rather tough-talk her, like she was a rookie soldier and he a seasoned general. He says, 'You made this deal, Isobel, not me. Like I told you, there's a charge for everything in this world.'

Isobel says, 'Don't suppose I could get it on credit?' but he doesn't laugh.

When he is gone, she puts herself to bed. Even though her heart is beating hard, she forces herself to close her eyes. She remembers the first time she met Jon Duke, in the corner of a restaurant on the King's Road. Terracotta walls and faux-Moroccan drapes, lots of ladies with thin, tanned shoulders. He was the bit of rough, the cheeky chappie someone had picked up. He hadn't really been on brown then, uppers were his thing. Anything to keep him perennially cheerful, always reaching for the brightest star or the highest apple on the tree. That night in her apartment his white skin had shed light sweat against hers, their waists the same size, his flimsy fingers around her wrists. He had seemed harmless at the time. He was meant to have been the shallow, hedonistic counterpart to her clever, sharp froideur. The joker to her queen. She had thought she could use him to facilitate her entry into a stylised, Mafioso world that seemed more interesting than the one she was used to – a world of midnight poker games and neat whisky. But, she realised, he never had the balls. Faced with a choice between a big-scale criminal rip-off venture and a series of pathetic, seedy transactions with twittering coke fiends, he would always pick the latter. He'd thought his residency at the King of England gave

15

him a certain kudos and made him into a local character, but she saw the place for what it really was: a smoky hovel with torn seats. She wasn't cut out for the life of a heroin addict, or a heroin addict's girlfriend. It was like being a vegetable in a hospital: dead in all but name. Isobel was too shallow for this world. She liked clothes too much. She liked having good skin, eating good food, and being able to speak without that hard, tight, junkie voice.

Isobel is rigid beneath the sheets. She has a strange, claustrophobic sensation of her destiny. Of it being the only possible solution to what she's done. The front door buzzer sounds and she leaps to her feet, every bone cold as steel. She creeps along the hall, takes a deep breath and swings the door wide open. On the step, bathed in yellow light from the porch, stands Alun, the top two buttons of his Hawaiian shirt undone and grey chest hair ruffling over it. Alun the Dragon and Isobel Aurora Paine stare at each other for a few seconds. His eyes are empty and he doesn't seem to be smiling so much for her as for himself, like a boy who's buried something special in the garden. Already her fear is underscored with a kind of lunatic happiness that Jon Duke has been erased. Eliminated! Just like that. And she has organised it. She is caught between wanting to push Alun away from the door and run straight on past the overflowing bins and broken street-lights until he is a spot on the horizon, and hugging him to her chest like a returning war hero.

But his smarmy, weathered face prevents her from thanking him or even enquiring about Duke's death. He looks like an insolent, plotting servant who's come to collect his month's payment. 'Not going to ask me inside then?' he winks. 'I been workin' hard all night.' He struts past her and sits on the sofa in the lounge. He starts drumming on his thighs with the palms of his hands, making that thick identity bracelet clink. 'Pub's got a

16

brand-new sign,' he announces casually. 'Well, not really the picture, you know, more the way it hangs. Got a lovely chain now. Swings like a kitten in a hammock.' Yes indeed, for the instrument of Jon Duke's sad demise now suspends the inn's board – a shining, narrow gold crown on a Union Jack background – from a black iron bracket. Isobel's gut turns to ice and she tries to laugh. The details of the execution come to her in visceral detail – Bald Kevin's bruised hands, the thick links of the chain, and the cramped back room of the King of England. Her throat clicks soundlessly for a while until Dragon springs to his feet and she jumps and screams, unable to help herself. He moves forward step by step and she moves back instinctively.

'You didn't look very pleased to see me, when you opened the door. Think I'd forget, didja? Think you could go blubbing to Marlon and he'd give you a little pat on the bottom and make everything better?' He's swaggering from side to side, his barrel chest taking up most of the corridor, his arms held out a little. Swinging from the hips. He continues: 'Rather have Jon back, would ya? Treating you like shit. You know you're better than that.' Isobel's knees are shaking. They go into the bedroom, she still taking steps backwards until her calves hit the end of the bed. He takes a single stride forward, punches her in the stomach and follows her down as she falls onto the mattress. He says, 'Except you're not better than that any more, really, are ya? I think, Isobel, that you've lowered yourself a little in the last few weeks. I'd say you've finally come down to our level. Bit of blood on your hands, isn't there?' Nearly sixteen stone of hairy-backed, tattooed brawn lying straight over her thin body. He sticks out his tongue – flat and short, and coated in yellow scum – and wipes it over her lips and cheeks. Saliva hangs out of his mouth and trails across her face. 'I've wanted you for a long time, but this feels a bit like sullied goods to me. It's not as romantic as I thought it'd be. You feel a bit dirty. Feels like you got some secrets behind that little white face of yours,' he whispers. 'After I leave tonight, I'm not going to want you any more. You're going to be like a little piece of shit on my shoe. Yeah?' Isobel nods.

She is only wearing a man's shirt and knickers. He puts his palm right in the centre of her face and grabs the edge of her underwear with the other hand. She's not moving, not even resisting. She stares straight up and thinks of Jon Duke. Dragon slides two fingers inside her crotch and she's as dry and rough as crocodile skin. Isobel thinks of Jon Duke and the easy, natural way he lied about everything. The way he thought he was a drugs-trade kingpin when he was just like all the others, getting cheap thrills from the knowledge that they were doing something slightly naughty and illegal. To make him no longer exist, she'd pay any price. One little fuck for an entire lifetime of knowing that Jon Duke was, as they say, not in service. One fuck, and she need never see or think about Jon Duke, Alun the Dragon or Marlon again. She wins. Dragon spits on his hand and pulls out his purple, rough-hewn cock. It's been with him for half a century, so it's looking a little the worse for wear. Isobel looks at it, then at his face. This ugly old man thinks he's the king of the castle, with all that cold-blooded Krays crap about sullied goods. Who's he kidding? He shoves his cock hard into her. Sweat drips from his armpits as he stares down into her eyes. She sneers with contempt at the entire bad-boy drama these people are playing out: Marlon with his shiny suits, Dragon with his cheesy tattoo. 'You stupid, old, fat fuck,' she whispers inaudibly as he comes.

Marlon and Dragon carry on running the King of England. A couple of times that summer, people ask about Jon Duke and

18

the story is he got busted. It happens all the time and after a while the enquiries trail off. December comes and the trees along Oxford Street are ringed with Christmas lights, then winter slowly turns to spring. Ever since the Jon Duke incident things have been preying on Marlon's mind, prompted by Isobel's horror at discovering that she was just like him. It made him see himself as some kind of animal, hunting people down with unerring hunger and extracting the price of their sins. Usually when he thought like this it gave him a twinge of pride. But he's slowly beginning to see the truth: he's turned into somebody no normal person would ever want to know. He's seen the stuff of kiddies' nightmares: a body landing onto concrete from a height of fifty feet; bone exposed through skin; a hand with a clear bullet hole. Nothing from the normal world excites him any more. He doesn't read. Music's boring. Violent films just make him laugh.

One Friday in April, Marlon's lying on the futon after work. From one of the neighbouring flats he can hear some sort of party in progress. He sinks down, pulling the covers over his head. It sometimes disturbs him to find himself acting like this, stroking his own face and kissing his own hand, hugging the duvet like a baby with a blankie. The phone rings and he groans. He doesn't want to speak to anyone else tonight – no more hard men with their tough requests. They all seem to read from the same gangster-movie script. But the phone keeps ringing. Eventually he picks up and on the other end of the line a garbled voice mutters, 'You bastard. You *bastard* bastard.'

Isobel hasn't left London. Instead she lives just twenty yards from her old flat, though she has never bumped into Marlon or Alun since July. After that night Isobel found terror invading her nights. She had thought that once Jon was out of the picture – she liked to think of him as having disappeared, like an unfortunate citizen in a dictatorship – she would sleep the sleep of the just. Instead, guilt gave her lucid, continual, long-haul nightmares. She spent her days expecting to be struck down by a bolt of divine lightning. She'd thought she had some time and money to play with, since the flat wouldn't be reclaimed for a month, but as soon as people heard Duke was off the scene, strangers started knocking on her door. Big men with suspiciously good clothes, scrawny men with cuts on their faces and box-fresh trainers, all crept to her to claim hard cash for the stuff Duke had bought on credit. Hands with chunky sovereign rings and gleaming watches nabbed their share from the box in the top drawer. Isobel took to the streets with ten twenty-bags of brown on her, thinking she could flog it. She wanted it out of the flat but didn't hate drugs enough to flush them down the bog. Instead, the police caught up with her, wandering about at two in the morning, casting shifty glances at the people around her. They asked if she was OK, and from her guilty, sleep-deprived stare they thought she might be what they termed, with a cynical wink, 'a good girl turned bad'. So they took her in for a check-up and a little TLC, and two hundred quids' worth of primetime entertainment in clingfilm wraps tumbled out onto the table. Because they were sure she was just a Sloane who'd fallen by the wayside for a time – which was true enough – and because they liked her face, and were sure she was protecting some man who'd organised the whole operation, she spent just one night inside and paid her way out. Within ten days of Duke's death she had no money whatsoever. She began to understand the depraved things people did when they had no other option; she wanted to go into restaurants' bins to see if they had any food in them, or risk stealing some from a shop. In the end she sold all her jewellery – the gold bangle and earrings, the necklace with a single diamond – and used the money to rent a studio the size of a cupboard. She handed Sleaze into a pound. He had to be dragged there, whining and pulling back, and the last time she saw him he looked at her sadly with a naked, human eye.

Marlon waits outside Isobel's warped door. The buzzer doesn't work. He knocks but nobody answers, even though there's a low mutter coming from inside. After a few seconds of staring at the illegible neon graffiti on the walls by the staircase, Marlon turns sideways and sends a straight waist-high kick, heel-first, against the lock. The door swings open with barely a sound, releasing the dense smell of sweat and dust. It is just one room, a kitchenette and shower area, which doesn't have a door, only a matted piece of cloth as a partition. Isobel is on the bed, legs wide apart, covered in blood. It's not like you see in the movies: this matter is uneven in texture, slimy, clotted. It smells. Her groin resembles ripped sponge. Marlon retches even as he approaches her. Her eyes are like a mad dog's and her skin is grey. She reaches out with one hand and grabs his T-shirt: 'Take. It. Away,' she says.

The baby's not making very much noise, but Marlon's vision has suddenly narrowed to that warm, wet mass supported by his two palms. He doesn't notice that Isobel is leaning away from it, the muscles in her face contorted with horror. She has lost so much blood her lips and feet are turning blue. Marlon just sees ten tiny fingertips curling from hands like sea-shells, a face like a damp flower. 'Put it in a plastic bag and throw it away,' says Isobel through a mouth full of hate. 'Kill it and put it in a bin on the street.' But she might as well be talking to the empty air. 'Hey, you,' Marlon greets the smudged face in his hands. The little mouth opens and squawks. 'Come on, you're a fighter, you're the number one

21

… You're lovely … you are,' croons Marlon, completely lost, his face soft with tenderness. His eyelashes are wet. 'You're a survivor – you're the king.'

1

At Kensington Shooting Range the guns are dented, the clientele badly dressed, the lighting a flat shade of orange.

The instructor rearranges his baseball cap and pushes his glasses back up his nose. 'When you're shooting a gun,' he says to the assembled class in the demonstration room, 'it's not really about technique or skill. Forget all the stuff you've seen on the telly about control and mastering the firearm.' He has a nasal, Dagenham-Dave-type voice. 'Life gives you a choice. You can either win or you can lose, and having a gun makes that choice a little easier. It's not just about accuracy or skill. Raise it to shoulder height, relax, straighten the spine, release the safety catch, cock the hammer and remember: you're not shooting at an outline of a man, you're shooting at every kid who bullied you at school, every arsehole who didn't give you a job.' He lifts his arm sideways and fires an entire round to the end of the range where a paper silhouette hangs, scored with demarcated damage zones: heart, head, lungs, groin.

The sound of the bullets fills the watching group with a sense of anarchic glee. The sheer noise of those speeding metal pellets – a kind of exhilarated, metallic explosion – makes them itch with impatience. When the instructor has stopped shooting, the paper silhouette spools forward, up the range, and he tears it off and shows it to his pupils, pointing at various holes. 'That's for my second wife. That's for the little shit who keyed my car last week. You see? You have to imbue every bullet with meaning.'

Now it's the teenagers' turn. They are a group of society's

least wanted: eighteen-year-olds about to be released from care into the welfare state. They have all known each other since early childhood. They go through to the range and one by one take their places opposite a paper target. In front of each of them is a shelf at waist height, a revolver chained to a post, and a pair of headphones to muffle the noise. There is sallow Neela, her short black hair crudely shorn; Gavin, runty and rat-like, with acne; pale, lupine Lukas, clowning and taking pot-shots at imaginary baddies; and finally Rex, tall and broad, very quiet, with a startling, translucently pretty face. He backs out of his booth, hands deep in pockets.

'I can't believe I let you talk me into this,' he says to Neela. 'They'll go spare. We're supposed to be at the bowling alley.'

Neela sneers. 'They won't go spare. They don't give a shit.' She has a flat, elegant voice which always sounds mocking: 'Think of it as the best skill there is, Rex. The one from which all others follow. If you want money, mug a businessman. If you want to have dinner at a top restaurant, shoot the doorman. You don't need A-levels when you've got perfect aim.'

The instructor comes up to her. 'Well, since you're so enthusiastic, why don't you begin?' There is something special, personal in his tone. Neela wonders what he sees when he looks at her; maybe a little capering monkey, something escaped from the jungle.

The four youths wait and watch. They have all been in love with the ritual of a shooting since they were old enough to watch the television. They have seen it all before: the sharpening focus of the shooter's eye, the arm, steady and straight, the reflected light sliding across the length of the barrel and the finger against the trigger, tensing, tightening. As Neela takes her place, the scene has a familiar, ceremonial beauty. She is small, with a bony, asexual face. The skin is stretched very tight, giving her features

24

a depraved look. The instructor claps his hand on her shoulder and she flinches. She hates being touched. She turns towards the target. She can feel the heat emanating from him, and senses rather than hears his nasal, laboured breathing.

'Now, look at this,' he calls to the other three. 'Often with girls, especially the petite type, their aim goes a bit funny. They're not really able to handle the weight of the gun as it kicks back in their hand. Of course, you can get firearms specially made for women, but we like to teach you the proper techniques here.'

Neela takes a deep breath and narrows her eyes so that the only thing in her sight is the hanging target, the long corridor leading up to it and her outstretched hand clasping the revolver. It is cold and far heavier than it looks. As soon as it is aloft, it seems to gain a life of its own. Her wrist aches just keeping it upright. She begins to understand the idea of a gun being loaded – not just with small, squat bullets, but also with a kind of unstoppable desire to expel them. It feels as though the weapon positively reverberates with the need for someone to pull its trigger.

She fires once, then again and again until the hammer clicks hollowly against the empty barrel. Her fingers ache. Her ears, even through the headphones, are filled with exquisite, rebellious, ricocheting noise. She looks round and everyone, even the instructor, is standing or crouching with their arms over their head. She feels her face burning with embarrassment.

The instructor gets up, takes the gun out of her hand and puts it back on the wooden shelf. 'Right everyone,' he calls out jubilantly, not looking at her. 'I think you'll all agree that was a classic example of how not to shoot. Yes? The terrible stance, weak hand-hold, careless positioning and, above all, the closed eyes are not conducive to a neat and efficient execution. As I said, women often find this kind of highly skilled task difficult, so we shouldn't be too quick to criticise. And I must add, people, your reaction was excellent. In the event of any similar hazard, get down low and protect your face and head.' He presses the button which spools her target forward: the very edges of the sheet of paper are slightly rucked, but the black ink man is picture-perfect.

Rex takes his place in front of the target. He has a powerful, underwater way of moving his limbs. His crystalline beauty makes him seem untouchable. Neela, in her silky way, calls him The Virgin King. But his personality is that of the court comedian – or so he feels – a desperate, joke-telling buffoon. He has a surprisingly high, reedy voice: 'I really don't want to do this. It's 2001 already, surely human beings have found a way to settle their differences without the use of an Uzi. Until I came to this place I didn't even know there was such a thing as a magazine called *Guns'n'Ammo*. It was in reception. A hundred pages of really violent weapons with loving captions like, "This serrated twelve-inch Apache warrior knife is guaranteed to cut through wood, steel and human bone with minimum abrasion to the all-steel shaft".' The others laugh. All his life, Rex has been the performer. He was the kid with large, brimming, love-me eyes. He was hugely, grossly overweight until he was fifteen, some three years ago, and he still can't look in the mirror without seeing his pubescent self and its attendant rolls of blubber, thick glasses and stretched, fat-boy clothes. The aristocracy and villainy mingling in his blood have produced a cushiony pair of lips, broad cheekbones and cherubic thick hair, but all he can see is the fat boy, who looks back at him with a doleful look and a mouth full of doughnut. So he likes to keep the laughs coming. Sometimes when he goes too far, Neela breaks in with, 'I think someone's doing the validation routine' or, 'Look, Mummy! I'm dancing!'

If he were alone, he would never touch a gun. His quavering, hysterical nature recoils at the sight of such a device. It is more than just a machine fashioned from metal in a factory, one of thousands exactly like it. It is the embodiment of a system of emotions and motivations alien to his understanding. A gun makes it easy for man to access the darkest regions of his psyche and expel his malice in a deadly, physical form. All it takes is a moment's pressure against the trigger and your malevolence is out in the open. To touch it would be to ally himself with what it represents, to be swept up by the power of its mythology – assassin, cowboy, cop – and break the seal he has placed around the boundaries of his lower nature.

Looking at it, he has the same feeling as Neela – that it is somehow already alive, in control, and simply needing a human hand to raise it before it jerks and sprays bullets from its mouth. But there are three pairs of eyes watching: Lukas, rooting for him, Neela and Gavin waiting to see how good or bad he is; maybe they're the kind who laugh when old folks stumble in the street. They like to discover the flaws in human nature, just for their own information. Rex takes just one bullet and snaps it into the chamber. Time seems to pass excruciatingly slowly as he stares at the object in his hands. Once again, he has a disconcerting sensation of the gun being aware of his presence, of it gazing back up at him, like a chess piece in Alice's looking-glass world, and sniggering to itself. He wonders if all the revolvers at the range were bought new. They appear battered. Knowing this place, they were probably the result of a police weapon cull in the area – the instruments of countless petty criminals' late-night attacks. He straightens and braces his shoulders. In the orange light, his hair looks like a coronet of woven platinum and his eyes are a crisp, iridescent silver. He can feel Neela's eyes on his body. She has a way of looking at him that reaches into the darkest ante-chamber of his personality and fixes its sights upon the one thing he wants to hide from the rest of the world: Neela has seen fat boy. Neela knows fat boy.

Rex faces the target head-on. He closes one eye and raises the gun. He wonders who he should visualise: the gym coach who made him do it in his vest and pants because 'they'd never find a kit big enough'; the care people, who couldn't bring themselves to hug him, or if they did it was with infinite pity; the hundreds of girls who didn't reject him, who didn't put the phone down on him and didn't cheat on him, because they never noticed him in the first place. He pulls the trigger and a bullet sails into the centre of the paper brain.

'Ouch!' yells Lukas joyously. Rex can see Neela nodding appreciatively. For some reason, her approval means more than Lukas'. It seems to wash over and through him like liquid gold, gilding his bones.

He fires the other seven bullets one by one, and each time his aim is robot-precise. The instructor has come in, along with a group of kids for the next shooting session, but he doesn't notice them. In his mind, doughnut guy is picking off the countless figures who made him cry into his pillow – the teachers, the fake friends, the strangers. But the others see something quite different: six feet of taut boy flesh. There is something grand about his performance, a kind of animal grace and nobility as he slowly lifts the gun and squeezes the trigger. After he has fired the last bullet there is silence. Everyone waits, watching, as Rex lets his arm fall to his side for a moment, then raises and inspects the gun closely. When he was shooting, he had felt something take him over. Dark and arrogant, from the very lowest layer of his personality, an egotistical voice which had been lying dormant his whole life seemed to yell hallelujah every time a bullet pierced the paper. His nerves were flooded with the power and simplicity of it, and his hand ached pleasurably as it absorbed the kick-back. He feels the adrenaline draw off a little and turns to face the others. As a joke, he takes a theatrical bow, but nobody laughs or smiles. Instead, they stand grave and admiring.

Gavin takes up his gun. Its black form appears far more substantial than his skinny arm. He looks ridiculous with it, his spine and rounded shoulders bent all the way back, as though the gun is actually holding him and he wants to get away. But he shoots with all the viciousness and accuracy of a boy who's spent his life casting stones at birds, and making bows and arrows of twigs. When he was a kid, the people in care could always find him at the bottom of the garden torturing caterpillars and worms with sticks. He used to catch birds by luring them into bird-houses in the winter, then shutting up the entrance. At the end of the season he would open them up again to explore and dissect the starved, wizened corpses he found. He was the type of child who was never scared of hurting other people, even adults, in quiet, nasty ways, by biting or scratching. At the range, the paper target comes back shot through the groin and midriff, not the heart or head, except for one single bullet lodged in the throat.

'God, Gav,' says Lukas, only half-jokingly, pulling his dark hair back into its ragged ponytail. 'You really know how to make a man suffer, don't you? Wouldn't like to meet you in a dark alley.'

Gavin never speaks without first looking at Neela to check if it's OK. Often, Neela talks for him, but this time she is grinning, going along with it. 'You'd make a great serial killer,' she says to him. 'You'd really know how to torture someone. Do you like the feel of that gun?' He looks down at the dull, scratched barrel and slightly worn trigger and nods. 'Wanna keep it?' Neela coaxes. Gavin nods again. Neela looks at Lukas and says, 'Get the gun for him.' She has a way of impelling people to do things, just by staring at them. People find it hard to meet her eyes, because whenever she wills it to, the Medusa flame begins to flicker in her pupils. Lukas looks at her for a second, then snaps into action. He gets Gavin to hold the gun at arm's length so the safety chain pulls taut across the range, then steps behind him with his own revolver and blasts the chain to pieces. The gun is free and untethered in Gavin's hand. 'There you go,' Neela says, as he strokes the piece, looks round to check the instructor isn't watching, and then tucks it into his waistband.

The instructor walks up to them after Lukas has taken his shots. 'Now, you've all had your turn. Well done. Especially you.' He indicates Rex. 'You're good. Lots of panache. It seems to me like you know how to treat a gun. You're welcome back here any time you like.' Neela looks at the instructor with gathering venom. No matter how poised she seems, she goes through life with the savage consciousness of a Cinderella, born for greater things but somehow denied them. Made for the light, but pushed into the shadows. As soon as people cast their attention upon her she feels like she is shrivelling, a violent, clumsy, self-hating animal. She wishes she had friends. She wishes she were beautiful like Rex, charming like Lukas. She doesn't wish she was anything like Gavin. Gavin is her hope, her sidekick, proof that there exists a person lower, uglier, nastier than she.

She can feel anger spiking her blood as she watches the instructor chumming up with Rex. Toys for the boys, is it? Bitterness is the only thing that keeps her going – she knows that, she isn't stupid – bitterness and malice. Occasionally it occurs to her that this is no way to live, marking out time as a series of masochistic episodes or revenge acts, measuring success by the degree to which she has victory over others. Her thoughts are interrupted by a startled cry from the opposite end of the range. Gavin has wrestled a gun from one of the boys in the other group, emptying it of its bullets. He scurries back up to her and pokes the instructor in the belly with a sharp elbow. 'Go on, show the fat ginger bastard,' he says to her.

When anger courses through her body it feels as though every nerve is alive, every muscle primed and strong. She feels truly like an animal when she is acting out of anger; as though she could hear a whisper in the trees two miles away, or trace the movement of a bug in the grass. She loads up and faces a new target. Her eyes glitter. She leaves off the headphones and cracks the knuckles of both hands. She wants to hear the sharp, joyous sound of metal in the air. She takes her gun and raises it high. The target appears to her to be extraordinarily clear, and very close. There is no distance between them at all, and the paper man seems to call to her. The gun feels as though it wants to pull free of her and race forwards. She tightens her grip and squeezes the trigger four times, in quick succession: heart, heart, stomach, groin. A white smile splits her narrow, high-cheekboned face as she masters the bucking, weighty machine. At the other end of the range, Rex and Lukas have broken out into broad grins and Gavin is casting sly, contemptuous looks at the instructor. Neela grimaces, closes her eyes and fires three more times: lungs, head, throat. She is breathing hard. She pauses for a second and realises what she is about to do. She lowers her arms and shoots the last bullet, away from the target, right into the instructor's left ankle. He stares at her blankly before the blood drains from his face and he swoons, hitting the floor with his whole weight. 'Thank you so much for your guidance,' she says to him, as he comes to, groaning, his blood pooling on the lino.

That evening is the farewell feast. Farewell to the home, the bright, moneyed Kensington neighbourhood, the buildings with their wedding-cake whiteness. Neela watches Rex as he hands out plates bearing pizza slices and uncracks a beer can from its plastic holding. She raises her camera and takes a photograph of him. She would like to be popular. Yet whenever she looks in the mirror she sees a strange creature, like those rare, hairless cats. As soon as the flash goes, Rex – as always – begins to hunch his shoulders and duck away from the lens, but by then it's too late. She photographs Gavin and Lukas rolling a joint at the other end of the table. It will be a relief to get out of this place, with its tired Seventies carpet and Oxfam-shop paintings on the walls, the depressing board-games and nylon bed-sheets. They have all outgrown it.

In a month their gang of four will be moved into the West Central Estate, blocks of red-brick flats arranged in a circle, facing inwards, with two wrecked cars and a skip in the middle. The estate is directly opposite a row of Grade II-listed Georgian houses. 'God, it's just a place where cookers and Ford Fiestas come to die, isn't it?' said Rex, the first time they went to check the place out. They had paced around in dead silence, despite the main road only yards away. 'Don't you notice something in the atmosphere?' Neela had asked him. 'It feels like nobody really lives here at all. I mean, humans inhabit the flats, of course, but it's really the buildings which are historic and alive and breathing, and if people move in they're somehow opening themselves up to the influence of the estate itself, not the other way around.'

Rex's voice jolts Neela into the present. He is holding his beer can high, calling for a toast. Neela lifts her glass of water. Rex yells, 'To our future!' but Neela slams down her glass before anyone has a chance to second his cry.

'You're joking, aren't you?' she spits, and everyone at the table freezes. 'We don't have a *future*, not like you mean. Those girls we see on High Street Ken have a future. We know how they're going to turn out: they'll have jobs, and cars, and houses in the country, and clothes and partners. We're about to move into a fucking council estate. We're not exactly making plans for our lives. All we've got is our *destiny*. All we've got is what life throws us when it's not busy giving other people promotions, and happiness, and money.' There is a brief silence.

'God, you're right,' says Lukas, sarcastically. 'Let's just kill ourselves now. I mean, since we all know how to shoot guns we can stand in a circle and execute each other.'

Unlike the others, Neela has never expected anything from life. She enjoys pointing out to the rest of the group just how meagre their beginnings were, and how narrow and dry the path before them lies. Tonight she drinks the clear water of truth while they swill cheap, intoxicating beer around their mouths. Let Rex and Lukas continue their charade of cheerfulness if they wish. It is a pretty enough illusion. They are possessed by the whimsical notion that the pursuit of happiness is worthwhile, even though their own history indicates the precise opposite. It has not been a past full of spectacular destruction, but quieter tragedies of pathos and torpor. The boys believe they love each other as brothers when in reality they are merely clinging together out of desperation, like shipwrecked sailors cast adrift in a convulsing dark sea. Neela likes to frighten them; at times it is as though she is observing their lives from a vantage point most untouchable and high, with an opinion wise and immutable. Occasionally, her intellect will attempt to liberate itself from the fatalism which she has adopted. Those moments are like chinks of sunlight between leaves. But more often the undertow reclaims her.

Lukas looks at Gavin, Gavin at Rex. It was as Neela said.

Whenever each of them tries to picture the coming years, all they can see is the tight circle of the estate, its black shadows and dank, echoing stairwells.

Marlon is forty-four years old. He now has many lines on his face. But the charged, athletic walk of his youth remains. He navigates the Kensington streets, his eyes shining with expectation. This is his city. There is not one corner of it he doesn't know. It feels as though his footsteps are shaking the pavements, jarring the earth, and that this mission, driven by colossal will, is not carrying him towards the home but rather thrusting *it* closer to *him*. This is the moment he has waited for, for eighteen years. Marlon will divest himself of his riches. It will be an act of mesmerising generosity for which he expects profuse thanks: a gift of crushing weight – wealth and power and pedigree. The legacy of his devotion. He breathes in deeply. The air has a chilly, overwhelming density. The dark winter night and the empty streets seem to be ready for him, ready for this encounter. Tonight, Marlon's appointed successor will undergo a ceremony of bequeathal.

Isobel died that night, while Marlon was in the room. She had lost so much blood that the entire bed was soaked. She clutched Marlon's arm for a moment, took a lucid, long look at the baby. Then her eyes turned glassy and her features stiffened as she fell back with a sharp jerk. It was the only time that Marlon had ever been disturbed by a death. All the petty killings he'd done by hand, as it were, and he'd never batted an eyelid. But this death was primal and vicious – it seemed to forcibly wrench Isobel out of the living world, giving her a tantalising glimpse of the child before tugging her back down.

He had known what to call Rex the instant he saw his face. The baby had a proud, somehow stately look. It seemed to genuinely *see* him, and had patted him upon the chest with his minute fist, as though giving benediction.

Marlon, whose body had been constructed for conflict and force, found himself cradling the child with excessive delicacy while trying to prevent himself from gathering it up in one hand and crushing it against him. An atavistic urge for concealment and flight made him want to bundle Rex into his pocket and make away with him. What he felt was not really love – or not love as he imagined love to be – more a vigorous, proprietary instinct which shocked him with its fervour and suddenness. It was a palpable, greedy emotion that had seemed to have a definite goal – that of total possession. Yet at the same time Marlon would have made himself poor to make the child rich. He had surveyed the bloody sheets and squalid room. Although generally immune to the complex choreography of other people's thought processes, the unplanned violence of the scenario briefly jolted his conscience into a kind of fevered insightfulness. Isobel had summoned him for a reason – to execute Alun's progeny and terminate the proliferation of innate cruelty which must surely have made its lair in his DNA. To shear from Alun's corrupt empire that terrible symbol of futurity and continuity which the baby represented.

But Marlon would not obey. Once it was lying nonchalantly in his grasp, the baby seemed utterly free of the rancour and strife that had created it. The child was innocent, soft, malleable. Its existence spoke more of Marlon's power than it did of Isobel's spite or Alun's brutality. Though technically the child of Isobel, it appeared now to have been the sole, inevitable result of a situation he himself had engineered. The product of Marlon's machinations – the fruits of his labour. To kill it would be to deny and thwart his own greatness, in a way. And Isobel was guilty too. The horror did not come entirely from Alun's corner. When she allowed the iron chain to be tightened around Jon Duke's neck, she ceased to hold any moral influence over the situation. She became as marked and spotted as the chain itself.

The baby had looked up at him with large, trusting eyes. Life had not yet imprinted them with any understanding of betrayal or hurt. Marlon began to weep again. If he abducted Rex in a spasm of possessive haste he would have damned the child's future as surely as if he had indeed slain it as Isobel wished. Its life would be one of treachery and theft. A range of despicable images presented themselves to Marlon: the impossibility of concealing the child from Alun, who would make Rex either a cherished apprentice or an abused slave; the prospect of himself cast in the absurd role of gruff tutor and warden; the shaping of a boy immersed from his first day in a life which shunned all beauty and negated any chance of perfectibility. It was ridiculous. The King of England was no place for children. And in any case, the boy was *his*. He was birthed from the vulgarity of Alun and the loneliness and guilt of Isobel, but he need not return to gore and outrage. He had committed no crime yet. He was paying no dues. Isobel, Alun, Marlon himself were all beyond salvation, but Rex was not. Marlon would give Rex the power to rebuff the circumstances of his own origination. Rex would be returned to the normal world as though meant for it and made by it. The secrets of his begetting would remain until he became a true man, at which time Marlon would lay upon him the price of this sacrifice, and summon him to his responsibility. Marlon would shape Rex's future for him, and the boy would be the channel of his supremacy. In the space of one generation the fortunes of villainy would become the foundation-stones of legitimate enterprise, executed by Rex but engineered by Marlon. Rex would bring purity to the race of Alun the Dragon.

36

It has been a long, lonely eighteen years. The first ten were spent the usual way, with Marlon attending to the daily business of the criminal world. But everything that had once looked impressive and cinematic about his life began to resemble a series of shabby tableaux; the midnight phone calls, intricate plotting and knot of loyalties seemed like the flimsy, disposable machinations of a B-movie villain. He was tired of turning up at the King of England every night, pacing the bar like a guardian knight at the portcullis, with a fake I'm-your-man smile. As Alun grew older he slowly began phasing himself out of the shadier dealings; he handed control of the place over to Marlon, who bought it freehold and then just barred it up, sealing the windows and doors and retreating to his white flat. For the last eight years Marlon has taken on only big jobs for close contacts, strictly freelance, and saved his money with all the miserliness of an old man stuffing banknotes under his mattress.

Now it is time to give Rex his due. To bare before him the site upon which he must labour. In lieu of affection he shall receive money. He will be Marlon's protégé, his mouthpiece, his successor. Rex has had eighteen years in the world of the good; now he will bring his reforming influence to The King of England. Marlon's imagination, which is largely constructed of monolithic, almost primitive images, associations and binaries, savours the idea of that venue simply having been sealed up, awaiting a new hand to restore it to the light. Of it occupying its original plot and maintaining a thick, patient silence whilst all around it the world altered. The moment has arrived. The boy will be bright and fierce. He will love and recognise Marlon with a burning, worshipful passion. There will be no question of his valour.

Marlon approaches the broad brick frontage of the orphanage, but none of the lights are on. Strangely, even from outside, the very building, with its indomitable squareness, thick oak door and outsized brass knocker, doesn't seem to embrace children. He can tell it is a place where their games and exuberant cries would be stifled by thick carpet and acres of curtain-dust. Perhaps he should have stolen Rex away after all.

Marlon walks down the side of the building and comes to the orphanage's 'grounds', a cement yard with wire netting around it. And there are the kids – adults, really – looking grotesque, penned into the childish environment, with its hopscotch squares marked on the ground. They are kicking a ball around. There is a vigorous wolfish boy with long dark hair. He looks like a Russian horseman, with his sharp, glittering expression. Then another boy on the edges of the game, tiny, bow-backed and creeping. Marlon moves into a thick shadow at the corner of the playground, which is lit with weak orange street-lamps. They seem to be playing with listless movements, as though drugged. When Marlon was eighteen, he had made himself utterly available to what life had to offer. He was never cynical. But these people have the air of souls hanging in purgatory, resigned and weary. There is a strange androgynous girl, Indian or maybe Oriental, with a cold, haughty look. Then, Rex strolls out and joins the game. At this moment Marlon tightly grips the wire netting. He knows it is him. Rex instantly resembles Isobel. He has her grey commanding eyes. The silvery-blond hair. The fine skin. The broadness and solidity of Rex's body are Alun's, but everything else, the slow movements and long-fingered hands – Isobel.

Neela has stopped playing. The ball lies on the ground by her feet and she stands transfixed. Her skin breaks out in goose-bumps. At the other end of the playground is a ravaged face and pale hands holding onto the netting. The eyes wear an ancient, hungry expression. The knuckles are dead white. Lukas sees what Neela is looking at and says, 'Ignore him.'

Lukas turns away, but the dark, devouring eyes sweep over his back and he shudders. Marlon whispers, 'Rex', but nobody hears. Neela has always been sensitive to the things other people can't see. The overbearing presence in haunted rooms, the secret symbolism of dreams. She's superstitious. To her, Marlon's face resembles some ghoulish death's-head, a corrupt spectre come to chain a few souls. 'Look, he's still there,' she says. 'Look at the way he hangs against the wire. Get him to go away.'

Lukas calls over to Marlon tauntingly, 'Grandmother, grandmother, what big eyes you've got,' but there is no response.

Gavin, grinning, pulls this morning's gun from his waistband and raises it towards Marlon. Before he has the chance to fire, there is a whip-crack sound and the entire gun seems to explode in his hand and jerk out of his grasp. It falls, mangled, onto the ground. Everyone looks over at the figure behind the net. In one white hand is a gun, the trigger-finger curled and ready to send another blast into the playground. But the eyes are sorrowful. In Marlon's time, there were rules. You never shot anyone for fun. You never killed anyone who didn't deserve to be killed. You operated eye-for-an-eye. You showed regard where it was due. But this rat-like boy would kill because it amuses him. He could have shot Marlon and they would all have stood around his body, laughing as he bled to death.

Marlon had wanted to come in peace, bearing gifts. He had fantasised that a basic, powerful memory would stir in Rex's mind, like a shark on the ocean-bed, and awaken some kind of elemental devotion. He puts the gun away, back into the folds of his black coat. 'It's Rex I want to speak to,' he calls out. 'The rest of you, don't worry about him. I'm a friend.' Rex looks at Marlon. There is an appalled look in the older man's gaze, a disappointment of some kind. Rex does not feel afraid. The two burning eyes attract him like tunnels leading to the strange, magical destiny.

Rex approaches the wire netting. Marlon watches him intently. In the orange-tipped darkness, Rex's eyes are long shadows. His steps are hesitant and he holds one hand up in front his face as though shielding himself from a fire. 'Don't be concerned,' Marlon says, and he surprises himself with the gentleness of his tone. In another life, perhaps, it is the tone he'd use all the time – with his children, his wife, his friends. But here he is instead, standing in the shadows like a leper. Rex stands opposite him and links his fingers over the wires. 'Don't you recognise me?' says the older man. 'I have something for you.'

Rex shakes his head. 'Who are you? I'm not sure I want it.' They gaze at each other.

'I knew your mother,' says Marlon, 'and your father as well. I have photographs. If you come with me, I could tell you all about them.' He clamps his hands over Rex's. 'I was there when you were born,' Marlon whispers. 'I've been waiting for you for eighteen years. I have so much to tell you. Climb over the net. Please. I want to see you properly.'

The touch of the cold, strong fingers sends a shock through Rex's entire body. He feels as though Marlon has rooted him to the spot – that he has earthed him, like a circuit, and the same bizarre electricity relays between them. He is totally unaware of Neela, Lukas and Gavin as they watch the curious scene from the other end of the playground. He feels like he's been hypnotised. Without thinking, he braces his foot against the netting, reaches up hand over hand and begins to climb.

Marlon bends over Rex's body, his hand on the boy's neck. Rex's face is slack and greenish. They are in a residential square,

40

a manicured patch of grass with a circlet of oaks in the centre. Rex opens his eyes. 'Are you alright? You fainted,' Marlon tells him, stroking his cheek, and Rex closes his eyes again.

'Don't touch me,' he says, 'just take me back. I want to be with my friends. I don't want what you're offering.' He sits up and wipes his hand over his face. The grass is damp and fog hangs low on the ground. 'Why did you come here? Just to tell me I have a dead mother who didn't want me, and a criminal father who doesn't know I exist? How does that help me? Do you think I'm happier now than I was two hours ago?' Marlon reaches out to help Rex up but he slaps his hand away. 'I told you, don't touch me. Just go away. I don't want your money. I don't want this stupid bar you keep talking about.' Rex stands up unsteadily and begins to grope for the iron gate. The darkness disconcerts him but it is Marlon's element. The older man moves about in it like a bat, deft and unseen.

Marlon appears, suddenly, his hand on the latch, and says, 'I thought there'd be some connection between us. I know I make you sick. I can see it. You think I'm some kind of monster.' Slowly, great, heavy tears rise in the dark eyes and begin to drop, one by one, down the weathered face. They roll over his lips and drip off his jaw.

'Well, what would you think?' Rex retorts, unable to look Marlon in the eye, shivering as the damp air sticks his clothes to his skin. He doesn't want to touch Marlon or push him out of the way. He is afraid of this stranger's body. 'Only a monster creeps about in the dark and hunts people down for eighteen years.' He stares Marlon full in the face. 'Why are you here? What do you want from me? Why do you keep looking at me like that, like a dog?' Marlon grasps both his shoulders and Rex gasps. Once more, he has that startling, live-wire sensation of having been plugged into the earth. The mist rises higher, up to their shoulders.

Finally, Marlon speaks, with a bitter laugh. 'Sorry. Sorry for frightening you.' He sighs. ' I spent eighteen years waiting for you to grow up, and I never really thought about you once, did I?' He opens the gate and walks through it, waiting for Rex. They turn towards the shadow of the orphanage. 'On eighteen birthdays I lit a white candle for you in my flat and I wondered what you looked like. I used to wonder what it would be like meeting you. I thought we could be friends.' He laughs again. 'Maybe we'd play football in the park. Maybe I'd buy you a visit to a prostitute for your birthday. I don't know.' Marlon's face is blushing.

They approach the orphanage playground again. 'Can I tell you one thing, though?' Marlon asks. Rex nods but takes a step back. Something about the gangster's presence make him feel as though he is sleepwalking to the edge of a cliff; he has to actively stop himself from falling. 'You said that I was a monster, and you weren't,' Marlon says bitterly. 'Well let me tell you once and for all, you're of pure monster blood. You're monster through and through. Even your mother was a monster in her own way. She could have left her boyfriend. She could have simply saved herself, but she didn't. She wanted to punish him too. Then she wanted me to kill you and put you in a litter bin. How would that have felt? If I'd picked you up and deposited you somewhere, like dogshit in a Poopa-Scoop? It only takes one very small thing to unlock the ogre in the attic. Remember that. And look to your own friends before you start on me. If your little pal with the acne had shot that beaten-up, second-hand revolver of his, none of you would have said anything, would you? None of you flinched when he took aim. You were all watching. Waiting for him to kill me. What would you have done then? You wouldn't have called the police, would you? You wouldn't have summoned anyone to help you. You would have found some shovels and stood in the fog digging me a grave. It would have been your little secret.' His expression hardens. 'Show some respect, Rex. Don't treat me like some interfering teacher who's trying to give you life advice. I've seen some of the most horrible things human beings are capable of doing to each other. Believe me, the line between being civilised and being a monster is very, very thin. And once you cross the line you can't go back.' He shrugs, suddenly exhausted.

They are back at the wire netting. They both look up at the orphanage. The others have all gone in and the ball lies neglected in one corner of the playground. Marlon presses an envelope into Rex's hands. 'Don't turn your back on me. I don't want anything from you. If you take my help, that's it. I just want to set you up in your life. I want you to be good. It's not a deal with the devil.'

Two weeks later, Lukas, Gavin, Neela and Rex stand at the entrance to the West Central Estate, an iron-barred gate between two brick pillars. The gate appears steep and rusty before them, opening with a sonorous clang. The pillars spread pointed shadows across the central courtyard, where two burnt, bent cars have been dumped next to an overflowing yellow skip. Lukas' quick eye alights on the debris. 'Look in the skip,' he says to the others, 'it's full of children's toys.' The toys are melted and burnt but they can make out a wooden dog on wheels, a dolly with shining nylon hair, a red tin bus. 'And there's blood on the cars,' Lukas adds, his voice high with nerves. True enough, along the blackened edges of the junked cars is another, unmistakable substance. It clouds the shattered windscreen and patterns the side windows. Around the courtyard are identical red-brick buildings: blocks of four or five flats with steps leading up to the main door of each. The blocks are so tightly packed together that they appear to be leaning over and inwards, as though trying to peer into the skip.

'OK everyone, we've wandered into Satan's grotto. I'm not living here,' says Rex, backing away from the gate.

Neela gives him a look. 'Get real,' she says. 'What are you going to do, phone up the council and say "I'm terribly sorry, the free central London flats you gave us are clean, spacious and in perfect working order, but we don't like the contents of the skip"? Get over it.'

'Don't you play the tough girl,' Rex shoots back. 'You hated this place from the moment you saw it. You think the buildings are all watching you and the walls are eavesdropping on your conversations.' Yet even as he's talking he begins to believe her; as each word leaves his mouth it seems to be eaten up and carried away, not lifted upwards to the bright harsh sun but pressed down, into the centre of the earth. 'Hey, shout something out loud, Lukas,' says Rex.

Lukas shouts, 'Beelzebub, honey, we're home.' No echo.

They have no choice, though. Moving in is easy as none of them have many belongings, and at the end of the afternoon they congregate in Rex's place. 'It's usually proper to celebrate in situations like this, isn't it?' he says, tentatively.

'No, not situations like *this*,' says Neela.

'What are we going to do?' Rex asks. 'What if we spend the rest of our lives here? What if we die here and we're still signing on? Oh, God.'

'What d'you mean, what if we die here?' Lukas snaps at him. 'You know exactly what'll happen. Someone'll discover our bodies and dump them in the skip, where they'll remain for the rest of eternity. End of story.'

'I know what you should do,' Neela says, giving Rex her X-ray stare.

Rex had returned after his meeting with Marlon, white and shaking. The man's talk about deviant blood had made him feel that one day his villainous genes would get the better of him, it was only a matter of time. In his room the next morning he had opened the envelope. For the most part, it was papers documenting the progress of an account Marlon had set up in Rex's name. His eyes had widened as he realised how much money was there. Other papers proved Marlon's ownership of the King of England, and its subsequent transferral to Rex. Finally, there were two photographs. One showed Isobel, her grey eyes cool and defiant, her chin held high, leaning against the bar at the King. Rex brushed his fingertips over the image. The other picture was of Alun the Dragon, wearing his red Hawaiian shirt. Marlon was right. Rex's daddy was monster to the bone – 'monster' written all the way through him like a stick of rock. Monster in the narrow, glinting eyes and shit-eating grin. Monster in the chest hair.

Rex shrugs. 'I don't know how to explain it,' he tells Neela. 'He told me there'd be no comeback if I took his help. And I believe him, technically. Nobody's gonna turn up and ask me to give the money back or anything like that. But you didn't see him up close. Every time he touched me I had this feeling, like he was trying to drag me towards something I was magnetically attracted to, you know, attracted in my bones, even though I knew it wasn't right.'

Neela crosses her arms. 'Rex, you talk like we have an alternative, like it's a clear choice between Marlon's fucked-up low-life magnetic voodoo boys-in-the-hood shit, and – whatever – a series of top jobs in the City with a company car and a fuck-off pay packet. Don't be so naive. The choice is, we rot in this pit or we take help where it's offered.'

Rex has never been able to say no, especially to Neela. She

has a way of making him feel like she knows exactly what he's been through, even the feeling of being jolted and held in the ground, inextricably connected with Marlon and his world. 'So you reckon I should fuck the consequences?' he asks her.

'Fuck them up, down and sideways,' she says. 'What's the worst that can happen? You lose a load of money that wasn't yours in the first place. The bar turns out to be a dump or a flop or both. So what? We're not talking about raping and pillaging and pistols at dawn. We're talking about running a bloody pub.'

Rex looks at Marlon's hands in the wan November light. The knuckles are hard and rough, the fingers strong. They are hands made for gripping, breaking, punching. Marlon holds a crowbar and uses it to lever the planks off the door of the King of England. He grunts as he slowly works each plank loose. His entire frame seems to attend to the action, the muscles lean and efficient with that wiry, old-man strength, as though his whole body enjoys the movement. Watching Marlon gradually revealing the entrance to the forgotten pub, Rex has the impression of something bestial and unhinged lying close beneath the gentrified surface, and begins to edge away. 'I don't suppose you fancy helping me, do you?' Marlon grunts, and Rex starts forward again, embarrassed. They reach up and lay their hands on the last, highest board, gripping with their fingertips. The cords along Rex's arm stand out as he pulls. The board begins to work itself loose. Rex grimaces as he feels the grain embedding itself into his fingertips, and pulls harder, working the plank in small movements. 'You're strong,' Marlon says, from some distance back, and Rex realises that he has been watching him. The board comes free in his hands.

After eight years, the King of England is finally open to the world. Marlon and Rex let in the sunlight, harsh upon the damp floorboards and dated furniture. The long bar is thick with dust, behind it rows of bottles mired in grease. A long mirror stands against the far wall. The air is stifling. Strange artefacts, previously used as ornaments, lie broken in one corner: a cracked hourglass, its sand blackened and clotted; an intricate clock, like something a Victorian mariner would have used, with brass dials and a compass; broken picture frames. Rex and Marlon stare at each other. Marlon says, 'We killed your mother's boyfriend in the back rooms. I didn't see it. I was standing over there with her.' He points to the bar. 'I bought her a glass of champagne. We did it with chains. I bought them myself from a hardware shop. It's not there any more.' He walks alongside the bar, then back to Rex. 'This was my patch,' he said. 'If anyone needed anything, they'd come and find me here. Once, I had someone killed behind the bar on New Year's Eve. One bullet in the head, using a silencer. Everyone thought it was a champagne cork being released. We left him there till closing time and nobody noticed. People just thought he was drunk. They couldn't understand why we suddenly called it happy hour and started selling shots at half price.' He looks around. 'It seems a lot smaller than I remember it.'

Rex has backed away, towards the door. He feels like an archaeologist standing at the mouth of a tomb, fearful yet fascinated, trying to understand its dark, ritualistic significance. The sun suddenly bursts in from behind him, dragging its bleaching light across the rotten boards. 'Here it is!' Marlon suddenly calls, and Rex jumps. Marlon holds a thick coil of iron links in his hands. He shows them to Rex. Fat, black ovals all in a row, heavy and rust-bitten. Rex stares, then realises what they were used for. He wants to say something, but no words come out. Marlon says, 'We used this to hang the sign outside.' He winds the ends of the chain around his hands and holds the length out, horizontally. 'It's really simple. What you do, you get the person on the floor, facing away from you. Then you drape it around their throat, like you're helping them put on a necklace. But you've got to make sure the lengths cross over at the front. It hurts more that way. Then, you just pull.' He acts it out with such precision that the entire scene – Jon Duke on his knees, the chain cutting into his throat, his airways pressing in on themselves – assembles itself in Rex's mind.

'Marlon, I'm sorry,' he begins to say, 'I think I must have got the wrong end of the stick or something.' His fingers are gripping the door frame. 'I'm not sure … what you want from me.' He tries to lighten his tone. 'I thought you just wanted to help me, but the whole world seems to want to turn me into a renegade. First the trip to the shooting range, now you showing me how to do someone in.' He nods towards the chain. 'I'll probably wake up tomorrow morning with a severed horse's head lying on the pillow next to me.'

Before Marlon can answer, the door to the back of the pub swings open softly. A long shape emerges from the dark, swaddled in something shapeless and white. 'Hello, you fine, handsome gentlemen,' says an educated, melodic voice which rings in the air. It belongs to a tall girl in a padded dressing-gown, plump and very beautiful. She seems to be of mixed origin: caramel-coloured skin and tightly curled gold hair, with large, dense-lashed amber eyes. She wears a row of gold hoops in her right ear. She gives a lazy, slow smile before slipping behind the bar and producing from beneath it a new bottle of vodka and three clean shot glasses. 'I'm so happy you're here. I don't like to be without people for too long. Now, let's have a little housewarming party,' she says. Marlon and Rex move towards her. She fills the shot glasses. There is something sun-like about her, rich and chemically striking. Rex, through a hormonal fog, sees an exotic girl with a mane of huntress hair. Marlon, with a leap of recognition, sees something quite different. It is as though time has doubled back and he is once more returned to the bar of Alun's heyday. There is something in the girl's intelligent, immovable stare which recalls the ambition and ruthlessness of his former colleagues – those knuckle-breakers and kneecappers who, Marlon believed, had died out as soon as The King of England was entombed. Those who flouted the difference between right and wrong so often that they had ceased to be aware of the division at all. Their lives were a series of transgressions and deviations which they performed as they needed, entirely for their own ends, without any twinges of regret or conscience. And this girl is the same. She pours out the vodka and pushes two shot glasses towards them. Here is a person infinitely capable of stealing, lying and hustling to get what she wants. There is no grain of introspection or timidity in her aspect. She would raze an entire city and emerge composed and smiling. Something about the way she looks at Marlon, a particular appreciative knowledge in those honeyed irises, secures his opinion. He looks back at her and nods his thanks for the vodka. It takes one to know one, his look says.

'Do hope you don't mind,' she says to them both. 'I noticed this place was untouched so I broke in the back way and set up home in the flat upstairs. I could have slept on the streets or squatted with other people, but I'm afraid I don't like dirt. And no matter what they tell you to the contrary, homeless people are pretty damn dirty.' She smiles at them and drinks her shot in one go, then straightens her arm out and looks at a thick gold bracelet on her wrist. 'I like things to be beautiful.' She reaches behind the bar once more and pulls out a tin tray. She takes from it a tiny plastic bag, the kind you get spare buttons in, only it contains coke. She offers it. Rex seems to have been struck dumb. Marlon declines but then leans forward, his elbows on the bar.

'So, little Gucci matchstick girl,' he says, 'we could use someone like you. Are you interested?' The girl laughs and puts the coke away. She drags her fingers along the dust on the bar.

'You know what I mean, don't you?' says Marlon, and he can see that she does. They stare at each other for a few moments.

'My name's Janine' she says finally, 'happy to be of service.' She looks at Rex, but holds out her hand to Marlon. 'You stick with me, baby,' she says, with a Bugsy Malone swagger, 'and together we'll reach the stars.'

Marlon has taken Rex to a shady, private bar. It is dark outside and the wind strikes the blacked-out windows. They are sitting together, knee to knee, in a booth lined with burgundy leather. 'What's this all about? You're not telling me anything. You said you were here to help me.' Rex is frowning. 'You acted like you knew that girl. Why did she give you that little smirk? Tell me what you were whispering about together when I went to check out the upstairs. Tell me!' He suddenly flings himself back, exhausted. 'This is like a really bad trip. We go to the pub, but it's not actually a pub, it's some kind of front for a load of stuff I don't even want to think about, and you tell me you killed a bloke during happy hour. Then we meet a girl, but she's not really a girl, she's some kind of sassy drug lord of the underworld, or whatever. Then you say, let's go for a drink, but this isn't really a regular bar, it's full of diamond dealers and pimps, isn't it?' He looks around. The room seems to be crowded with rich-looking men, all men, involved in intense discussions. The decor is heavily screened, stultifying and red. The men seem to know Marlon – as he and Rex took their places the sleek heads, all in turn, nodded a greeting. Drinks came to their table unordered.

Marlon is looking at him. Rex says 'What?', then feels something nudging his knee before being pushed onto the seat next to him.

Marlon whispers, 'Don't look down, just slide your hand across.' Rex shrinks back against the burgundy leather and edges his hand along. Then he gasps. His fingers close around something so cold it feels as though it's burning his flesh and eating into his bones. The shape almost resonates with its own weight. The metal seems to have moulded itself to his fingers. Marlon glances round the bar, then says, 'It's OK, quickly, you can look.' Rex casually casts his eyes down.

And there it is, clasped in his own hand. Long, keen silver giving off its own fierce light. Rex tightens his grip. It is so heavy it seems to stick to the seat, talismanic and eternal. When he lifts it, it seems to rise with its own slow power, like a great crane raising something from the sea. It casts a light around the booth and onto Rex's face. 'It's totally new. You have to make your mark on it. I ... procured it for you. There's nothing else like it in Britain,' Marlon is saying. 'I can see you like it. Go on, pass it from hand to hand. Get a feel of it. Make it your own. It's fully automatic, obviously. The most efficient machine of its size and class. If you have something like that going through life with you, you don't need friends, you don't need family, you don't need anything. Makes you feel like an emperor, doesn't it?' Rex nods as though underwater. The gun doesn't actually feel like it's his. It feels like Marlon, rendered in metal. It feels like a message from the other side – Marlon's side – a missive both persuasive and beautiful, urging him to *join us*. 'It suits you,' Marlon tells him, with something like fatherly love in his eyes. 'You've got wintry colouring, like your mother. Silver looks good on you.' Rex sees that he's faced with a choice: he could hurl the gun away, turn around and run, breaking out of this mesmerising, fractal pattern where events seem to fold out

51

and multiply like an infinite chain, or – what? Already, that farewell dinner at the orphanage seems like years ago. He looks down. The gun almost seems to be aware of him. It is now warm and snug in his palm, less like a monstrous, gleaming lump and more like a pet puppy, or another hand. *You don't need friends, you don't need family, you don't need anything when you've got a gun like that.* 'It's the same temperature as you now, isn't it?' Marlon is asking, his dark eyes massive in the red light. 'I'm so glad you like it. I was certain you would. I picked it out myself.'

Rex looks at him, his face slack, almost stupefied. 'You shouldn't have.'

2

In a private ward in Saint Teresa's hospital, Mayfair, Alun the Dragon lies back against the pillows and thinks to himself: I had a good run. I had good times. His tattoo now resembles a shrunken worm and his aged torso boasts shrivelled tits. He reaches over and takes a long, grateful pull on a cigar. Lung cancer or no lung cancer, Alun's going to have his smokes. A couple of months ago, during Christmas, he undertook the strange experience of organising his own funeral – where his body would go, what would be done to it, what sign would mark the spot. 'Right, that's my final project,' he had said at the time. 'I've worked hard enough these last seventy years, and this is the last thing I'm going to do. I even know what I'm going to wear in me own coffin. Now I deserve a break.' So this is his holiday, his time to kick back and spend some lazy days watching the surf and conversing with the ladies. This is Alun, sittin' in the dock of the bay.

He thinks back on his life with satisfaction. It only started to happen for him maybe in the late Seventies, early Eighties. Before then he was strictly small-time and his haunts were seedy, dirty, damp bunkers, the city's shabbiest drinking dens, where he would flog shitty drugs and hot stereos, tacky imported Eastern ornaments, bad wine, fake jewellery – fake everything. He didn't have money but he had a reputation. The King of England was his making, the first time he'd felt he could show his face to the rest of the world and shake off some of the muck he'd been dealing in before. He was Alun, innkeeper to the undiscerning. He owned something, he could call himself a businessman, a real man with real work to do. Someone people looked up to. And by then there was this other guy on the scene. By his right hand there was always dark-haired, dark-eyed Marlon, who sprang from nowhere – so intense and sharp that talking to him was like stepping over broken glass.

They turned the King of England into a huge success. It began to attract all the types of people Alun liked, the ones who added a bit of colour to the world: Jon Duke in his green velvet-collared coat; Isobel, that poor, pathetic, beautiful bitch, with her frosty smile. The King of England had become the place where anything was possible – anything, that is, which involved harming, cheating, deceiving or tricking others. Alun's motto was: there's always a way. People would come to him with the queerest requests, and after fifty or sixty phone calls Marlon would find a man willing to do the job. Those were the glory days. Marlon and him. It'd felt like they had the ability to challenge Providence at times. The power to choose who lived, who died, who made a fortune, who lost it. There was an intricate system of conventions they had all followed which had nothing to do with what was decreed in the court-rooms and Parliament. Complex codes of honour and shame, respect and insult. Their line of business had the ability to undercut the petty movements of most of the population. Marlon and Alun had dealt with man's most primal, naked impulses: greed, revenge, lust. And it had been a thrilling ride.

In the end, they hadn't really gone out with a bang. Marlon's usual charisma had shrunk back and folded in upon itself. So many nights at the King during that final stage – '92 or '93 – Alun had glanced over at him from his usual post at the entrance to the back rooms, and spotted him, his fresh face made ugly and bitter. People were becoming scared of Marlon, the gossip said. Marlon was getting too big for the King of England. And by this time Alun was too old for the game anyway. There was a sickly, cold feeling in his lungs. His voice was disappearing. He couldn't concentrate on and didn't really care about keeping track of the petty rivalries which played themselves out against the pub's frosted windows and velvet banquettes. Alun retired, thinking he was giving Marlon what he wanted – full control over the King. Now he could make his bid for greatness, unhindered, while Alun himself began to live – legally – off profits from his other part-ownerships.

Alun finishes his cigar and coughs. It seems to come right from the centre of his body, husky and dog-like. Surprisingly, Marlon didn't carry on with the King, he just kept the freehold and had the doors and windows blocked. Obviously, he had his sights set on something even bigger. Alun's face contorts with disgust. He never liked that sort of naked ambition. Alun likes to think of himself as having been a people-person. The crimes were there, every one of them, all with the appropriate charge, but primarily he was in it for the social life. Marlon had obviously wanted to strike out on an entirely new path, unrelated to anything from the past, to wipe out any hint that there had been other people helping him. Alun received news of him frequently, over the eight years between then and now. How as soon as Marlon left the King he began calling in the favours from each one of his associates over the previous decade, and took on huge jobs single-handed. He was known and respected on both sides of the line – a celebrity crim who could never be caught.

Old Marlon, eh, felled in his prime. Alun wipes away a tear. Poor Marlon, he didn't go with dignity. It wasn't a high-speed limo chase through the streets of Milan that got him in the end, not a slick killing with an unregistered gun. Not even a crime of passion – stabbed through the heart with a lady's stiletto heel. Nobody stuck him in a bucket of cement and toppled him into the river. Just one month ago – curtains.

He only stepped out for a pint of milk. He shut the door to the flat and pocketed his keys and wallet. He walked down Old Compton Street and went to cross to the other side when a black cab shot in from Greek Street. At the same time, a courier on a motorbike – a particularly shabby motorbike – jerked away from the kerb next to him. Marlon reared up and stepped into the cab's path. What a way to go: the victim of a cabby's over-enthusiastic use of the accelerator. Buffeted by that black front, simultaneously mown down by a bucking Yamaha. Word is that he was actually thrown under the cab by the bike. Right underneath the wheels, his body caught in the hot, spinning rubber tracks. He didn't die instantly. He screamed for a full minute at least, a continuous scream, full-blooded and feral. There's an urban myth about a guy who threw himself in front of a train. He was electrocuted, then he was chopped in half by the train. But he was still alive. He lay in the tunnel for a while, then pulled himself up to the platform, gripped the edge and screamed his head off until he eventually died. The stuff of nightmares. Marlon screamed – with fear, with sheer pain. A ring of passers-by stood and watched. Marlon, flower of London.

Alun lies back and stares at the ceiling and thinks again about his life. He knows there are things he did wrong, things he missed out on. Things that the other people in the hospital – with their flower-strewn rooms and rows of get-well cards – take for granted. Alun, Marlon, Isobel, Jon Duke: leaving the world without knowing what it's like to be wanted, needed, adored, touched. Well, too late to think about that now. It's not long before he meets his maker, before he gains entry to the most exclusive party there is. He sparks up another cigar and turns his face to heaven.

'Where did this fog come from? It's like something from a horror movie.' Lukas looks out over the courtyard. 'Even the bloody fog looks strange on this estate. Usually it disappears by noon but it's been like this all today and all of yesterday, hasn't it? It looks solid – like you could stick a knife in there and it'd stay. Like ... I don't know, translucent cheese.'

Neela looks at him. 'Translucent cheese? I don't think so. If this place really is some secret diabolical enclave, I don't think the idea of coating it in cheese would really appeal. You think one of Satan's minions came up to him and said, "O dark master of the deepest pits of hell, I know what'll really scare 'em. Translucent cheese!" Please.' But Lukas is right. The estate is dense with a kind of solid, pressing fog. It has a distinct metallic smell. From the steps of Lukas' flat, they can't even see as far as the skip. The burnt cars are just dense, flat outlines, like cardboard cutouts. The fog has distorted their view, and even more than usual the flats seem to be in a stage of perpetual advancement – creeping closer, tightening the circle.

Neela and Lukas are painting his front door in an attempt to instil his flat with a sense of homeliness, 'or failing that, I'd just like it to look normal.' Rex is at the King of England. Neela dips her brush in the tin of paint and begins to stroke it onto the door. The colour is beautiful, a red so rich and bloody it makes her want to taste it. They paint in silence, their hands cold and aching on the brush-handles. Every so often, one of them will glance around over their shoulder. 'I feel like I'm waiting to be shot,' says Lukas. 'You know, face to the door, no idea what's behind you.'

Neela nods, concentrating, red on red. She has to keep

stopping herself from darting her head forward and licking those glossy stripes. Eventually, she sits back on her heels and lays her brush across the rim of the tin. 'I'm convinced we're being watched. I mean, regardless of the atmosphere of the buildings themselves, I think the other people who live here are also on the lookout. We moved in maybe eight weeks ago, right, before the New Year, before Christmas, and not a single person's made themselves known to us.'

Lukas gives her a look. 'Just tell me something nice. Tell me one nice thing. It can be about anything you like.'

Neela takes her brush and starts up again. She spreads the colour higher and higher until she is kneeling up and leaning her free elbow on one knee, like a troubadour. After a couple of minutes, she says, 'No, I can't think of anything. I've tried, but I just can't.'

Lukas sighs. He too is kneeling up and together they layer on more of the thick, shining red. Neela wants to press her whole body against it, pulling up her sweatshirt and laying her bare torso onto the cold, fresh paint. The door seems to glow in the fog. 'Oh, I can think of a nice thing!' Lukas suddenly exclaims. 'My little brother's going to be staying with me.' He stands up and frowns as he paints the topmost section of the door. 'His name's Victor. He's just come out of a detention centre. I think he's ripe for my reforming influence.' He smiles to himself. 'I love him.'

Neela snorts. Lukas has a striking, animalistic appearance which he does not seem to be aware of. When they are walking around town, the young man's energy and glowing paleness, and his dark, long hair, draw awed stares from teenaged girls. They think he will be one to serve them a little rough, randy love. In reality, though, he is of such facile and dependent mettle that Neela finds her voice heavy with scorn whenever she speaks with him. Once his devotion has hitched itself to something, be it a person or an object, it hangs there and cannot be budged. His open idolatry of Rex mobilises her with a feeling that is eight parts disgust, two parts wistfulness at Rex's privilege in being so glorious to another's eyes. But Lukas is, basically, a drip. He repeatedly presents his company and friendship to Neela, in the mode of a slightly stupid puppy, although he finds her frightening. She in turn likes to maul and tease him.

Lukas asks, 'Where's Gavin, today?' and she shrugs: 'Oh, he's off killing children, or whatever he does when he's out. I don't actually know where he goes.' She's about to say something else when Lukas suddenly elbows her in the ribs.

They both turn around. In front of them, all down the steps, is the rest of the paint. Even though they chose it themselves, and used it just one minute ago, it looks so much like blood that they're both struck dumb. The paint seems to gather and clot, moving lazily before settling. It spreads slowly, languorous as a femme fatale. They stare at it, transfixed. It isn't just one shade, but several, some deeper, others almost iridescent. They tell themselves it's just paint. But it looks so much like blood.

On one of the middle steps is a huge, fat man in a black T-shirt and dirty tracksuit bottoms. His arms are beefy in size and colour. He stands there, quite still. The fog blocks off everything beyond the steps, making it seem like he's standing in front of a blank screen. The man has an oblong face, a loose wet mouth and eyes small and sharp as iron filings. 'New meat,' he whispers. Neela shudders. The man has the kind of hissing, telephone-pervert voice that doesn't so much make a noise as press its words into her skull by suggestion or osmosis. 'New, dark meat,' he whispers again, looking straight at her, 'come to join our friendly neighbourhood. And you too,' he turns to look at Lukas. 'You, long-hair. What are you? Eastern European, is it?' Lukas doesn't do anything and the man continues, 'Shouldn't you be on the tubes? It's your peak hour now. Go on, long-hair. You can put the money in your empty paint pot.' The man smiles to himself and rubs his hand over his belly. His body is so fleshy it looks like a pornographic gesture. 'I'll tell you something, youse two. I've been here a fair while. We all have. And we don't like you people. That is to say, we don't want your company. We don't like the look of you refugee-types. I saw you on the first day, peering into my skip. Well, you're not going to find anything interesting in there –' He goes on. By now, he's simply mouthing the words, and without realising it Lukas and Neela have leant forward to listen.

Next to her, Neela can feel Lukas' confusion. He's naive. He has gone through life in his mercurial, happy way. He couldn't even begin to understand the fat man and his lisping, sibilant rhetoric. Neela has lived with fat man her whole life. Fat man in different disguises: shop attendant, bus conductor, partygoer, police officer. Cleverness doesn't work with them. It wouldn't matter what she was: writer, artist, politician. They just see a street-beggar. A boat-person. She takes a breath and finds herself whispering back, 'No.' That word unlocks her courage, uncracking the dryness of her throat. It feels so good to say no to the fat man. 'Can you hear me, bully boy? We're not going anywhere.' Now fat man finds himself leaning closer. 'Come on, ghostface, you listen to me for a change. We're here to stay.' It feels as though her whole body's pounding with adrenaline, even though they're just whispering in the fog. 'We're here now, and things are different. I promise you, white-o, whiteface, one day I'm going to round up all the refugee-types I know. Every nigger, every paki, every chink, every wog. It's going to be a fucking week-long refugee street party. Yes? And we're going to find you. You wait. We'll be at your door. I'm tired of people like you, paleface. One day soon there'll a backlash, a riot, something. We'll find a way. Every copper, every honky – we'll hunt you out, and when we're done there'll be nothing left. Nothing recognisable anyway. I'll find a huge, smelly, illiterate paki to fuck your corpse in every hole, and some niggers to shit in your mouth. How does that sound?'

The fat man and Neela look at each other in the mist. Their faces are close together, like lovers. A certain understanding seems to pass between them. Then the fat man starts to laugh. He throws his head back, and even though his whole body shakes with the hilarity of it, his laugh is the near-silent spittle-rattle of a cartoon snake. His hand shoots out and takes Neela by the throat. It tightens slowly. He drags her towards him. His slack, wet mouth is spread in a broad smile and she gets a good look at every one of his tiny, perfect teeth. 'No, little missy,' he whispers, 'I think you've got it wrong.' His massive hand takes up the entire space between her shoulders and chin. As he begins to squeeze, she feels the blood boiling in her face. She wonders how much time she's got left before she suffocates. Her temples start to throb. Fat man begins to lift her up, off the ground. Her hands are gripping his wrist and she sees how pathetic they look, tiny wan fingers against his red skin. 'I am the hunter and you are the quarry.' He's speaking very slowly, as if to a stupid child. 'It can be our little game. I'll find you, wherever you go. Every step, I'll be at your heels. Every time you look over your shoulder, I'll be there. You wait, Miss Thing. It won't be long. It may even be now. Feel that, do you? Go on, what does that feel like?' He begins to shake her. She flies back and forth like a rag-doll in his hands. She tries not to breathe, to simply go with the movement, but the way he whips her about makes her gasp with pain. She sees Lukas from the corner of her eye: fat man has him kneeling on the ground. He

61

grips him by the hair, like a caveman. Then her vision beings to cloud.

Fat man's hand abruptly slackens and Neela drops to the ground. Lukas also stumbles back, clutching his scalp. There is a tearing, gurgling sound and fat man takes one pace forward then plummets, his chin on the top step and his eyes wide open. At first it looks like he's got a huge red smile on his face, then they see: his throat is cut, ear to ear. He looks like the man with a flip-top head from the toothpaste ads except that in this case there is blood literally pumping out of the gash. It pumps so hard the whole scene appears to throb: the step, his face, his body all seem to be working, push-pull, to expel it. It mixes with the paint and spreads across the landing.

A hand reaches out of the fog. It is very beautiful for a moment, golden-skinned and strong, seeming to sail out of the hostile whiteness. Neela grasps it and it lifts her to her feet. The same with Lukas. Then a face appears, smiling, and Neela gasps. The stranger looks like her double, even his body, muscular and lithe. But his eyes are brown, not green. And, she realises with sudden keen pain, he is very beautiful; a millimetre's difference here and there results in her being hideous, he beautiful. Lukas is gazing up at him with utter, abject gratitude.

The stranger smiles. He holds a knife in his other hand, precisely the kind of serrated, gun-magazine weapon Rex had mocked at the shooting range. The blade is red with blood, as is the hand, and most of the golden forearm. Neela looks down and realises they are all standing in a shallow puddle of blood-paint solution. The stranger says, 'I can't stand violence.' Then he laughs gaily. He is a marvellous creature, Neela thinks with bitterness, so fiery and grand. Their physical similarity prompts in her an immediate unwarranted loathing of him. It is almost as though the stranger has been produced by witchcraft or by the elements, like a mirage or a hologram created in her form, simply to needle and torment her with his brilliance.

He introduces himself as Leo before reaching into his back pocket and taking out a packet of cigarettes and a lighter. He is wearing a fitted white T-shirt and expensive-looking grey flannel trousers. Of course he does not feel the cold, Neela reasons. Leo is obviously some kind of bionic man, who registers no pain. Come to the estate to help them, to redeem them, to save them. He says, 'If you're going to be violent, be cool at the same time, no? This person, he had no sense of style.' He nods at the fat man, then casually rests his foot on the bloody head. Lukas is by now behaving like a lovestruck schoolgirl – his mouth stretched into the wet, overlong smile of an imbecile, his eyes limpid. Neela can barely look at Leo any more. He radiates a virility which stings her senses and makes her want to back away from him. The intensity of her hatred for this newcomer startles her. It fills her so swiftly and completely, it is as though she had been storing it up for years, in anticipation of his arrival. Every beam of suppressed agony within her personality has immediately found and affixed its focus upon him. His face, his clothes, his friendliness, his utter lack of fear. His strong, knife-gripping fingers. Neela wants them all so badly that she instantly becomes repellent to herself, because she hates desperation. How can he cut someone's throat and stand there smoking a fag, making witty banter, his trainer poised on the dead man's head? She would look like a clown if she tried to emulate him.

They come off the steps and stand for a moment looking at the mess they've left. The entire estate seems to vibrate, appalled by what has occurred. The sense of people watching from behind their curtains is stronger than ever. A dislocating silver light is cast over the scene, making it look like Lukas,

Neela and Leo are observing a painting: the sprawled body facing the landing as if reaching for something; the red door like a defiant flag; the paint, or blood, whichever is which, pooling top and bottom – glistening, drying, textured.

'Put him in the skip,' Neela says. 'It's what he deserves. He said it was his anyway.'

'No,' says Leo, and Neela bristles. She wants to turn to him, her eyes glinting, and say, *Don't you say 'no' to me in that tone.* Instead, she just looks at the body as he continues, 'It'll smell. Just leave it to me. There's an industrial dumping ground quite far from here that'll be perfect. There's a hole in the fencing round the back. I'll stick him under some vats of caustic acid or Sellafield bubble-wrap or whatever people dump there. I can take him tonight in the van.'

Neela takes off her shoes and runs into her flat. She returns with her camera and starts photographing the flip-top fat man. Lukas looks at her with disgust, Leo with interest. They don't say anything. She raises the camera to photograph them and as she does so she swoons for a second. Her hands drop and her camera hits the ground. Leo darts forward and grabs her. 'Go and lie down,' he tells her. 'Lukas here can help me move in and get rid of the body,' and Lukas nods with exhilarated, ostentatious humility. Neela can tell from Leo's hand on hers that he is immensely strong. He delights in movement and force and action. When she picks up the camera and retreats in the direction of her flat she turns a final time to see him sliding open the door of his white van, straining his whole body into it as though he were furling the sail of a great ship.

Marlon's apartment doesn't seem like the abandoned abode of a dead man. It hasn't had time to settle into staleness and dust. It still smells of him. His clothes hang in the wardrobe. There is a dirty mug on the table, daily rubbish in the bins. An open book of colour-saturated photographs. Rex walks around gingerly, looking inside cupboards and scanning shelves. Marlon had meant to visit him one night a month ago, and he hadn't turned up. Rex had waited by the window all night. After three more days and nights of waiting, he went to Marlon's apartment where the door was opened by a woman with a cerebral, lawyerly face. She told him about the accident and he rushed out of the hall, blind, only to find himself standing on the street corner at the exact spot of the accident. He returned to Marlon's pad, to be told that it now belonged to him. At that precise moment, with the lawyer's eyes trained on him in an attitude of professional sympathy, he'd had the sensation not of liberation – since Marlon was technically out of the picture – but of being under his influence more strongly now than ever. Having passed out of this life, his erstwhile benefactor had now entered the realm of legend and myth. Marlon would come to represent an entire depraved milieu, a sphere which Rex was even now struggling to hold off even as he became more entrenched in it. The situation could not have been more successful in terrifying him if it had been deliberately contrived. Life was dealing him a series of impeccably vicious shocks. Rex liked to think of himself as a somewhat hapless protagonist, powerless to halt or hinder whatever befell him, but this was hardly an inconsequential pastoral adventure. Marlon would remain in the darkness, more sinister and terrible than ever before; his power over Rex would grow with infinite strength, unchecked by the deglamorising idiosyncrasies of regular interaction. It's like he was hearing voices in his head. He felt Marlon's presence burning right at the centre of his brain, willing him forward, pushing him, goading him. Decisions seemed not to come from him, Rex, but from Marlon. He went

65

to the King of England, found Janine, and offered her the flat in return for helping him to resurrect the bar.

Already, Rex has begun to think like a desperate man. He may not yet have committed any specific act which establishes his allegiance with the mores and subtle distinctions of Marlon's world. But the mentality is there. An extreme, paranoid anxiety has now been driven into Rex, prompted by the discovery of who his parents were. Precisely the opposite of what Marlon planned has happened. Instead of an urge to re-make the past, to not merely discard but actively amend it, Rex has submitted to it. He has surrendered himself with complete, though horrified, passivity. A particular flaw deep in his character – a slightly suicidal willingness to be mastered – finds the ruthless barbarity in the King of England's history equally abhorrent and difficult to deny. The tale of Alun, Jon Duke and Isobel chimes in his mind with a certain unconventional but clear logic. There is something almost comforting in the predictable pattern of devastation and reprisal. It is something that can be relied upon, like a family curse. It absolves one of responsibility. He could quite simply and easily sell the bar. Within one month, it would be off his hands. But somehow that is not an option, it is merely a technical possibility. There would be some kind of punishment, he is sure, if he denied his inheritance. From beyond the grave, Marlon would mobilise a plague or vicious scourge to indicate his wrath and displeasure. The windows and doors of the King of England have been unsealed at this time for a reason, and they will not again be barred until this chapter of its ongoing story has reached its conclusion. Janine assumed her new role not simply without demur, but as though she had been waiting for the call. Marlon had after all selected her specifically for such a task, since the two were evidently forged from the same gleaming ore.

Now Janine turns up at Marlon's place for the first time, startling Rex. 'How did you get in?' he asks. She grins and goes over to the futon, immediately reclining on it with her feet up.

'I picked the lock. Always remember, anything that's been made can be unmade. Locks, computer systems, any type of machinery. The chances are, the person who put them together in the first place was probably some antisocial geek with Sellotape holding his bottle-end specs together, and there's no way I'm going to let someone like that get the better of me.' Rex looks at her lazing there, her hair fanned over the white cotton. She has an indolent manner which makes a luxury of any activity, like a lion – languid and solid. She lacks any respectful sense of the flat having only recently belonged to someone else – someone, moreover, who died in tragic circumstances. As far as she's concerned, he's given it to her, and so it is hers, and the future begins with her. Janine's is the kind of anarchic, self-loving nature that can conquer Rex's own, make it weak, awe it into obedience. He realises that.

Yawning and stretching, Janine gets off the couch and goes over to the rail of Marlon's clothes. She flicks from hanger to hanger, her fingers delving into pockets and searching out labels. 'These are amazing clothes,' she says, 'you should take them.'

Rex says, 'Take them? Take them where?'

'No, I mean you should wear them. They'd probably fit perfectly. Come here and I'll tell you which ones to try. Look, hold out your arms. Then you can give me a fashion show.'

There is nothing Rex wants to do less than wear his dead patron's clothes. His first instinct is to burn them, but that, he realises, is precisely the kind of Satanic, after-hours, superstitious thing Marlon himself would have done. No, the normal reaction would simply be to wash them, fold them and sell them to the nearest second-hand designer label shop. 'I don't really want to, Janine. I'd feel funny about it,' he says, but she looks at him with genuine incomprehension.

'Honey, he's dead. He hasn't gone on holiday, he's finished, over, kaput. He only needs one outfit, and he's wearing it right now, in a box in the ground. These clothes are stunning. It seems simple to me. You can either throw them out or you can do the smart thing and gain from the situation.' Janine's life has been worse than Rex's, because its sudden downturn was so unexpected. She started out more privileged than most, the daughter of a Ugandan diplomat and an English teacher, from whom she got, respectively, her golden colouring and her plumpness. While she was growing up they had moved all over the world, two years or so a time, and there was a lot of money around. When her mother died, money taught her about good clothes and good food, and money was her constant companion. When she changed schools and bedrooms, money eased her troubles. In any new place, it bought her friends. To allay her shyness she gave herself the image of a little adult, someone well-travelled and debonair who could take on anything the world threw at her and had a soul as old and wise as the pyramids. Eventually, through sheer force of determination, she actually became the image, and it felt like there was nothing she couldn't do. She attracted attention – and bitter-sweet jealous gossip – wherever she went. Then her father died, when his chauffeur-driven car slid off an icy road and into a tree one night in Washington. The chauffeur survived, her father was killed instantly. She will never forget that call: 'Sorry, miss, I have to tell you something … the road was very slippery, it was dark, and there was a tree.' If it had been someone else's father, it might have seemed laughable. In shock, Janine bought herself a plane ticket to London where she rented a fabulous Hyde Park-side apartment until her money ran out.

At the lowest point in her life, Janine bought six grams of coke with the last of her money, thinking that if she was going to end it all it might as well be in style. Instead, she gatecrashed a do at a Soho drinking club, had the night of her life and managed to sell the stuff at a profit. People were willing to pay more than usual simply for the novelty of having a dealer who was 'walkable' – that is, someone they could bring to their own parties, who wouldn't embarrass them. Someone beautiful, talented, witty, clever, educated, just like them, but with the bonus of that essential link to another, shadier world. Magazine editors and corpulent coke kings alike patronised her, and her business grew. She had very little money but a high profile. And now here she is. About to give the dealers of London a new focus for their work. 'You're not getting this place for free, you know,' Rex had warned, and she had said, 'I know that. You just have to leave it to me. I'll make you a success.'

Rex comes out of the bathroom in one of the suits Janine has given him. He felt like some kind of morbid pervert, sliding his feet down Marlon's legholes. Usually he's in sportswear, nondescript boy clothes which only look good on him because of his height and body. He feels like a child who's been trussed up for church. He stands bashfully as Janine looks him up and down, then gets him to give her a twirl. 'I like your looks,' she tells him. She takes him and places him in front of the long mirror in the living room. He stares at himself and doesn't say anything. Janine appears behind him in the reflection. 'Tell me you don't like it. Just say the word and we'll pack them all up and get rid of them. Tell me you think you look ugly in them and we'll forget the whole deal.' Her voice is like a chant. 'There are coats, belts, casual stuff. This guy really liked his fashion.' He

69

continues staring. She gets exasperated: 'Are you blind? Don't you like being beautiful?' Yes. Yes, Rex likes what he sees. Like Narcissus, staring into his own reflection, closer and closer, falling into danger and pleasure. He had thought that after care he might get a job in a shop. There was an entire range of no-brain things he could have done: bartender, postman, kitchen-hand. Now he is wearing a three-thousand-pound bespoke suit in dark, smooth silk. He stands staring out of the window while Janine dresses him, sliding a belt through the loops, brushing down a woollen coat.

'It's so gloomy out,' he says dreamily, a few times. He tries on every single item of clothing in a stupor, drunk on his emergent vanity. Eventually the ring of his mobile phone breaks the spell and he talks – it's Lukas with a strange story about a serrated knife and some paint – while Janine trawls through the rest of Marlon's belongings, deciding what she's going to keep.

Lukas and Leo are on their knees, scrubbing like scullery maids. The fog seems to have thinned. It's beginning to get dark and all they have is the light from the landing. Their lungs are full of white spirit fumes. 'It won't come off,' says Lukas.

'Yes it will, I've done this a million times,' grunts Leo, a film of sweat on his forehead. Lukas looks at him for a beat. 'No, not the blood. The paint. We'll just have to leave it. Anyway, I feel a bit wobbly.' He stands up slowly and then sees a figure coming in the gate. In the black suit and long winter coat it looks exactly like Marlon when he came to the orphanage playground.

Standing between the two stone pillars Rex can identify the precise point at which the atmosphere of the street changes to the atmosphere of the estate. The smell, the temperature, the sounds are all different. The courtyard seems to have something else in it making the place seem even smaller: a dirty white van.

He sees a movement and a light, and realises Lukas is waving and calling to him: 'Hey, smoothie. Nice suit. Thinking of picking up some laydeez and going on to a casino later?' Rex smiles and waves back. All the way home, people were taking little looks at his clothes, he was certain of it. He thought he noticed a distinct difference in the way he was treated in shops, too. Lukas continues, 'So, where's this superwoman we've all been hearing about? Don't suppose she got killed too did she? We could make it a hat-trick. Marlon, fat man and super-woman.' Rex begins to explain, coming forward, then notices the figure next to Lukas. On first glance he thinks it's Neela. It has the same runner's body that gives the impression not so much of brute strength as agility, pulsing, drawing forward and back as he scrubs. The stranger has glossy olive skin and large, well-articulated, masculine hands.

'Oh,' says Rex, 'you must be Lukas' knight in shining armour.'

Leo stops his work, turns around and grins, 'Yeah, but I don't have a white horse – only a van with Help Me written in dust on the back.' He gets up and they shake hands, smiling at each other. Leo is shorter and narrower, with a hard, keen country boy look where Rex is pale, broad and classical, but they seem to complement each other, Leo the gold and Rex the silver.

They go to Rex's place and start drinking. Leo exhibits an ability to talk at length without requiring any external encour-agement or response, and Rex watches the handsome smiling mouth as it produces anecdote after aphorism. He, like Lukas, will be happy to place himself beneath the tutelage of this new arrival. There is something in the stranger's demeanour which dulls the intensity of the fatman's death and refigures it as theatre or performance. Lukas tells Rex in greater detail about the events of the afternoon – the man in his dirty jogging bottoms, the unexpected incision and the tumble on to the stairs – yet the shock he feels manifests itself in a perverse urge to laugh. Here is a new type of thug, a different breed from Marlon's humourless ilk. One who cloaks his misdeeds in comedy and farce, embellishing the raw details of each episode with irony. A child of the carnival. Leo is the type who would commit an act simply for the storytelling possibilities it could incur. There is no psychology at work behind the actions themselves, Rex believes. They seem like sport to Leo – a brief but acute joy, as in a dance.

Their new neighbour has a taut, trip-wire quality to him that produces a sharpening effect on Rex's mind. He has a sensation of being utterly alive. He realises suddenly how far he, Lukas, Gavin and Neela must have allowed themselves to become affected by the estate's spectral atmosphere, with its implication of an imminent uncanny, doomed fate. The arrival of Leo will bring with it, he is sure, a return to felicity and mischief. He may even provide a means to break the chafing cord Marlon has strung between Rex and the past. He seems a character free from the dogma of ancestral fear. 'So,' Rex asks quietly, 'I take it that throat-slitting's one of your party pieces?' Leo grins. It is difficult for Rex to look at his face clearly because it is so similar to Neela's, like a reflection in slightly rippled water. But Neela's strange green eyes are hot, crystalline with secrets and unvoiced feelings, while this man's brown ones are opaque. Leo shrugs: 'I've worked as a bouncer in clubs. A trouble-shooter. Not one of the beefy types you get on the door. They can't really move fast, only punch you so hard your face turns inside-out. But they pay people like me to stay on the edge of the dancefloor, inside. We're meant to blend in with the crowd. If there's any trouble, we've got an open brief.' He has a habit of smiling and talking at the same time, all in an impersonal, undulating, generalised tone. The eyes are flat and do not become suffused with merriment when he laughs. It is part of their beauty: they remain slightly cold.

They carry on drinking in silence, until Lukas exclaims, 'Oh, hey, Leo, show Rex what you did today.'

Thus Rex receives his second lesson in how to eliminate an unwanted person. Lukas acts as the fat man, and instead of the serrated knife – which is soaking in Leo's sink – they get a long vegetable knife from the kitchen. Leo, like Marlon, has a kind of fierce, double-jointed quality to him that makes every action look a little too convincing. Rex sits on his dingy sofa, wincing, as Leo stands behind Lukas, grabs his hair and pulls his head back. 'Right, the best way to do it,' he explains, 'is to kick the guy in the back of the knees so he's below you and you can get some leverage. Now, you press the point of the knife into the neck just below the ear, on this soft bit here. Push it right in as far as it'll go, and keep the blade high, as close to the jawline as you can get. Then, you have to make like you're slicing up a huge melon. Get a firm grip and sweep the knife all the way round as smoothly as possible. Don't forget, the point stays at the back of the throat and you slide the rest of the blade round until you're at the other ear. If you've gone too low and you meet resistance, or if you're using the wrong knife, you'll have to do a bit of sawing, but that's the general principle. After that, the head should flip right back. You gotta mind out for the blood though. It really pumps, and if you're holding the body upright you'll cop it in the face.' Rex notices that Leo's face has become animated by passion, and that he handles the knife with small caressing movements. The smooth pallor of his tanned skin gives way to two rosy patches on his cheeks and his ringing voice takes on the exaggerated aspect of a puppet in the role of a diabolical though sardonic foe. He is enjoying this little

73

show. Suddenly, Leo's nature becomes transparent to Rex. He sees it clearly, almost psychically, the absolute boisterous enjoyment the newcomer takes in carnage and war. In that moment, Rex becomes totally convinced that Leo has arrived to take up the position of accomplice, to complete their faction – although against what he doesn't know – and effect the group's final severance from the laws and lores which restrain the rest of the city. Yet he does not find him foul. Leo's frank physical beauty alchemically converts his savage charade into a wry masquerade, mannered and comical. He exerts his dominance over the rites of sacrament and civility which surround death.

They go down to the courtyard. The paint residue on Lukas' steps looks macabre, and less like the remainder of some unfortunate domestic event than a curse or blight on the flat, placed there by God. 'I don't fancy stepping over that every time I go in or come out,' Lukas says, staring at it. 'It looks like a huge bloody hand's going to come out of the red and pull me down.'

'Oh, for fuck's sake,' says Rex, angrily, 'how did we get to a point where I'm wearing one dead person's clothes, we're about to look at another dead person, and the only things we can think of to talk about are guns and blood and killing? I don't understand how this happened. We've killed someone. Leo did it, but he's one of us now. We're killers. We don't even feel guilty.'

Lukas looks at him and his eyes go cold for a second. Then he shrugs, 'You said it, Rex. We don't feel guilty. That includes you. So, you tell me.'

They're interrupted by the noise of the van door. It slides open and Leo stands deferentially, presenting the body then moving to one side like a cabaret compere. 'Jesus.' Rex moves in closer as he eyes the recent corpse. They are in the big league now. Rex stares into the van. The slit neck alters the proportions of the fat face. His whole neck seems to be smiling with uncontainable joy, and then there is a smaller, stranger mouth above it, stiff, blue and stretched. No more hissing words into people's brains. No more threats in the fog. Rex can't tear his eyes away. Now they are killers. Rex steps forward and slides the door shut. 'Go on,' he says to the other two, 'take him away. And make sure you hide him well.' He too can feel strangers looking at them from their windows, straining to see in the dark.

A week later, Leo is standing in the front room of the King of England, looking around thoughtfully. Where Rex sees only junk and dubious stains, Leo notices the high ceiling and the sun's perfect aim into the room, lush white light making the old furniture look stark. 'Yes,' he says, 'I could really make something of this – I mean, we could make something of it. How much money are we talking?' Rex shrugs and hands him a pile of papers. Leo looks through them and then stares at Rex. 'Coutts. You're banking with Coutts. It's the bank for rich people.' He sits down at one of the old tables and starts writing down lists of numbers, a look of barely restrained greed on his face. 'What d'you fancy?' he asks Rex. 'Ten BMWs or five Ferraris? A prime-real-estate palace in Beverly Hills, plus staff, or an entire sprawling Continental home carved entirely out of white marble. Or a lot of prostitutes. The choice is yours.' A moment later, he adds, 'This is all set up as a business account. You need to go and certify who's allowed to access it. Whoever sorted your finances out, they totally knew the score.'

Rex had received all the documents in the post a couple of days ago. When he saw them, he just wanted to put them in the bin and forget the whole thing. He has never, not once in his life, desired to be a businessman or an 'operator'. He wanted a quiet, background job where people tell him what to do.

Something where he has to wear an apron and a servile expression. Now he is pacing his business premises, casing the joint. And who are his staff? Leo and Janine, who appear to have no discernible moral standpoint; Neela and Gavin, who will do whatever causes the most damage to the greatest number of people; and Lukas, who's out of his mind.

They go to inspect the other rooms, armed with architects' plans of the place. It is a lot bigger than Rex had thought: there are two decent-sized rooms out back, and a staircase leading up to a sort of living quarters. 'We should get the licence extended, knock through all the interior walls and create a kind of private drinking club with two huge, open-plan floors. Good plan?' Leo asks. It is he who belongs here, standing on the stairs, his face and body so lean and prepared for labour. He would be magnificent, his shirt off, hauling furniture to and fro in the sun. Rex is tired just looking at him. Coming back to this place without Marlon's protective company, he has been instilled with an agitation that borders on insanity and is so extensive that it overtakes him completely. It presses deep upon his greatest flaw: the tremulous passivity which evokes a near-narcoleptic condition. He understands how someone could faint from terror alone; this primal fear infects him with the urge to fall asleep, to disconnect himself and plunge into an unthinking void. Most menacing is the knowledge he has of this enterprise being his by force and not choice. It has been thrust into his hands. He has been selected, hunted, named. It is not simply an architectural undertaking, as Leo sees it – a jape, to be enjoyed and relished with a competitive, tigerish spirit – but a clear reinstatement of power that has been eighteen years in the making. He is being returned to the place of his spiritual if not physical conception. The site where Jon Duke, Alun the Dragon, Marlon and Isobel Aurora Paine came together one summer night. Today there is no precise source to his unease, only the distressing images conjured by his own imagination. In place of memory a series of sordid fictitious scenarios and desolate queries speculate upon the lives of his predecessors. Rex does not know what he dreads, exactly, only that he has permitted himself to be governed by something at once instinctive and yet strange, numbing, *other*.

He says, 'Leo, I have to tell you something. I'm fatally complacent about these things. Just do what you like and if you need something official done, then tell me. Otherwise, please just have a little consideration for my laziness.' Leo looks incredulous and begins to head towards the landing. 'All I want to do,' continues Rex, 'is go to bed and sleep for a really long time and hope that when I wake up, Marlon never existed, this place is owned by someone else, I'm not living where I'm living, and your van doesn't smell of a dead fat man.' There is no answer. Leo is standing on the staircase looking up. Janine has materialised on the landing. Both hands resting on the rail, she stares down with an enigmatic smile.

Rex is frightened of her. She wears the grin of an executioner, practised and complacent, humorous in a specific, mordant way. At ease with the world, her finger poised above the fatal button. He wondered what it was he felt for her: maybe he wanted to be her friend. Maybe he was in love with her. Now he realises. Janine scares Rex. It's in the way she seems to know everything and be everywhere at once, unimpeded by laws and locks. All with that half-dressed, careless smile. She's like one of the bully boys at school, impossible to deny, blessed with a talent for finding his hiding-place.

Leo and Janine look at each other. The sudden, instinctive mistrust that always occurs between people of a similar type strikes momentarily into the air between them, from his golden face to hers. They look like a king and queen from the same suit of cards. Then they do something strange. Leo climbs until he is just one step below her. She holds her hand out on a slant and he takes it. He bows deep, and she curtsies low.

'What are you doing here?' Rex breaks whatever cute little scenario they're acting out.

He comes up to join them and Janine tells him, 'I'm collecting some of my things. And I want some stuff from downstairs, like that weird marine clock with all the dials.' Janine shouldn't have that clock. That clock belongs to his father. Rex doesn't like to think of her moving around downstairs, deciding what to 'take'. Touching things, sizing them up according to how useful they would be. None of it is hers to take. But he can't say no. The clock was due to be thrown out anyway, why shouldn't she claim it? That's what her argument would be.

Instead, Rex says, 'Leo, Janine. Janine, Leo. Leo's masterminding the renovation and design. Janine's in charge of, er, personnel.'

'Personnel? I see.' Leo's looking at Janine, sizing her up. She looks back defiantly.

Watching them, Rex feels himself dissipating and becoming dull. The presence of these two strong, luminous people engenders in him a sudden start of precognitive angst. As Leo and Janine introduce themselves to each other more fully it is as though Rex can see, in a series of painted tableaux before his eyes, how together they have a force of ambition and deviousness which could eventually begin to feed upon his own more vulnerable nature. Rex will always succumb automatically to the stronger party. There is a solidity and immediacy to both of them which disturbs him, though he has no strength to reverse his position. Leo and Janine are creatures of display and performance, he of contemplation. Nothing in him could possibly lay its claim upon them. They were created in luscious forms that favour wanton pleasure and luxury.

Rex begins to daydream as Leo and Janine go on talking. Words seem to tumble out of their mouths like silk streamers – showy, dazzling, rapid. He imagines with delight an earthquake ripping through the city and casting down the King of England. It would be a glorious stroke of luck if the place were to tumble, beam upon beam, and lay its history to rest through no work of its own. Yet just as he constructs this fantasy, his daydream ceases abruptly. It is as though his thoughts have been repelled by a great kick of electrical energy. Marlon's desire is evidently so strong in his mind that it can conjure and cancel images at will. There is no choice but to submit himself to it. He must take the King of England as his, because it has been assigned to him. No matter how repellent its legacy, Rex must embrace it, and in the place of atrocity offer festivity and good will. He feels rather like a drowning man who's been thrown not a rubber ring but an anchor. He sighs, then clears his throat: 'OK, people, I need you out. I have stuff to do here.' Janine and Leo glance at him, startled, then begin to make their way past him, down the stairs. With a feeling of petty triumph, Rex realises Janine has forgotten about the clock she wanted.

Outside, the day is crisp and white. Leo and Janine yawn and stretch as though they have just awoken. The sunlight ushers into both their bodies an instant sense of contentment. Janine gives Leo a frank, appraising glare. Sheer physical beauty has a way of unlocking in her not just appreciation but true happiness. All must be well with the world, if it is capable of creating things which sparkle in the mind's eye. Though Leo does not resemble her, she sees, as Rex did, a person most like herself reflected in him. Someone free of the carping, grieving emotions and fancies which impede one's progress in life. Janine has always allowed her eagerness for rapture and experience to direct her. Those with acquiescent, inert personalities – those such as Rex, in fact – must exist in a deadened universe where everything is lifeless and null. Janine paces out her days with a roaming, blithe curiosity. In a way, she has spent her whole life on an expedition, first as a little rich girl going to bars and restaurants and galleries in cities all over the world, and then again, after her father died, slightly grief-numbed but still inquisitive about what the streets had to offer her.

It is good to have met Leo. Janine finds that life has a tendency to throw allies, partners and co-conspirators into one's path precisely when they are most needed. And this one is a fine fellow. She assesses him with an objective but eager gaze. She has imagined someone like him many times. Not in the role of lover but of sibling, for she has never felt the true unwavering devotion of a brother before. In her mind Janine is not Janine as she sees herself in the mirror every morning: powerful, dusky, heavy. She would rather be a tomboy, hard-kneed and white-toothed, with short, straight hair. She wishes for a playmate to cavort with, not in the ambiguous sexualised sense of infantile exploration, but as a true companion. Together they shall enjoy playing pranks or tricks on people, and indulge their taste for jeopardy and mirth.

They undertake an adventure around the city, visiting studios and stores. The King of England will be throwing out the old tat, which makes it look like a mad widow's attic, and will have reinvented itself by autumn, two spacious floors toned in sleek, low-slung, smoky red, and nearly all – from floor to ceiling, from the bar to the bathrooms – in shining, warm-to-the-naked-body leather. They pick out narrow, long couches, stark angular chairs and curly-backed loveseats. They visit design agencies to brainstorm a new 'bar concept'. Within twenty minutes of entering some starving joiner's draughty workspace, the three of them will be sitting there, and the joiner will be saying, 'Leo Jago, is it? Whereabouts are you originally from – Spain? I thought so. I've been to Spain, just after I left school, worked there for a while ... which part of the country? Oh yeah, I've been to Bilbao ...' People are charmed by Leo. He doesn't even have to try. He has that rare talent of seeming to be a little more stupid than he actually is, simple and boyish and ready to be wooed.

They are standing on one grey stretch of Old Street when Janine says, 'Look, we don't really have to go back and check in with Rex, do we? I mean, if he calls up, we can just say we're still looking for light-fittings or ashtrays or bog rolls or something. Let's go back to mine for a cup of tea.' Fifteen minutes later they get out of a cab on the corner of Old Compton and Wardour Street. Janine pays. 'We could have taken the bus, you know,' Leo says. He was never rich, like her.

She grimaces: 'Oh, sure. We could have done lots of things. We could have walked. We could have taken our shoes off and walked barefoot. We could have bought a few thousand rusty nails and walked over those, all the way home. God invented cabs for a reason.' She takes Leo up to the flat, makes him tea and shows him round, or rather points out various aspects of the room: 'This is the chair where I sit and read, that's my desk, that's Ferdinand the cactus – not the best flatmate in the world. He's prone to bouts of depression, and he gets separation anxiety.' There are special touches everywhere – the chair isn't really a chair, it's a laundry basket in disguise, a wooden box with a padded top-side; the coffee table is a plate of blackened glass balanced on some salvaged lengths of iron tubing. 'So, do you like my decor?' Janine asks.

'Isn't it that guy Marlon's?' Leo says, without thinking.

Janine stiffens: 'Yeah, when he was alive it was his. Now it's mine. And Ferdinand the cactus was always mine.'

That evening, Leo is walking back to the estate. He comes in at the gate and sees his van, pale in the dark. There is something wrong with it. Its lines have been wrestled out of place. One entire side has folded in on itself. It doesn't look like a heavy-weight vehicle made of metal and rubber so much as a giant crooked paper cup. Inside the bend is nestled an even more damaged black Golf GTi, its bonnet corrugated against the shattered windscreen. Leo's first thought is that the open feud has finally begun between them and the estate's other, unseen residents. He straightens up. He spots two figures brawling half-heartedly in the darkness behind the van. They're whispering to each other rapidly. 'You stupid little shit! That's Leo's van!' 'How was I meant to know it was parked there?' 'You weren't meant to know anything, you fucking idiot. You're thirteen years old! You weren't meant to have stolen a car and you weren't meant to be joyriding in it in the first place!' 'Don't touch me. I could stab you, I'm good at that.' 'No, you need to be hit. You need discipline!' By now they're laughing, weak-bellied. Their voices are full of love for each other.

Leo approaches, a quizzical frown on his face. They haven't seen him. He creeps up, then claps a hand on Lukas' shoulder. Lukas yells and stands bolt upright, then looks sheepish when he realises who it is. 'It's not my fault,' he says. He grabs the other figure and drags it into sight. 'If you want to punish anyone, punish him.' Leo looks down at a gangly kid with pallid, still-developing features set at odds with each other. 'Leo, meet Victor, my little brother.' Leo nods and Victor's mouth slowly lifts into a hesitant, enchanting curve which transforms his looks. Leo finds himself beginning to grin back foolishly. But the boy's mouth doesn't stop there. It stretches and grows, wider and wider, and opens, and reveals canine teeth, elongated and sharp, somehow not part of the surrounding face, like a vampire's.

3

Neela looks around Leo's flat, camera in hand. She slides her hand along his bed, then smells the pillow. She opens drawers and scans the bathroom cabinet. Tonight, Leo is hosting a drinks party to celebrate his arrival on the estate, or, as he puts it, 'To commemorate the marvel and wonder that is life with me.' At eight-thirty, his friends started to arrive. First Raymond and Alexandra, then Corinne and Luke, then Jay and Julia, then Paola and Carla. They look like a Benetton advert – all different colours, but essentially in the same league. Neela never liked gangs. They look with one eye and speak with one mouth. When she sees them, she wants to turn her face to the window, beat through the glass and dig a shelter for herself deep in the ground.

On Leo's bed is a patchwork quilt, a series of interlocking hearts in shades of yellow and green. On the dresser is a picture of him at an early age. He looks grumpy and shy, but holds his hands up to his head like bunny ears. She walks round, photographing all his belongings. The camera was Neela's way of snatching life back when, at thirteen or so, she realised she would never be like the people around her. She tried to endear herself to them, but they could tell she was acting. It was something to do with her sharp face and deceitful, elongated eyes. Everything she said came out like a snide, nasty joke. Next to them, she felt mute and hunched, like she had a club foot for a tongue. So she made herself even more different – hostile and possessive, with her shutter clicking greedily, taking in a pinch of light and storing it away. She began to snatch what she liked from them, frame by frame. She took their tiny triumphs, their naive jokes, their easy, white-on-white couplings.

Neela listens to the talk coming from next door and can't believe what Leo is like. So naive! He makes such facile small-talk, such lame jokes. He and Rex would be perfect friends. They could spend hours impressing each other. They laugh a lot and Neela hears it through the wall. Then there is a brief silence.

Leo appears, leaning in the doorway of the bedroom. 'Hey there,' he says, 'not feeling social? I can't tempt you with some cheap plonk? Guaranteed to give you absolutely no pleasure upon drinking, and a ball-breaking hangover the next day.' Neela doesn't say anything, just stares at him. She watches him cringe and diminish, ever so slightly. He doesn't like being looked at. He doesn't like silence. It's always the way, with people like him. You get them alone and they turn into the ugly, unlayable freak of their secondary-school years. Give them a weekend with no parties to go to, no friends to visit, no pals to invite over, no caning sessions to conduct, and they go demented. They can't stand to be with themselves. Neela feels a stroke of pleasure. If there's something she has a talent for, it's being alone. She can out-wait anyone, she can sink low in her flat and close her eyes, and Monday to Friday will go by without her moving. Let the world perish and Neela will take one step back into the cold, into the dark, and outlast everyone.

She flashes him a smile and says, 'I'm fine. I'll be through in a second. I just wanted to see how you'd done your place up.'

By the time she returns to the living room, the others have arrived: Rex right beside Leo, quieter than normal, Lukas his usual glittering white presence, Gavin hunkering in a corner like a mangy, chastised dog. And there is someone new, Lukas'

86

brother, a boy constructed entirely of bones and joints. Now, that is a person she could take an interest in. He has the same scavenging look as she does, the same utter obvious disregard for anything of delicacy and propriety and grace.

Neela gets up and forces herself to try and talk to some of Leo's other friends. But within five minutes it is like she is thirteen again, sitting on the edges of other people's conversations. Their talk is littered with references to a life that she has never known: jazz festivals in suburban parks, countryside retreats and weekend breaks to the seaside, matinees and ice-creams, roof-terrace drinks and summer Pimm's sessions. Neela feels her heart burn with jealousy and curiosity. Their lives seem to have been studded with so many small happinesses. Neela wishes she could tell proper anecdotes with a beginning, a middle and a wry, ironic end. She wishes she could hit upon something to say, an inspired joke or tale, which will make friends out of some of these strangers. At the same time she would like to see one of them, alone at three in the morning, trying to find their way home from a shopping-centre car-park in Zone 6. She would like to see one of them hauling a girl's body out of the toilet cubicle at a party and checking her cold neck and wrists for signs of life. She would like to see one of them with not a single piece of paper to their name – none of the film diplomas or design degrees and Eng. Lit. BAs – treading the pavements of London in the same trainers they were wearing three years ago.

Lukas comes up to save her. 'What do you think of her, then?' he asks, and points. Neela strains to see who he means. The room is full of smoke. Everyone is drunk and she is sober. Then she sees her: the crinkly, heavy gold hair; those strange clothes, like a work of art, white gauze folded and padded around that already substantial bottom. 'Wouldn't you like to have a bite of that particular apple?' Lukas leers.

'She's not my type,' Neela murmurs, but still she keeps watching. Prom Queen Janine. The most popular girl in the school. Janine goes from person to person, singling out every one of Leo's friends in turn and making them smile, nod, laugh, gesticulate, like an expert. Cheerleading Janine, with her bountiful breasts, loved by the masses, feared by a few.

Leo stands up and calls everyone to attention. He has an unattractive red, bloated look. His eyes have a slight film over them. 'Now everyone's here I'd like to propose something. Naked Twister!' Nobody laughs. Nobody even smiles. He continues, 'No? Only joking. Actually, I bought some fireworks, so if anyone knows how to set them off we can have a little display.' Victor and Gavin dart forward. Little boys love to play with matches.

Down in the courtyard, the group splits into Leo's old friends and Leo's new friends. Being outdoors in the frosty air has killed the party atmosphere. The guests are no longer required to mingle. They eye one another and smile politely. Leo's van and Victor's Golf have disappeared. There is only the skip full of its sinister junk, and the bloodied cars. Suddenly, the sky divides with a scream and a scorching line of red sparks. Everyone begins to smile and crane their necks. Neela stares at her trainers. She hates the sight of a group of grown adults oohing and aahing over some colours in the sky. They don't die of astonishment and wonder every time they turn on a light-bulb, do they? Pricks. Victor and Gavin are crouching, grinning at each other. They let off another firework, a knot of white shards which pops then springs apart and blooms into a dozen smaller clusters. Then a series of screeching blue bullets which soar straight up and explode. Then handfuls of pretty golden starbursts, momentary and silent. They sink and dim, only to be replaced by a dozen thundering magnesium white flares. Neela glances to the side and sees that three other people aren't watching. Rex is staring at the skip and the cars, totally absorbed in his thoughts. Leo and Janine are looking at each other.

A week or so later, Janine waits at Great Portland Street tube station. This is what would technically be known as a business trip. Janine has come to procure the most basic ingredients of her recipe for success, in accordance with her sole business dictum: where drugs are, people follow. 'I don't care what you do, just make me a success,' Rex had told her and Leo. They showed him the architects' plans. He barely glanced at them. They kept a record of their expenditure – Janine working under a spurious 'Entertainments' account – but Rex just said, 'Look, how much can things cost? They can't cost more than I've got. And anyway, I trust you.'

They have set themselves up with temporary offices at the King of England. Every day on the phone people attempt to sweet-talk Janine into letting them come to the launch. She is always amazed at the depths to which people will sink. They wheedle, they cajole, they lie. They treat her like their best friend, asking 'How are you?' with honey in their voices. Janine has magicked up some 'competition' for membership, and she and Leo enjoyed devising the selection criteria. To be accepted, you first have to be nominated by three people who're already members. Then you have to write a begging letter or two. Then come in for an interview. 'Maybe we should make them sit some kind of aptitude test,' mused Janine.

Now she is doing the actual work. The score. A white Ford Escort with mud smeared over the number plate takes the turning outside the station and just manages to avoid the security railings. It parks haphazardly on a double yellow and a bloke with acne and puppy fat gets out. He winks at Janine and says, 'Alright? Come with me.' Once they're in the car, he reaches across her lap and opens the window on her side. 'Got some good stuff, you'll like it.' Janine knows not to say anything. She has to play the dumb bitch before she gets her treats. It's a shame about this guy, Mark. He's eighteen years old, from a good family, He's funny, smart, caring. His whole personality's been mangled just because of some grains of stuff on a bit of tinfoil or a spoon. It doesn't seem like a good enough trade. Just eighteen. When she was that age, she stole occasionally, she vandalised occasionally, she did it without a condom. They were spoilt-girl misdemeanours. But there wasn't a fundamental problem in her soul. She didn't get out of bed every morning needing one particular thing she couldn't function without. The most she did was smoke cigarettes all night, or eat too much.

Mark drives like a maniac. He gets close to the car in front, then shines the headlights full-beam into their mirror. He doesn't brake for anyone, even when it's in his own best interests. That says it all about heroin, really. It wouldn't mean anything if he died. Nothing matters – nothing. The gear is all. They turn into a perfectly nice middle-class street with nice middle-class houses, and pull up in front of the only one with thick black bars across the door and windows. Janine sits meekly in the car while Mark goes to speak to someone inside. Every so often, she looks behind her, but eventually gives up the watch and picks up an old copy of the *Sun* from the floor.

It isn't a big job, but then it never is. Janine covers her tracks well, double- and triple-dealing. She has a roster of dealers all around London, and she visits each of them just like all the other creeps and credit-takers out there. She's prepared to do the whole act – whining at the door, phoning mobiles in the middle of the night, pleading poverty and then begging just another gram or tenner's worth – just so they believe she's working solo. Some of the middle-men, like Mark, they're proper friends with her and they know the reality. They work for her – with her – because she gives them what they want and she doesn't insult their machismo in the process. She invites them to parties, introduces them to pretty girls. She offers them a bite of the life they always imagined for themselves. Mark comes back to the car and she puts two hundred quid into his hand. He pats her on the head and then disappears back into the house. Then she waits for another hour, staring down the street, listening to the rain beginning to fall.

Mark gets back to her, gives her a handful of cellophane wraps and says, 'He gave me a bit extra cos it's a decent-sized order. But I'm keeping it.' Then he says, 'Can I borrow some money? Pay ya back later.' Mark currently owes Janine a couple of hundred quid, which he calls 'petrol money'. But it goes with the territory. They jerk away from the kerb – not that they were very close to it in the first place – and drive back down the street, then turn without looking and head towards the station. They're taking a loose curve at the roundabout when something butts the car. They laugh. Something butts the car again, then a pulsing blue light fills the back seat area. Janine and Mark lock eyes and freeze.

PC Plod had been having a shitty evening until he saw the Ford Escort. PC Plod is breaking up with his wife, his daughter treats him like a freak, and the other guys on the force don't respect him as they should. He doesn't get paid enough, he has to do all this bloody paperwork, and he doesn't get his teeth into any real action. No chance to be a hero. So the sight of a car, number plate obscured, lights off in the dark, hugely over speed – it makes him cream his pants. Both cars pull over. Plod arranges his face appropriately and strides out, over to the window of the poor little bastard whose misfortune it is to make his evening so very sweet.

Janine hisses to Mark, 'Don't you dare tell the truth, OK?' and Mark nods, calm, because this has happened to him so many times before. So when Plod comes up and starts asking them questions, they lie every way they know how. Plod makes them get out and give him their details. He checks the car and jots down every single thing that's wrong with it. Then he gives it a good hard kick in the driver door. Now, that Ford is Mark's pride and joy. That car has taken him on missions all the way to Brixton, where the real bad boys hang out. It was the site of his virginity loss, not so long ago, and also the venue of his break-up with his girlfriend, the latter incident not unrelated to the former. So when Plod gets the toe of his little boot right into the enamel, and across the panel, he's really buggering about with the whole of Mark's history, his hopes and joys, his identity.

Then Mark does something intensely stupid, which Janine cannot prevent. He lunges forward and clips Plod around the face, saying, 'You aren't even close, mate.' Then he stands back, whips out his handful of wraps and says, 'This is what you should have been looking to book us for, you blind git.' Janine groans and slaps her hand over her face. All Plod's Christmases have come at once.

Luckily for Janine, it's true what Plod thinks about the other blokes not respecting him. The three go to the police station and, basically, everyone there laughs in his face. Under the fluorescent lighting, with Plod's fist around the collar of his old puffa jacket, Mark looks like a callow sixth-former. 'Let's face it, it's not exactly Carlos The Jackal and Myra Hindley, is it?' sniggers the guy behind the reception desk. They think Janine's just the obligatory daft, pampered girlfriend and get set to give her a caution. They don't even search her. She goes off to take a piss before her bollocking, leaving Mark alone. She tries to pass a look to him but he doesn't notice.

A young whippersnapper of a PC, by the name of Shane Chisholm, catches sight of Mark by the door. In the bad old days, Shane knew Mark. In the bad old days, Shane and Mark were mates 'n' muckers. They spraypainted cars together. They went joyriding together. They stole together. They went to tacky clubs and groped girls together. They sniffed glue together. They did things, sexual things, together, in the first flush of pubescent curiosity. They started taking drugs together. So Shane's on the inside track, as far as Mark's concerned. For many months now, a special group of keen, red-gummed young policepeople has been following a white Ford Escort driven with unbridled enthusiasm hither and thither, from shady lock-up to council-housing rendezvous, from under the railway bridge to behind the community library car-park. Shane comes forward and touches Mark on the shoulder. Mark turns. He's caught off guard and smiles and begins to say, 'Shane, mate –' when his grin slips and he understands what's going on. Shane takes him by the wrist and slings him into a little room with no sharp edges before coming back out.

When Janine gets back from the bathroom, Mark is gone, and Shane is there. But she is, she thinks, one step ahead. She saw him notice Mark and inferred the rest. Shane has that special forces, undercover look to him. He looks like the kind of person who'd be good at waiting, tracking, hunting. She went into the toilet, fished a condom out of her purse, stuffed the wraps into it, knotted it and forced herself to swallow the bundle. Now her mouth tastes like nonoxynol-9. She knows Shane will figure out, at least roughly, what she does. Any woman who hangs around with Mark is in it for the drugs. Smack addicts can't fuck, eat or drink. They can't even talk properly. No woman – especially one who looks like Janine – would actually be friends with Mark.

Shane comes up to her with a swagger. 'I wouldn't say you were Mark's type,' he says, and he has an East-End brawling-geezer just-you-try-me voice. He looks her up and down. She keeps her face expressionless. 'Oi! Lenny!' Shane calls to his sidekick, a skinny, tall guy with luscious blonde hair and an earring. 'What d'you make of this one?'

Lenny ambles over. 'She's a bit heavy, isn't she? Anyway, I don't like nig-nogs.'

'I do,' says Shane. He turns to Janine: 'You gonna give me a bit of that Caribbean flavour?' He purses his lips and makes little kissing noises.

'If that's what you want, why don't you take her to a holding cell right now?' Lenny asks Shane.

'Nah, Lenny,' Shane replies, 'I believe in waiting.' Janine recognises that this is a routine they've been through many times before.

Lenny is saying to Shane, 'So, what are you going to do, then? Climb in her window and fuck her while she's asleep? Hold her down on the bed with one hand over her mouth? And I can come in and watch while you do it.'

And Shane says, 'No you're not, you're going to help me break in and she's going to make us both a drink, and when she's in the kitchen I'm going to come in and hit her and she'll go down. I'll pull her legs apart and pin them with my knees and do it to her on the floor and then when I'm finished we'll leave her there crying and screaming and you and I can go for a night out in town.'

'And that's how you'll fuck her?'

'Yeah. On her back with her wrists above her head. And every so often I'll pause and hit her across the face, a backhander, closed fist.'

Shane pauses for breath, and that is when Janine slams her hand between his legs, grabs his bollocks and twists. Lenny stands there, stunned, even smiling a bit, while Shane, without a sound, goes purple in the face and doubles over. It really hurts. This is celestial pain, pure as an angel's aura – glowing, brilliant, pain singing hosanna to the skies. All the movies, all the self-defence classes, all the revenge fantasies don't even begin to express how much it hurts to have your nuts wrung. By the time he regains his senses, Janine is out the door.

Late that night, Shane gets ready to visit Mark in his cell. He gets a pair of knuckle-dusters from his locker. When he was fourteen, he ordered them from a magazine. Shining steel with short spikes on the outside, enough to give a little bit of texture to the face of one's opponent. He would slip them on, and then walk around with his fists balled up in his jacket pockets. He was too much of a coward to use them, he just showed them to his mates. He's not a coward any more, he doesn't think. Now he's on the other side of the law, and people steal fearful little glances at him when he walks the streets. He shows them to Mark. 'Remember these?' he says. 'A tenner, *Combat Magazine*. Bloody bargain! Shall we see if they still work?' While Janine rides back into Soho in a black cab, Shane duffs Mark up. In Shane's hands, Mark turns from a tough yoof into a veritable poet, a chorus of revelation embellished not only with names but also dates and places. Information. Beans.

By the end of the night, Mark and Shane are friends again. Mark smiles at him through his broken teeth, winks through the bruises, and says, 'Look, you were always my best mate. You're just doing your job. No hard feelings.' Shane prides himself on his ability to put business matters aside once the main issues have been addressed, and opens his heart to his ex-play-mate once more. Now the girl is done for, the boys can be buddies. They have found their scapegoat. They shake hands and clap each other on the shoulder, standing on the steps of the police station.

Then Mark goes home and phones Janine, and they plot their revenge. She can hear how much pain he's in. 'Don't worry, honey,' she says, 'I'll talk to my friend Leo. I promise you, we'll get him.'

Late that night, Leo, Lukas, Rex and Victor are on their way into the estate, beer bottles in hand. They form a loose, silent group. Occasionally, Victor and Lukas josh each other, trying to break the atmosphere, but Leo and Rex are too busy thinking about the King of England. 'This is the stuff legends are made of,' Leo had proclaimed when the builders moved in and started knocking through all the interior walls.

'What? Rubble?' said Rex.

Now they are each wondering if the other was right. Janine has submerged herself in a series of bizarre suburban encounters with small-time dealers and their flunkies. The phone in her 'office' rings constantly when she is away. Neela and Gavin occasionally drop by to pick through the site listlessly, whis-pering comments to each other. There seems to be nothing for them to do, and yet the bar is just naked brickwork and dust.

The estate is the same as always, night-loving and secretive. In the daytime it seems to shrink away from the sky, bleached and airless, but as soon as the sun is down, the skip and the cars take on the aspect of towering sculptures and the red paint on Lukas' steps glistens below his landing light. The group enters between the pillars. There is someone waiting for them behind the gate, a short, boxy man with a flesh-coloured eye-patch and stringy, long white hair. He comes to stand in front of them and they look down at him. Lukas laughs, 'Great! Ambushed by Captain Pugwash! It doesn't stop, this place, does it? It's like Pandora's fucking Box.' The man does look as though he's stepped from the pages of a fairytale, blessed as he has been with a grizzled, goblin's face and stumpy limbs. He's the sort they'd fire out of a cannon at the circus.

Max Stein runs the estate. He also organises the drugs that are bought, sold and resold from it. This is his patch. He has been watching these new arrivals. They could have submitted to the place and been broken by it. Instead, they have brought with them that girl, the dealer, and that boy, with his deft knife-hand – and Max Stein is still very much in mourning for his old friend the fat man.

Max addresses himself to Rex. He has a clipped, smarmy voice. 'So,' he says pleasantly enough, 'I hear you're relaunching the King of England.'

'That's our plan,' replies Rex shortly.

Max Stein nods. 'I knew the previous owners, you know.' Rex freezes. ' I'm very old. Seventy-something. I don't look it, do I?' He puffs his chest out. 'Alun the Dragon took my eye out. Want to know how he did it?' Rex doesn't, at all, in fact it is the last thing he wants to know, but Max Stein continues. As he talks, he gradually becomes less monstrous. He is civilised. A gentleman. He certainly belongs to Alun's class and generation, Rex thinks. Max is saying, 'He got me by the face and before I knew it he'd stuck the tip of his thumb into the socket. After that it was only a slight shove that knocked it out. No force required. It didn't hurt. You'd think it would have but it didn't. The main nerve was still connected. I thought I'd got away easy, I'd just run home and pop it back in. Then he held me down and Marlon cut the nerve with a pair of scissors.' The entire group

97

winces and, as one, puts their hands over their eyes. Max starts chuckling: 'Yep. Now, I've felt pain before. I've been shot, stabbed, strangled. I've climbed the outside of a building for four storeys. I've fallen off a building about the same distance. I've even been electrocuted, though I suppose that one was my own fault. But I tell you, having one of your nerves severed with a pair of scissors beats them all. And you want to know why they did it?' The group nods like a bunch of nursery children during storytelling hour. 'Because I tried to muscle in on their trade. Now, I'm not presuming to know what your business is, but I'll let you in on something. I was pretty ecstatic when they closed the King of England down. Once that place was gone it opened up a whole host of opportunities. If ever you're in this area and you see a junkie sitting by a wall or a cokehead trying to cross the road, you know they've taken a trip to Max Stein's. That's me. Max Stein. Welcome to my kingdom.' He holds his arms out in a gesture of all-this-is-mine. 'I wasn't too bothered when you came along, you know. I was thinking, maybe I could do a deal with them, see if they can teach an old dog like me some new tricks. But now I'm finding out all sorts of things. You're trying to edge me out of the market, you and your lot. You think you're going to do what Alun did all over again –'

'No,' starts Rex, suddenly, but Max Stein looks genuinely puzzled. 'No, but you are like those people. You're those people all over again. Doing the same thing in exactly the same way. You even look the same. You look like Alun. So don't tell me it's not just the same circle turning.' Rex looks away. Max Stein takes a breath and then says, 'So what I'm giving you is basically a gentle warning. Drugs is my business, right? Substances, quantities, prices – that's all my department. And this estate is my headquarters. Everybody who lives here, they do so because I granted them permission. Now, pulling pints is your business.

Your business and my business can go alongside each other just fine, if you respect your limits. So I'll tell you what to do. You find that little friend of yours, her with the hair, and give her a little talking to. Put the fear in her, yeah? Let her know – and tell her Max Stein advised you on this – that if she carries on upsetting my cronies and confusing my clients – cos junkies don't like to have to make choices – I'll get her. And it won't just be a broken arm or a few bruised ribs. I'll make it so she never walks again. I'll pound her so far into the ground you'll need a potato peeler to scrape her off again. Once you've done that, come back to me and we can start talking.' He finishes off with a big smile, then adds, 'Tell me something, Rex, how old are you?' and Rex, his voice cracked, whispers, 'Eighteen.' Max Stein cocks his head to the side. 'You've got your whole life to make enemies. Best not to start off on the wrong foot, eh? And a word of advice: try not to let any women interfere in your business. You can't trust 'em as far as you can hit 'em, and I should know.'

Max Stein gives them a congenial wave and then turns to leave. His composure is breathtaking. His hunched, inefficient walk seems to carry with it an atmosphere of utterly secure power. Rex is frozen to the spot – *don't tell me it's not just the same circle turning* – but he sees Leo dart forward to block Max Stein's way. He holds his beer bottle in his hand, by the middle, not the neck, illuminated by the one courtyard light that works. Rex, Lukas and Victor watch Leo as he raises the bottle so that it catches the yellow beam of the bulb. Max Stein's head also tips up to see it, like a magpie's, attracted by the brightness. As though in slow motion, the group watches Leo's fist quivering as it tightens around the bottle until, with an almost musical shudder, it blasts apart. Splinters cleave the air, catching the light. Max Stein is mesmerised. Leo reveals his palm, in which numerous segments of curving, sharp-edged glass are embedded. He looks at it for a second, then slams his hand into Max Stein's face, turning it strongly, screwing the glass into the face. He pulls back and nonchalantly starts removing the glass from his hand, angling the pieces slightly to dislodge them.

Max Stein has fallen to the floor. He kneels there, not making a sound, with his hands held up to his face but not touching it. He is trembling, but he doesn't say anything. Rex stares. Lukas and Victor have run forward. They start kicking – savage, considered kicks to the stomach and kidneys. Ribs and cuts can heal, but you can't use a sticky plaster to stop internal bleeding. After several minutes, Lukas looks up at Rex in panic. 'Can't you do something?' he asks. 'He won't die.'

Rex moves forward. His eye-sockets and cheeks look totally hollow under the light. Maybe we shouldn't do this, he thinks about saying, but it is too late. He can't think of a precise point at which he could have stopped it, but there must have been one. No, he could have said. I don't want this to happen. That point is long gone. He reaches down and takes hold of Max Stein by the collar of his black jacket. The head lolls back and the eye-patch has been wrenched to the side, revealing an empty socket clamped shut by a yellow eyelid. Leo, Victor and Lukas fall away. Now there is only the old leader and the new. Rex reaches behind him, under his coat, and draws from his waistband the gun Marlon gave him. The others gasp. The machine emits its own white rays. It seems to pull forward, almost out of his grip, and align itself with the goblin's ruined face. Rex squeezes the trigger. He means to release just one bullet but forgets that the gun is an automatic. Within a few seconds, he has propelled ten bullets into Max Stein, at point-blank range. Rex's arm reverberates with the force of the blasts. It feels good. Blood, skin and brain fly up and streak his clothes, his face, his hair. When he is done, there is no face left, to speak of. The skin and bone seem to have peeled back. There's just gristle, blistered and raw.

Then they are left with a body. 'What am I supposed to do? Take it to the dump in a cab?' Leo sighs, and the others laugh, subdued. The courtyard smells of blood. The body is still so solid, the arms and legs so intact, that it looks like it might get up, dust itself down and walk off at any moment.

Victor says, 'We can burn it right here. It can act as a warning to everyone else on the estate, not that anyone's going to bother us now, if he was the main guy. But it can be, like, a symbolic thing.' Everyone looks at him.

'You know, you really have a nasty streak,' says Lukas, ruffling his hair. Victor grins his bat grin. He fishes a packet of cigarettes out of his jacket and passes them round. They all stand puffing thoughtfully.

Leo goes into his flat and returns with a biology-lab flask of white spirit. 'It's my favourite all-purpose substance, this,' he says, before pouring it over Max Stein.

By now, it is two in the morning. There is no sound anywhere, neither on the estate nor on any of the streets surrounding it. Victor sets light to the body. They stand back. Instead of the solid, flowering form of a bonfire, Max Stein burns in a particular shape – there are his arms, there his legs. The flames don't connect with each other and rise up in an undulating orange column. It looks as though Max is writhing on the ground. Rex stares at it, then glances up and realises Neela and Gavin have arrived. 'It's not going to work, Dracula,' Neela tells Victor. 'You can't burn a body down to ashes like that. You have to really incinerate it.'

'Yeah, well, just you wait,' retorts Victor, looking worried.

So they wait. Everyone is swaying with tiredness. Max Stein's clothes burn down but his bones don't. His flesh barely chars. Reduced and blackened, surrounded by ashes, the body looks like something caught in the fallout of a nuclear bomb. It is raised up, the legs tensed, the arms somehow reaching and flexing, trying to climb out of the flames. 'He's changed position,' Lukas muses. 'Maybe he wasn't totally dead when we lit him up?'

'Nah,' says Leo, 'it's just a chemical thing. Something that happens when it gets heated up. Maybe the flesh shrinks and draws the limbs up or something.' 'What're you gonna do now, Little Drac?' Neela asks, not bothering to hide her smile. 'Why don't you take him back home with you? You can prop him up in a chair and deal with it tomorrow. Or make some kind of pie out of him.' Victor gives her a look so intense it could reignite the fire, before turning on his heel and trudging back to his flat. 'Don't forget your friend!' Neela calls out as he goes. 'He's losing his head without you! He just goes to pieces when you're not around!'

Within minutes, Victor is back, and in his hand he holds an iron bar shaped into a wicked hook at one end. 'Bloody hell,' says Leo, staring at it. 'Where the fuck did you get that from?'

Lukas says, 'We picked it out of a salvage yard years ago. Most kids attach their sentiments to a cuddly toy. Vic here has a length of bent metal.' Victor approaches Neela and presents the implement for her inspection. She reaches out, shivering in the cold, and slides her fingertips along the curve of the hook. The very end of the bar has been sharpened to a point. Neela smiles and wraps her hand around it as Victor holds it. She lets go and makes a movement with her head, as though assenting to whatever he is about to do.

Everyone stands back. Now the fire is finished, the cold blasts wakefulness into them all. Where the flames gave them something to wonder at, like children, with their shifting colours and dense heat, the mangled body and ashes merely look sordid. They have killed not in self-defence but, in a sense, in jest. Leo and his stunt with the bottle. Rex, not one bullet but ten. And then came the burning. It was a damn good show. They should feel guilty, they know, but they don't. Neither guilt nor fear at what they have become. Victor stands over the body, his legs braced. He takes a breath and raises the bar above his head. He gets his focus, then, using all his force, he drives the hook down in a whistling arc, smashing it into Max Stein's rib-cage. It lodges there, splitting the bones, clawing against the roasted heart. Victor withdraws, then strikes again, groaning with the exertion, and attacks the spine. Systematically, turning the hook and its point this way and that, he rips Max Stein to shreds. The only noises on the estate at that time, in the thick of the night, are Victor's brief shouts as he brings the bar down, and the muted, husky creak of Max Stein's body as it fractures.

Everyone stands with heads bowed. Eventually, Neela looks up at Victor. Gavin gives him a thumbs-up. Lukas hugs him. Leo and Rex linger together. Max Stein is destroyed. Over. Not a single identifiable particle of him remains. Already the wind is sifting the ashes, ushering them along the ground. Rex realises he still has the gun in his hand. He sighs. Slowly, they go to their flats to rest for what remains of the night, the new kings of West Central.

4

At nine-thirty on an October night in central London, a thick-set bouncer at the King of England observes the dressed-up crowd shivering outside. They look like schoolkids queuing up for their lunch, pasty and dull. Music pounds through the entire building. Inside, the stairs and corridors are teeming with guests, touching, gossiping, giggling. Victor and Gavin are dancing. The toilet cubicles are jammed with people in their twos and threes. Neela's sprawled across one of the couches talking with a girl in a lilac dress who's kneeling on the floor hanging on to her every word. Lukas lies twitching on the opposite couch, coked out of his brains. 'God, that Janine really pulled it off big-time,' he says to no one in particular. 'There's so much of it floating around I should have come dressed in snow-boots and ski goggles.'

Janine, Leo and Rex are in the private rooms at the top of the building, watching the party through Securicam monitors. 'Yum,' says Janine appreciatively, 'I do like to garnish my parties with a sprinkling of fine young men. You need a bit of fresh boy sweat to add that special tang to the air.' Leo laughs. They've made it. The leather flooring, the two elongated storeys, a bar on each, joined by a wide watch-me staircase. Dim, tiny lights studding the ceiling. It has all come together. Janine adjusts her dress – white silk cut into a bastardised kimono – and pours the champagne. Rex watches them. This is their domain. They look like show horses: groomed, glossy and primed for performance. Arrogant. Expectant. Easy on the eye.

Leo fishes a wrap from his pocket and unpicks it. 'Want some?' He holds it out. 'It's a speedball. I mixed it up before I came out.'

Janine shakes her head: 'I never indulge in the product I sell.'

'Why not?' asks Leo, as he tips his head back and unloads the bag into his nose. Any dust left on his face, he pushes it over to his nostrils. 'Because,' she says, 'that'd make me the same as them, and if I ever found out I was anything like those freaks out there' – she nods towards the monitors – 'I'd kill myself. And I'd never touch heroin, anyway. It turns you into a thief.' Like all dealers, Janine loves to relay her statistics: where, when, how many, how harmful, how exquisite. Stories of death and disease through pipe or crumbling line.

Leo shrugs, his feet up on the table. 'So what? Nothing wrong with having a binge occasionally. You don't have to keep your head all the time.'

Janine drinks her champagne and pushes a glass over to Rex. She watches Leo for a while then says disgustedly, 'You should see the fatuous smile you've got on your face. You look like a bad actor who's been told to show what it's like to have a drugs experience. Come on. Get up. We have to go and greet our fans.' She stands up and starts pulling Leo's wrist. He laughs and puts his arm around her waist. She draws her hand back and slaps him half-jokingly around the face. 'Leo, we have to leave now.' A look passes between them. Whatever they have planned, Rex doesn't want to know. He watches them go.

Outside in the corridor, Leo pulls Janine back. 'J, seriously, do you think we should tell him about the job tonight, since he's paying for it?'

She turns to him scornfully. 'Oh, get off my face. Don't tell me you're losing your bollocks. It has nothing to do with Rex, and anyway, he has so much money he doesn't know what to do with it. If we told him we're about to deliver some meals-on-wheels to a policeman he'd just go through his Hamlet routine. He's got no right to play the morality game with us. Only a few months ago you stood and watched while he shot ten bullets into the face of a four-foot man, and you told me he looked like he was creaming his pants while he did it. Who's he to judge? He's the one with the gun and the bank account. He's the signature on the cheques. He could have taken control of everything himself and opened a children's playground, or a nice library, or somewhere people go to buy plants and garden accessories. Don't let yourself be swayed by his pillar-of-society shit. He's got schmuck written all over him. We've talked about this so many times: people like Rex are there to be used. This is our bar now, that's our money. Now come on.'

They enter through the first-floor bar and stand in one corner of the room looking around them and nodding greetings to the acquaintances who approach with almost slavish expressions. Everybody wears a hungry look, their fingers itching to reach into their wallets and pay whatever's asked: 'Janine, hey, how's it going? It's so good to see you. We were just wondering where you were tonight, maybe you could help us out ...' Always chasing the tail of pleasure. Janine and Leo are both jumpy. Tonight, PC Shane Chisholm will learn that there is something greater than the law. They have organised the sweetest send-off for him – a single drive-by bullet racing through the night to meet with him at a private meal Janine's hosting to celebrate the King of England's relaunch. The only thing Shane Chisholm will be swallowing tonight is a mouthful of metal; his date will have to check the old hood and scythe at the cloakroom, and his after-dinner mint's going to hit him right between the eyes.

People start queuing outside Rex's door. A cast of characters impervious to the dancing and the basslines: old, fierce, gnarled. Some have pieces missing from their bodies – a hunk of flesh, a finger. They've come to pay their respects. Now the girl and her faggoty friend are gone, it's time for Rex to meet some of Alun's old associates, man to man. Time to rekindle the flames of friendship as they stood circa twenty years ago.

Rex receives them. What astonishes him is that these people – this parade of freaks – treat him like an honorary son. Like actors in a ghoulish, hammy comedy, they sidle up to him with obsequious smiles on their warped visages, introducing themselves, offering services of various kinds. Women, weapons, musclepower. All the little essentials that never made it into the Yellow Pages. Rex pours them glasses of champagne and tries not to put his foot in it. He is convinced people can tell that behind the wide, silvery eyes lurks fat boy, his palms sticky with sugar. Fat boy, high on orange squash.

Out in the corridor, Terence Blackheath knocks on the door. Terence could really do with joining a gym. Too many biryanis in front of Ceefax have rendered him pot-bellied yet thin and bandy. He resembles a gravity toy, a pin-head weighted in the centre, impossible to knock down. He has a globular white face and a harelip. He talks with a lisp. He wears an expensive suit which looks like an Oxfam bargain buy, and bespoke leather shoes which resemble old potatoes. His genuine Rolex looks fake. He's glad the King of England's starting up again. He did a lot of his most delicate work for those guys – some of his finest commissions. Now he can see if he's still got the touch. He opens the door and there is the boy, all clean and broadly handsome with his rolling pale hair. Now, Terence Blackheath likes beauty. Even though nature has damned him with the kind of form on which a monarch's ermine cloak would look like cat-tails and curtain-cloth, Terence has the eye. 'Well, you're a fine piece,' is the first thing he says to Rex. 'A real young man. Marlon was quite right in choosing you. Time we injected a bit of glamour back into the neighbourhood.'

Rex takes in the soft voice and thin, hairy ankles below the trouser cuffs. The stranger wedges himself into the chair oppo-site him. He looks like a pervy uncle, the kind who touches you a little too high on the leg.

'I've come to offer you my services.' He extends his thin, wilting hand and Rex shakes it, repressing a shudder. 'Terence Blackheath is my name,' the stranger says, 'but I'll let you call me Terry.' He takes a pouch of tobacco and papers from his jacket pocket and meticulously begins rolling a cigarette. All his movements have a wet, clinging quality to them – the way he stirs his knuckles around the tobacco, touching every corner of the packet, then fingers the papers until they're limp and damp. 'Nice place,' he says, his head down, 'very modern. You'll get a lovely rich young clientele, with all your leather and what-have-you. A new crowd.' He looks up and watches Rex for a few seconds. 'You'll probably not be interested in what I've got to say for myself. You don't seem the type. Don't like to get your feet too muddy, am I right?'

Rex laughs vaguely and says, 'I'm sorry, I don't know what you mean.' Terence Blackheath talks like he's feeling you up at the same time, with a knowing, sexual, only-I-can-tell tone.

He shrugs diffidently: 'You're a sort of hands-off person is all I'm saying. Don't want to get too close to the action. Little bit squeamish.' He lights a match and applies it to his cigarette slowly, then watches it burn down. Rex freezes. The flame licks Terence's clammy fingers before dying out. 'I'm offering you my services. You can call me, any time of the night or day. I'll be looking forward to hearing your voice.' He takes a delicate, shallow drag and exhales. 'If you ever want anything a little bit special. You know what I mean, something people are going to remember.' Terence lights another match and throws it at Rex's face with a flirtatious flick of his wrist. Rex jerks back and leaps to his feet. Terence laughs. The match falls to the floor and goes out. Rex wishes he could yell for someone to come but the music's too loud. Terence lights another match and pulls over a magazine with his other hand, pacing each movement like a stripper. 'I know all about you. I think I know what you'd like. I heard about the little bonfire you had, over at your place. I thought, that young man's got some style, he really does. I thought, that'll be someone I should get to know better.' He sets fire to a corner of the magazine, and within seconds all its pages are splayed and blazing. Terence has a wide smile on his face. 'Fire's my thing. If ever you want someone smoked out of their home, burnt in their bed; if you ever want to put the heat on someone, you give me a bell and it'd be a pleasure. Truly it would.' Rex is standing with his back pressed against the far wall. Terence is still holding the burning magazine. He says, 'You know, fire is so noisy. That's one of the many things I love about it. You might think it was the colour, but to be frank it's that snapping, creaking sound you get. Like twigs in a forest. There's really nothing else like it. Look at it … You're not looking.' He holds it out to Rex. 'Fire makes things come alive, don't you think, in four dimensions. I can teach you all about fire, Rex. Anything you need, I'll find a way. People, places, children. I'm not particular. No questions asked. Of course, it'll cost you, but I'll give you the best service. One time with me, and you'll never look back. Any environment, I'll work my way in there somehow. I can wipe out a whole block of flats if you give me due notice.' He drops the magazine. Rex darts forward and stamps the fire out. 'Look at your face,' says Terence Blackheath fondly. 'Like a high-society miss who's seen a rat at the opera.'

Outside the restaurant, Leo turns to Janine. 'I'd better go home,' he says. She stands inside the doorway, about to go in.

'You don't want to stay for one drink?'

Leo grins and shakes his head. 'Don't pretend like you want me here. This is your moment of glory. Anyway, we don't both want to be at the scene of the crime, it gives too many people too much opportunity to speculate. Go inside and have a good time.'

Janine takes a vintage 1920s enamelled compact from her pocket and checks her face. Running a fingertip under her eye, she says, 'Did you call them to check everything's in order?'

Leo nods: 'Yeah, course I did. It's all set up. But you've got to make sure everyone's in the right place, it's going to be one shot into the restaurant. I've got to say, it was pretty difficult finding a female hitman. Hitperson. Whatever.' Janine looks at him. 'I like to think of it as affirmative action. It's a very male-dominated line of work, you know. Anyway, women are quicker and more savage. And we never get caught.' He moves to kiss her on the cheek but she ducks back inside the doorway. She pushes him away with her foot. 'I'll call you when it's done.' He gives her a sarcastic salute then ambles off down the street as she enters the restaurant.

'Good evening,' says the maitre d', taking her coat. 'I believe your friends have already arrived.' Janine has always adored restaurants. She is Daddy's little princess, in love with the spectacle – the gossip, the dressing up. And her flesh loves to be fed. Meat almost raw, oozing pale blood on the plate; ornate chopsticks sinking into sushi; raspberry sorbet, dense purple. All washed down with champagne, cold, sharp and expensive as a glassful of crushed diamonds. She walks in and people automatically turn to look at her. White is her favourite colour. People don't usually wear white. Too scared – they think they're going to spill something on it, as though they're babies.

She looks around. It is a perfect place – seating arranged around crescent-shaped benches, golden prettifying light, and one window running the entire length of the room. One section of the restaurant is taken up with Janine's guests: Neela, Gavin, Lukas, Victor and Mark are all there, and so, thank God, is PC Shane Chisholm. Even in his normal clothes he still looks like a policeman, with that barely-civilised, scrubbed look. 'He's not really a human being,' Mark had told her through his split lips immediately after their encounter. 'More like a very stupid dog. You make nice with him and he makes nice back to you. You kick him and he attacks. That's all you need to know about Shane. But you have to get it right, OK? I endured a pulping in the faith that you would come up with something really vicious. Now you have to give him his payback. We have to do it so he has no opportunity to strike back. A no-returns purchase. It has to be a bolt from the blue.'

Janine approaches her table. 'So? I take it we're in the mood to celebrate our success as club entrepreneurs.' She doesn't look at Shane.

Lukas looks up and says, 'Hey! The woman of the hour. We were just talking about you. Sit down and get some grub in you.' Victor waves. Gavin sneers, his version of a smile. Neela greets her cautiously, not quite meeting her eyes. She is what Janine always wanted to look like – fierce and nasty, instead of cheap and fat and slothful, which is what she feels like in the girl's presence, all fleshy and desperate to please, like a past-it comedian.

She takes her seat, between Gavin and Mark, opposite the

window. She watches the street for a few seconds, scanning the road.

Mark whispers to her: 'Are you OK?' and she gives him a smile and nods: 'You?' Mark shrugs.

'Remember me?' Shane has leant forward and stuck his face into hers. She jolts back but remembers to smile.

'Yes, of course. So nice to see you and Mark pals again.'

Shane claps his buddy on the shoulder. 'Yeah, well, life's like that, isn't it? But just cos him and me have made up doesn't mean to say me and you are done.' He's looking at her with his mouth in an ugly snarl. The rest of the table is watching. 'You thought you were being clever,' he says. 'Where'd they teach you to go for the guy's bollocks? Self-defence class, was it? Or some bint on the telly giving ten tips for every girl's safety on the walk home?'

'Oh yes, sorry about that,' says Janine, looking around for the waiter. 'I don't quite know what came over me.' She relives the feel of his nuts in her palm, like quail eggs, silky and crushable.

Shane jabs his finger at her. 'No, don't look away, I'm talking to you.' He reaches out and picks one ringlet off her shoulder. He pulls it slowly till it straightens, then keeps pulling until her head tips forward. She is looking at him, mystified. Fisticuffs and hair-pulling: the two rare high-level combat techniques required for a career in the Met.

She yanks her head back, picks up the menu and flicks it in his face. Then she angles it and stabs the corner close to his eye. 'Behave. And don't touch me.' He looks at her for a second and then abruptly sits back.

The food comes, great glossy plates of caveman grub, slabs of meat all round. Shane eats with his head right down. Gavin and Victor both eat like children, snapping open mouthfuls and swallowing without tasting any of it. They don't care for restaurants.

Lukas eats like he does everything else, in his interested, intense way, darting pleased glances at the other diners. Neela is only picking at her food, her shoulders hunched and miserable, even though she is very hungry. She doesn't like eating in public. Her tongue dries up and she becomes clumsy. Mark doesn't order anything. Janine tries to get him to share her meal but he shakes his head. 'How can you not eat?' Janine says, her voice sad, and he replies, 'I don't want to. Even looking at food makes me feel sick.' He pushes her plate away from him. 'So,' she presses, 'you can't eat, you can't sleep, you can't piss, you can't fuck. What can you do?' He shrugs: 'Take brown.'

After the main course Mark sidles away to the toilets, ignoring Janine's look. Once there, he sits down and reaches inside his jacket. He was always addicted to something but heroin is the glorious city, the end of his travels. He has the look of the immovable addict that others instantly recognise, that passive self-satisfied vortex-pull of junkiedom. No fear. He takes out a pristine square of tinfoil and carefully tears it in two. He would never jack up. He would rather steal money to get a bigger smoking hit. Jacking up is for council-block tenants whose mothers are prostitutes. It's a low-life method. Mark's mum is a psychotherapist from Kent. He rolls one piece of tinfoil into a cone shape and holds it between his lips. He folds the other piece along the middle, then runs his lighter under it. People come and go outside the cubicle door. He unpicks a ten-bag and empties it into the groove. He tries not to breathe on the dull, clotted brown powder as he holds it under the end of the cone. He runs his lighter under it again. It burns down in a split second, smoke rising in an uncontrolled burst, whitish and airy. Mark breathes in great lungfuls. The smell of charred wood fills the cubicle before being swamped by that characteristic odour, caramelised and cloying, dense like discount perfume.

Janine feels sweat running between her shoulder blades. Mark hasn't yet returned. Her mobile's in her coat pocket, in the cloakroom. Neela and Gavin are watching her curiously. Where did Rex find these people? In all her life she's never had friends like this – always vigilant and hostile, like crows gathering on a roof-ledge, incapable of taking sheer physical enjoyment from life. She could never imagine one of this lot, Neela or Gavin or Victor, smiling at the feel of a fine gold chain on their skin, or a perfect mug of coffee on a snowy afternoon. If you gave them a gift they'd look at you suspiciously, wondering if it was a trick. Shane Chisholm, his cheeks bloated and red with drink, crashes into Mark's place beside her. He slams his hand onto her thigh. 'Not having any fun? You look a bit knackered.' His fingers dig into her skin. He takes his arm away and then tries to push her back into the seat. 'You should lean back. Relax your spine.' He presses his chest against her to wrestle her into place. People like him make Janine believe in original sin. They are totally devoid of conscience. She can see exactly what he was like as a child – a pathological liar, a dare-maker, a pincher. She pushes him away roughly and he comes back, his shoulder right in her chest, with twice as much force. He is smiling. 'What's wrong?' he asks her. 'Not in the mood to be friendly? I'm not going to bite.' His breath smells of wine. Janine raises her hand, fingers spread. She puts it over his face and shoves him back.

'Shane, you're in my seat.' Mark's eyes are hooded and filmy. He slurs his words. Janine looks up at him. The nights spent sprawled on the couch, the depressing sorties around the city, the before-dawn timetable of seedy meetings, it's all written there in his clogged junkie irises.

Shane gives him a big smile and says, 'Sorry, mate, you'll have to take mine. Me and Janine are just having a little discussion.'

Mark shrugs and makes to sit, blind and deaf to everything around him except the warmth of inhaled contentment saturating his cells.

Janine springs forward, reaching out, and says, 'I –' before Shane puts his hand on top of her head, forcibly turning it to face him.

As soon as Mark sits down, the window running the length of the restaurant breaks. Everyone flings themselves back in reflex. The glass bends and shatters in slow motion. It seems almost to freeze over and form a mosaic of icy nuggets before some pressured kick from the outside sends it blasting horizontally through the dining hall. The glass doesn't come loose in shards but in innumerable pellets, flat on the sides and sharp all the way round, impossible to hold. The pellets slice people's faces and embed themselves in the far wall. The remaining parts of the window shiver and cling to the frame. The diners cower, exposed to the street. The road is empty except for a black car sailing away, its lights intense in the dark.

All at Janine's table have thrown their arms across their faces. She raises her eyes and peers around the restaurant. It is deathly quiet, save for the whimpering of people who caught it in the eye. All the yellow light has dissipated, drawn off by the October frost. The place is wrecked and ugly, the diners not the glamorous beauties of five minutes ago, but small and grey and cowardly, their mouths a collective 'oh' of shock. Shane's head is leaning on Janine's shoulder. She pulls a face. She isn't squeamish but she hadn't quite planned to inspect her victim at such close range. She doesn't want to be face to face with her crime. Gingerly, she reaches round and grabs the head by the hair. She raises it up and cautiously turns. There it is: eyes wide open, skin pale, mouth frozen in a wet smile. Her trophy. PC Shane Chisholm, leader of the pack no more. No more nights spent watching the cons. No more little victories over the under-world. Shane, poor dumb Shane, receiving the kiss-off a policeman deserves. Janine experiences the feeling Leo described to her once, of superiority and power, of being on the other side of the mirror and breaking through into total light. She observes the lashes, blonde at the tips. The veins in the eyeballs. The fine lines in the skin. The face juts forward and lands a smacker on her nose. 'Alright, sweet thing,' he says. Janine lets go of Shane's hair.

Next to Shane is Mark, a neat red hole between his eyebrows. The hole looks as though it's been stuck on, so perfect is it. Real talent went into creating that crisp-edged crimson circle. 'Hey Janine,' Lukas says, 'your friend Mark may need some Nurofen.' His voice is cold. The back of Mark's head has been blown away. The sofa-back is soaked, not just with blood but with actual pieces of gore.

'Wow,' says Victor, picking up a chunk of mingled meat and glass with his dessert spoon, 'actual brain. Jesus. Gavin, look. I've got actual human brain in my spoon.' Janine knows her brief reign is coming to an end. She has suffered a certain loss of prestige. She was once the mysterious stranger who promised untold riches. Better-dressed than them, better-mannered, better-connected. Only marginally sinful, not mired in it like they were, not steeped in bad deeds. Now she has sent a bullet scorching into the midst of their little group. Their allegiance, so shaky from the start, is now ashes under her feet. They don't know what went on between Shane and Mark. They are pack animals committed to jungle protocol, sticking close to their leader. Gavin, Lukas, Neela, Victor. All basically the same breed – narrow, sallow – with minor differences: Victor's sharpened incisors, Neela's knife-nick eyes.

Neela fastens her gaze on Janine's face. 'Judging by your

expression I take it there's been some kind of mistake,' she says, her voice low and triumphant. 'Which one of us was it you wanted?'

Lukas is looking out at the street. 'You're very stylish, aren't you?' he says contemplatively. 'You do things with panache. I like that.' He turns back to face her, 'But you're an amateur, Janine. You shouldn't try to extend your expertise. There's nothing wrong with doing something purely for effect, but there are rules. The main rule is, never let your ego triumph over the occasion. Don't allow the quest for personal glory to dominate the search for greater good.' He looks at Mark, then reaches over and unfastens the dead boy's watch, putting it on his own wrist. He continues, 'Look at him, poor creep. What do you want us to do now? Give you a round of applause? Call for an encore? The broken window's pretty spectacular and everything, but it's not exactly energy-efficient, is it? I mean, you have to think about these things.'

Janine interrupts him, scowling, 'Spare me the schpiel. I don't see any movie cameras here. Last thing I heard, they weren't reshooting *Goodfellas* in the area. One night in front of Sky Moviemax and you think you've got a bit part in *Pulp Fiction*. Save your breath.'

Janine does not fear Lukas. He is like an overgrown child, bounding and ungainly but easily mastered. One word from Rex and he will be knocking at her door trying to be her friend again. Gavin and Victor are just kids – sidekicks, hired assassins. They have no intellect. It is Neela who scares her. That observant, all-despising mentality, the force of self-loathing behind everything she says. Janine could never outwit Neela. Every lie and deceit would be discovered. It is only a matter of time now. She will have to start running, with the pack snapping at her ankles all the way.

118

Shane is looking at her intently. He seems to be on the brink of laughter: Shane Chisholm defies death once again! Instead, he puts on a mock-mournful face. 'Shame.' He reaches into Mark's jacket and takes out his wallet, pocketing it. 'It's always tough when you lose a friend. Anytime you need counselling, drop by the station. We'll fix you up.'

Janine looks from face to face. She too wants to laugh. It's as if they're all attending some kind of diabolical banquet – the blood on the plates, the dead, brained boy in the place of honour, the glass studding the napkins. All they need now is for the head waiter to reveal himself as half man, half goat. She looks down and realises Mark's goo has dappled her outfit. Nobody else in the restaurant has noticed them because their table faces the street. She stands up and makes to leave. The glass crunches under her feet. She doesn't go towards the door. Instead, she walks out through the shattered window, stepping down onto the street. It is just past midnight. Goosebumps rise on her skin. People she passes turn curiously at the sight of her. She is moving very slowly. Her mind turns doggedly. Rex will do whatever he is told to. In the self-defence courses she sat through at school, they told her: if ever you feel threatened, find a friendly-looking woman and ask if you can walk with her. Call a friend for assistance. Don't start to run. Don't look over your shoulder. It has all been a misunderstanding. But they are there, on her trail. They don't need a reason. She is their new toy. Gavin and Lukas would love to shred her. They would laugh and bicker while they destroyed her face. But they would never touch Leo – that is what stings most – because everybody loves Leo. So brave, so funny, so handsome. It is women they want to hurt. And Neela, tough, hard, repressed Neela, who can't quite look her in the face, she would want it the most. Janine shivers. What can she do – just say no?

119

By four that morning, Rex's skin feels grainy with tiredness. He has finally finished organising the clear-up operation after the King of England's launch. It is still dark outside. He flops onto one of the sofas in the ground-floor bar. He never had much physical stamina. Sleep is what he loves, over all other activities. Sinking into the bed, the covers heavy on his limbs, feeling rational thoughts slowly unknot themselves. He closes his eyes. They made money tonight. Money and contacts. Rex is a success. His head throbs.

The next thing he knows, there is a shadow and a weight at the end of the sofa. Rex cries out and sits bolt upright. He gropes in the dark but the figure twists out of his reach instinctively, before advancing again. It is Neela. They are lit only by the street-lamps outside. She holds something up to him: 'I had a copy of the back entrance key made.'

Rex rubs his hands over his face. 'How long have you been here?'

Neela shrugs and looks around. 'Not long. I didn't want to wake you.' Rex slides away from her, then stands up and goes to the opposite couch. Neela has a way of claiming the air around her – stray too close and you get ten thousand volts. She makes him uncomfortable, moving unimpeded in the dark, her senses primed. Night-vision is what she has. 'We need to hurt Janine,' she says. 'She's making a fool of you. She's taking your money.'

Rex groans and lies down on his couch. 'I don't want to hear it. Let her make a fool of me if she likes,' he puts his arm over his eyes, 'I don't care.'

Neela goes and stands over him, knowing it will disturb him. 'Look at me,' she says, and he turns his face away. 'Look at me,' she urges again. 'I need you to find a way to harm her. She needs to be stopped.'

Rex sits up grumpily. 'She's not doing anything, Neela. Just let it go. Anyway, I'm a firm believer in the theory that if you wait by the river long enough, the bodies of your enemies will float past.'

Neela holds something up, cupped in her palm. 'Have you got a light?' she asks, and Rex fumbles for one, saying, 'I thought you were a health freak. It must be bad if Janine's induced you to start smoking.' He holds the flame up, thinking to light Neela's cigarette. Instead, in the girl's small palm is something red and slightly wet, the size of a mouse. It looks solid and alive. 'Neela, it's the middle of the night. I'm not playing guess-the-object with you now.' Rex sits back and crosses his arms.

'Go on, just play it once,' Neela says, pushing her hand in front of him. In the lighter's flame her eyes seem to pulse – grey, green, yellow. She is excited. 'Have a few goes, then I'll tell you what it is.'

Rex sighs. 'Sponge, a rag soaked in something. Offal –'

'Nearly!' Neela shrieks. She holds it even closer: 'Smell it. Go on, smell it.'

He shoves her hand away by the wrist. 'Please, whatever it is, just leave me alone. I don't want to know. But it does stink. I don't know. Steak that's gone off? Something you found in the gutter?'

Neela smiles. 'Rex, meet Janine's friend Mark. Mark's very happy to make your acquaintance. He's out of his mind with joy. Believe me, this is the proof.' Their eyes meet. Neela raises her free hand to the meat and begins to stroke it. Then she licks it. Then she kisses it. 'Mmm! So juicy,' she mumbles. Blood squeezes out onto her lips. Rex lurches forward and dry-retches loudly. Neela throws the brain-part onto the floor and grins. 'Pretty gross, right? That was one of her best friends. Maybe she meant to get him, maybe it was meant for one of us. But the point is, she'd kill her own friends. And you know who paid for it?' She bats her eyelashes and points at him theatrically. 'You, you gorgeous great hunk of blond stupidity.'

Rex gets up and shuffles over to the bar. He grabs a bottle of whisky and drinks, rinsing his mouth out and spitting into the sink. Neela comes up to him. He can see dried blood on her lips. Every exchange he has with her, he seems to get weaker and she stronger. He is already half-convinced. He can imagine Janine, laughing at the restaurant, her neck stretched out long and flirtatious, as her best friend jerks and expires on the seat next to her. None of the others would carry out a killing like that. It is too civilised. They would choose slow, painful, bygone methods – beatings, knives; rape and broken bones. He looks at Neela's taut skin, the cheekbones sharp in the darkness. Neela would choose rope.

She hoists herself up on one of the bar stools. Then she climbs onto the bar itself and lies down. She takes off her jacket. 'You're such a reptile,' Rex tells her as he stands behind the bar, 'You like the cold and the dark and the damp.'

Neela turns onto her side and looks at him. 'Janine's making an idiot of you,' she taunts. 'She's trying to break us all up. You don't get it, do you? She runs this place, not you. She controls the money, not you. She has the contacts, not you.' Neela stretches and turns her face to the ceiling. 'Oh, you're so fucking stupid. I'm trying to help you. Out of all the people in the world, who would you say are your friends? Out of your entire life, who's stuck with you? Me, Lukas, Gavin. Victor and Leo too, now, maybe. We love you. We respect you. We've never bullied you, have we? We've never laughed at you. We're like family. It's Janine who's laughing. She thinks you're weak. She's telling people right now – See how stupid Rex is. I do these things, and he doesn't notice. I take his money, and he just smiles.'

Rex laughs harshly and swigs more whisky. 'Neela, look me in the eye and tell me all of that again. You've never loved anyone in your entire life.'

Neela is like a lizard. She thrives in the dry winter. Whenever she can't get to sleep, she imagines that she's trekking alone across a great slab of ice, the air blazing cold on her face, before and behind her only white upon white. It always relaxes her. She looks at Rex's silhouette, so plainly grand. A real man. But when she looks a little closer there is fat boy, bullied boy, lowest-marks-in-the-class boy. Always desperate to belong. That veneer of bravado – so excruciatingly thin. She sits cross-legged on the bar. Now their faces are at the same level. 'No, you look me in the eye, Rex,' she says. Her voice has dropped to a hypnotic murmur. Rex finds himself suddenly scared. Despite those young court-eunuch looks there is something about her that resembles a seaside fortune teller, wizened and ancient in her incense-heavy hut. Something claw-like and grasping which will lay its hooks into his soul. Neela speaks: 'Don't you recognise her? Doesn't Janine remind you of anyone? Haven't all those years spent alone in a corner of the playground taught you anything? When bullies grow up, they turn into Janine.' Rex turns away but Neela lays her chilly hand on his throat. 'What does a bully do? Let me tell you. He singles you out and makes you pay. He separates you from your friends. He's better than you. Craftier, quicker, more nimble. He finds a way of doing things to you, secretly and slowly. Mental things, physical things. He enslaves you without your noticing it. Doesn't he? He makes it so that wherever you turn, you see him. Every option you thought you had, if you pull the string for long enough, he is always at the end.'

Suddenly, Neela gets off the bar. She removes her hand from his neck, picks up her jacket and puts it on. Rex falls back as though released. But Neela hasn't finished talking. She prowls the room. 'You paid for tonight. You realise that, don't you? You paid for Janine to kill her friend. A foot to the left, and you would have paid for Lukas' death. Don't you see? She's already at the end of the string. She's already on the other side of the door. Don't kid yourself that you have any power here.' She stands by the door. He can barely see her. Her voice carries, firm and controlled. It seems as though the whole room is talking to him. 'I do love you, Rex. And I know you love me, because without me and Lukas and the others you'd have nothing. I know you realise that. Without us, you'd be alone, and you hate being alone. The phone would never ring. You'd have to walk the streets all day, and nobody would say a word to you from the moment you woke to the moment you went to bed. If you were ill, nobody would help you. We brighten up your life. We laugh at your jokes. We help you. You need us. And now Janine has come, we're worried about you. We don't want to die, one by one. We don't want to see your money drained away. How many people does Janine know? Hundreds. They all came here tonight, and they drank your champagne. Imagine each one of those people laughing at you. The sound would be deafening. She's a bully, Rex, just like all the others. But now you're older. You have things. This is your chance. Nobody's going to give you power. You have to take it. Every revenge fantasy you had, you can play out. Everything you never did to those people, do to her.'

Neela yawns and stretches. The night makes her confident. It hides her ugly face. She feels things more keenly in the dark.

124

Over behind the bar, Rex is completely still, the whisky bottle gripped in his hand. Neela smiles to herself. She knows she has very few talents. When they were handing out charms and accomplishments, she was truanting in the local shopping centre. But she can press herself into people's fears. Rex has been listening to her. When she was talking, she could sense his nerves straining to hear. Now he puts down the bottle and clears his throat. Neela opens the door. She raises her eyes to the moon, steps out and doesn't look back.

Rex is already dialling. He raises the receiver to his ear and listens for a moment. Then he says, 'Terence?'

The sun begins to rise. The air is misty and white. On Soho's Berwick Street the market-stall cages stand black and rusted. The city hasn't woken yet. Occasionally, a cab with its light off coasts past. The area is anonymous and silent as a satellite town. Outside Janine's flat is a winding, reaching line of smoke. It floats upwards, thin and fine, a whisper in the fog. It doesn't make a sound.

Terence Blackheath is shapeless, ugly, repulsive, but he can move in the night. He is the main usher: he holds all the keys. He slips under windows, inside locks, between bricks. He owns things. He owns people's homes. When they need to piss in the dark, and reach for this switch, they shine the bulb full in Terence's face. Outside Janine's flat the trail rises higher. A drunk homeless woman draws closer, talking to herself. She's wearing a tattered winter coat and shiny, brand-new trainers. She sniffs the air and sways. She tries the door and reaches to grasp the vapour in the air. The door swings back. Fog meets fog, mist meets mist. Terence has been visiting. Say hello to Terence!

Janine is fast asleep. She is curled, her flesh heavy and warm, under a quilt. Dancing with the sandman. Her soiled dress is in the bin.

Old Compton Street waits. The homeless woman waits. There is perfect silence until, with the sweetest noise, the glass in the windows explodes and falls. 'And Snow White broke her stepmother's mirror, and it shattered into one hundred thousand pieces, each like a diamond,' says the homeless woman in a cracked, theatrical voice. It's not so quiet any more. It's like a rock concert, in fact. Black smoke pours from the windows. Fire. Fire is here. Prehistoric man discovered it, but Terence bought the rights. Janine's things are turning to nothing – corners and ends and stumps. Her clothes burn. Her papers burn. The futon is a cube of flames. The chair seems to dance orange and red flamenco steps. The ceiling turns black. Another life in the city, unwinding quickly, disturbing the night, breaking up the fog, backing away, filling the final supply of air with smoke and long, low, cornered, claustrophobic cries.

Six hours later, Leo is queuing up at the Authentic Neighbourhood Coffee Vendors for his Saturday latte and croissants. He knocked on the others' doors but they must have been comatose after the party. He hums a tune to himself and greets the other people in the shop. They all make small-talk with him; everybody likes Leo. The folks who vend the Authentic Coffee keep a little powder-blue plastic Fifties-style radio on the counter, and the news report winds up with the sombre tale of a fire in central London, address so-and-so, and a woman dead. Death by misadventure, they're calling it. The people in the shop are all tutting and shaking their heads – a woman dead, her organs roasted, her eyes gone, found crouching in a corner, brittle, skinned, mouth open. Shock sprouts like cartoon icicles all over Leo's body, turning him numb. He pays for his order and walks back to the estate. Everything seems at one remove. He somehow gets the key into the lock and himself into the flat. His mind seems to race and be frozen at the same time.

In the kitchen he lays out his stuff. The telly's on, and sunshine comes in at the window. He calls, 'Hey, you'll never guess what. I just heard that you were dead,' and Janine, coming in from the bedroom with the patchwork quilt still around her shoulders, takes one of the coffees and a croissant and says, 'No way. What a total bummer,' in an impeccable Valley Girl voice.

5

The next day, Janine is walking in Hyde Park. There is a lacerating wind. It seems to charge down the pathway and hit her face-first. A couple of rollerbladers barrel past, but other than that there is nothing but the flat, dry, tended template of grass and gravel. As soon as she is back on the streets she is returned to the game. It used to be that she was free. Circulating amongst the scum, serving the scum, friends with scum, but not scum herself. The shadow-life was something she dropped into occasionally for her own diversion. It excited her to have a roll-call of bandits and renegades in her address book. She had always thought failure was Rex's destiny; he had the sort of nature that cried out to be dominated, to be made the mouthpiece of others' ventriloquism. But now she sees there is something about him. He attracts trauma. The creeps of the universe find themselves inexplicably drawn to his kingdom. The contacts she so carefully built up have advanced themselves, entirely and immediately, for Rex's patronage. Men seem to be in love with other men. That is something she never believed before. She took success as though it was owed to her. Now she has experienced their way of moving – collective, sudden, secretive. All with that safety-in-numbers supremacy.

Janine is wearing new, expensive clothes. After leaving the restaurant, she didn't go back to her flat. She called Leo and told him to run a deep bath. When she arrived on his doorstep he took one look at her and led her in without a word. She tried to wash her white dress but the blood wouldn't come out, so she went to town and bought cream cashmere, pale butterscotch leather and sapphire studs. It was the least Rex could do, after sending Terence Blackheath to lay his torch-touch on her. She loaded up on exquisite underwear and perfect shoes, and for lunch she bought herself a towering portion of cake, icing-dusted berries perched between leaves of white chocolate. She had heard about Terence and never really believed he existed. He formed part of a rumoured roster of idiosyncratic, one-trick mobsters, gossiped about but never seen. She can picture him now as a teenager, bandy-legged and asthmatic, bunking gym to play with matches.

There were certain trademark methods known to belong to certain people, and in this case the trail of cinders lay straight back to Terence. Janine laughs as she imagines what Rex must be feeling at this moment. He believes she has perished. That her broad back and rounded legs have been returned to the dust. He did not see that this could never be possible. Janine is immune from ignoble death. She will never be dragged into the farcical and unclassy demise of a grudge-job. It was not black dust she came from, like him, but grains of gold. It will be great sport to pounce upon Rex, to torment him a little. She will come to him all sorrowful, or vengeful, or perhaps giddy and gay. His limp, spineless nature dredges up from the very bottom of her soul an exultant feeling of raw superiority which makes her want to provoke and destabilise him for her own diversion. At heart she does not care what becomes of him, or of the others, with the exception perhaps of Neela. Of the entire crew, that one girl has the power to unsettle Janine, for her motiveless wrath and fury at the world seems to pierce all times and conti-nents. She has been afflicted with a personality so damaged and demonic that it could burn a hole straight through history. The girl obeys no laws of psychology or personality; she is a siphon through which vast abstract impulses charge. But Neela is the only one. For all their intensity, these months have a quality of impermanence about them. There is no doubt in Janine's mind that she will eventually snap the fine net of enmities and warring parties, and that the entire structure of her life at the moment will shiver and fall to her feet in feeble threads. The hazards and dares that have formed a customary part of her existence are just like intervals or dreams which interrupt but do not impinge upon reality. They do not cause Janine any real fear, because they are ephemeral and inconsequential. Somewhere on the horizon awaits, she is sure, an adventure which will cause her to feel, to be infatuated, enraged, ecstatic. But this is not it.

She walks very slowly, thinking. She doesn't like the cold. It makes her feel like a beached seal-cub, immobile and swaddled in blubber. Slowly, she becomes aware of a heat and solidity immediately behind her. The wind seems to be moving around it. She walks a little faster. It is a man, vigorous and silent, someone very fit. Janine can almost feel the muscles working along his legs and torso. She doesn't want to look round. A very small, lazy part of her wants to be shot and thrown away like a sweet wrapper. At least it would end the matrix of backstabbings and mouse-hunts that constitute her current life. Eventually, though, she sighs and whips round. 'Oh, piss off, you,' she shouts at PC Shane Chisholm. 'I saw you at Harvey Nicks, I saw you on the King's Road and I saw you in that taxi. Now, why don't you go back to your office and file your expenses?'

Shane Chisholm considers himself a hard man. Infallible, unfellable. Rippling in the sun, stony and colossal in the rain. And Shane believes in revenge. There is a delicate, ritualistic beauty in wronging the person who has wronged you. A neat cancelling-out of debt. He has given this one her chance. She could have proved herself to be sympathetic to his point of view. But no. She is wayward. Her list of crimes – generally, plus those specifically against him – is a mile long. He could have her on any number of drugs charges – up there, pleading her case to a judge, dressed in her church-going clothes. He could knot her up in laws and litigation. Or he could have her for himself.

Janine stares him out. He isn't wearing a scarf or heavy coat. He stands legs parted, planted like a pillar of salt, raw, white and dry. The bones in his face are wind-whipped. He seems not to inhabit but actually embody the cold. The cold seems to come from him. She watches him, as if in slow motion, as he braces his shoulders then bends his elbow and draws his fist back. It shoots out, not the aimless slug of a streetside brawler but trained and sharp and proud, employing all the shoulder and back muscles, before snapping back. Strangely, being punched in the face doesn't hurt. Everything goes starry white then black. When Janine opens her eyes she is looking at the sky and her cheek and eye are numb. Her tongue smarts where she bit on it. She has flown about five feet away from Shane, who now approaches. He hauls her up by the coat collar.

'We have a saying, down at the station. Fuck or fight. We give people a choice. We fight them or we fuck them.' He sets her on her feet and holds both her hands in his, like a priest. He wears a square silver ring which presses into her knuckle. It is clear from his grasp that she cannot get away. His thick fingers seem to lock her arms into place. She can feel his body opposite her, straight-backed and wide, ready to break into an even, sweatless sprint if she bolts. 'Let me talk you through the procedure,' he says. He begins to walk slowly back in the direction from which they'd come, dragging her with him – back down the pathway, past the leafless trees and riverside cafe, the damp and empty benches. 'If they opt to fight, they have a chance. Heavy, big guys do well if they fight. The ones who've got forearms like joints of beef. Some of the little, tough ones are tricky too. You've got to watch for them. They'll scratch, bite, anything. They could take your eye out with some of their moves. They could turn you into one of them eunuchs. But generally speaking we've got the upper hand.' He snorts then turns his head sharply to the side and spits on the ground. 'By the time we get them in a cell they're stripped down to the basics – two arms, two legs. And if they're handcuffed they've got even less to work with. But we've got the whole armoury. Sharp objects, blunt objects. Things for cutting, things for breaking. And we're trained. There are pressure-points. All you do is give 'em a prod and they go down, cold. Most times we win. Once in a while we lose, and it's big news. But we take it in our stride.' He takes one of her hands and places it on his waist so she can feel the outline of his gun. They are nearing one of the park exits, the turning at Marble Arch. Bands of traffic wait at the junction. Now they are off the grass, walking through yellow dust towards the iron railings. Janine's hands and face are hurting. She is getting irritated. His voice goes on and on, dropped-t after glottal stop. A dagger in the temple would be such sweet relief. Shane continues: 'What we prefer to do, though, is take the fuck option. Now, to you fucking someone means one certain thing, doesn't it? But to us, it implies a whole range of activities. When you hunt someone down and give them a threat, like you're standing at the end of the bed when they wake up, that's fucking them. Or when you pick off their friends and family, that's another good way to fuck them. In our book, fucking someone means to harm slowly, over time. You plot each move. It's a full-scale operation. Do you get what I'm driving at? I'm just trying to make you understand my vocabulary. What I'm saying is, Janine, you tried to fuck me but now I'm fucking you back.' He raises one of his hands to grab her hair and steer her towards a blue Nissan parked high on the kerb. It has a parking ticket attached to the windscreen, which he ignores.

Janine looks around. Leo should be here but he hasn't come. He should be waiting by the gate. Leo, all limber and hard-bodied. Her best friend. Maybe he is tired of her. Maybe he has tricked her. They were meant to meet and talk. They would have reset the pattern of grudges in their favour. Now the Nissan's rear door is open and Shane is levering her in, pushing her head down close to her breastbone. It's a clever manoeuvre: try to resist and you wind up breaking your own neck. The car smells of stale burgers.

At least he has stopped talking. Any more prime nuggets of that cable TV crime-series script and she would have begged him to execute her. Janine watches his strong, square hands gripping the wheel. He has a fine clean neck and small ears set very close to his head. In her experience it is mistakes that cause the most harm: the furtive Chinese whispers of rumour and repute; the blunt idiocy of a mutual misunderstanding. This daylight abduction is too perfect. They are waiting at the lights. Shane abruptly turns the radio on and it blares through the speakers right behind Janine's head. She looks out of the window and there is Leo on the street only a foot away, just about to cross. He is looking over the car's hood and scanning the park railings, his eyes narrowed. His cheeks are red. He doesn't know what Shane looks like. His torso is level with her window. Shane is busy gearing up to launch the Nissan ahead of their neighbour. Janine carefully winds the window down a couple of inches, all knotted eyebrows and wincing, mincing movements. She reaches out, index finger extended, and prods Leo in the stomach. He frowns and looks down, then his face changes into comic incredulity. It makes Janine grin to see it.

Leo's smile fades when he sees her swollen face. As she takes a breath to whisper something, the lights are suddenly green and with a jerk she is thrown back into her seat.

Shane Chisholm drives like he's running an obstacle course, full of deft, last-minute moves. He watches her through his mirror. Every time she looks up, he winks at her. They drive northwards out of the city centre, into Finsbury Park. Janine stares at the streets, at once wide and dirty, grand and defiled. She knows the area. The properties are broad-fronted and imperial but their front gardens are loaded with stinking bins and old bikes, boxes and battered chairs. This is one of her main recruiting posts for dealers: an old duffer in the High Street fighters-and-pukers pub, a dapper boy in one of the Victorian houses. A lot of the faces and wares at the King of England come from here. The car turns into one of the uglier streets, a thin strip of brown terraces with mean cement paths leading up to each front door. Janine's quick eyes take in at least two cars with slashed tyres. The pavement is strewn with carrier bags and soggy pizza parlour circulars. Shane parks but doesn't get out. He toys with the central locking – the locks flick up, then down, and he watches Janine in the mirror, as though she's meant to make a grab for the door-handle when she can. He turns around to face her, his gun in his hand. It is an automatic like Rex's, only smaller, and black, not silver. It seeks her out, alive, with an interrogative look.

'You know,' says Shane, 'all that stuff I told you about the difference between a fuck and a fight, and the difference between a fuck in your language and a fuck in mine? I'm not sure I should have revealed all the secrets of the trade. I think it might've been better if we'd stuck with the original definition. A fuck is a fuck is a fuck. Whaddya reckon?' He looks straight at her crotch. She can feel it, even through her layers of clothes.

She knows from Mark what he was like before – before the Force came calling. A tube-train creep, all eyes; a voice on the phone line, husky and unafraid; uncouth in a disco.

Shane gets out of the car and walks round to her side, the gun low and trained on her face. He opens her door, grabs her by the neck and pulls her upright. 'Smile,' he whispers to her, 'the neighbours are watching.' Inside one of the nearest houses she sees the twitch of cheap curtains and the pulsing light of a television. From another, the low-pitched shout of warring parents. Shane is unlocking the door, still with one hand clamped around her neck. He has tucked the gun back into his waistband. The top half of the door is taken up with a stained glass window bearing the picture of a sunrise. 'You'd fit right in, here,' he is saying. 'Lots of people like you in the neighbourhood. Odds and ends from all over the world. All sorts of colours, talking in their language at the tops of their voices. You come to this country, you'd think some of them would learn to speak English.' He opens the door and pushes her inside.

Janine scans the place for a second. It is clean but ugly. The air is dull and shaded. There are little touches which remind her of a programme she once saw about serial killers and their foibles: the row of polished, identical shoes; the visible lack of any dust; the plastic runners covering the hall carpet; the cheap calendar in the exact centre of the wall. Shane is fastening the door with an old-fashioned chain. Janine reaches over casually and takes his gun. It is warm from his body. She weighs it in her hand and laughs. 'That was easy,' she says. Shane turns round. There is something in his face – the prankster caught. Janine looks at him for a second, then puts the gun in her mouth and pulls the trigger. It clicks. She pulls the trigger again. Nothing. It's not loaded. She stamps her foot with irritation, stuffs the empty weapon in her pocket and heads straight for the door.

She looks like a debutante whose credit card's been rejected. 'You really are a timewaster, you know that?' she spits at him. 'I was having a great little day out before you decided to come up and play the big bad wolf in the woods. Then you drive me to this dump in your shitty fourth-rate Nissan, and you threaten me with this.' She pulls the gun back out and waves it in his face. 'You know my theory about guns? Gun is to ammo what ego is to dick. A man with an automatic, he likes to think he can do it hard and fast. That's his dream. A man with a revolver, he wants to take his time. He's strategic. He's the Barry White of gun owners. But someone like you,' she pulls the trigger a couple of times, listening to its ineffectual, hollow sound, 'you're all for show. You're what I'd call a cunt-tease. You get the vibe, you set the scene. You make all sorts of promises. But at the end of the day you're just a dickless wonder. You make all the right faces, but you're shooting blanks.'

She reaches for the chain on the door but he throws her back. It is almost pleasant to sail through the air. Janine usually feels cumbersome but in his hands she becomes liquid and light. Shane takes up a kickboxing pose, arms raised to block his face, back leg sprung, torso side-on, chin lowered. He is backing Janine down the hallway, past the stairs and the entrance into the front room. 'Come on, Bruce Lee,' she's saying, 'show us some of your moves.' She realises she's stepped onto lino. The kitchen is spartan and neat: mugs on a hook and a rack of knives in a row. 'What're you going to do now?' Shane taunts. He's still in the hallway. 'Cook us up some tea?' Janine sticks her tongue out at him, then simply reaches to the side and shuts the kitchen door in his face. She leans against it, giggling to herself at the absurdity of the situation. The door jerks.

At the other end of the hallway a fist wrapped in a winter scarf punches through the stained glass window, which breaks with a cheap, thin sound. Segments of the sunrise fall to the mat: burnt orange, scarlet, gold. The hand flexes, then reaches down and disconnects the safety chain from its bolt before turning the catch to open the door. Leo stands there on the step, shaking his scarf free of glass. He looks inside the house. He is sorry to be late. As Shane's car had sped off Janine had turned to stare hard at him, and he'd got the message. She would never voluntarily go anywhere in a Nissan. It was harder than he thought it'd be, getting a cab to 'follow that car'. Most drivers just laughed.

Shane hasn't noticed he's here. The policeman's face is red, braced against the kitchen door, which repeatedly gives a little then slams shut again. He is stocky and excessively built where Leo is sinewy and triangular. Shane is the type he terms 'Mighty White' – a white bread-buying, full-fat milk-drinking, Sunday lunch-eating bloke. All porno mags and pints. He's got that bulldog look, brought up on frozen fish-fingers and five-a-side. Leo can hear Janine's laughter from behind the door. He steps up to Shane and taps him on the shoulder with the tip of one finger. Shane turns and Leo headbutts him. The only part of them that makes contact is Leo's brow and the bridge of Shane's nose. One quick peck is all it takes to crush the cartilage. Blood, real inside-blood, thick and maroon, starts to slide from his nose. Shane's eyes keep crossing as he tries to look down and assess the damage. He is breathing fast through his mouth. His skin goes slightly green. Leo steps forward and knocks on the kitchen door.

Janine peers out. 'Hiya,' she says to Leo. 'Ta for dropping by.' In her hand is a Safeway's pain au chocolat she found in the bread-bin. She eats it slowly, looking at Shane, who by now has sunk, stunned, to the floor. 'Oh, I get it,' she says after a while, 'you don't like pain. You've got a low tolerance threshold.' She shrugs. 'Nothing wrong with that. Don't feel bad. It doesn't make you any less of a man. But it's interesting, all the same.' It is true enough. If there is a choice, Shane Chisholm would take a raincheck on pain. His nose feels as though it's been torn from a root deep in his brain, a wrench blasting saltwater into his eyes. The traumatised nerves in his face seem to pulse like the prongs of a tuning fork, hitting the highest note of pain.

Janine goes down the hall and opens the cupboard under the stairs, peering inside. It is as she thought; inside are all the tools of Shane's obsessive-compulsive trade: the earthquake survival kit, the holocaust pack, the power-cut candles, the household screws, large and small, all in labelled boxes. 'Now, let's see, you anal bastard,' she muses. 'If I were going to pick just one item, what would it be? Choices, choices.' There is a power drill, its cable neatly coiled. But Janine has her limits. She would rather not have to witness the application of a whirring drill-bit to the young man's face. If it was a hands-off deal, then maybe it would make a nice story. There is a sander and a jigsaw, for shaping planks of wood. Janine holds it out to Shane. 'How about that? We could slice you into pieces and market you as a jumbo puzzle. The whole family could play. You never know, it could be a hit at cocktail parties.' Then she spots it. Ignored and old in a compartment of the toolbox. Just an ordinary, domestic claw hammer, its handle smooth and worn. As she picks it up, Leo springs forward.

'That's it,' he says. He poses with it. 'As in fashion, so in violence, sweetie. Always stick with the classics.'

Janine sits down next to Shane. 'You know,' she says, 'life is so complicated. You fucked my friend, I tried to fuck you and it didn't work, you fucked me and now I've fucked you again. I don't know about you but I'm feeling pretty fucked out.' She motions to Leo, who reaches into his back pocket then throws her his cigarettes and lighter. She sparks up and takes a long drag. Leo swings the hammer in a low arc. Its weighted glide makes him want to continue the action, like a pendulum. Shane is still sitting on the floor. Janine gets up, the fag clamped in her mouth. She takes Leo's scarf and begins wiping the door locks with it. Then she runs it over the handle of the understairs cupboard.

The more time passes, the more Shane's face hurts. Once the anaesthetic of shock has dissipated, all that's left is sheer, dumb, animal pain, crashing through his senses, inexorable as lava flow. It doesn't feel like he has a body at all, only a face where all his sensations are located. The world revolves around his broken nose. 'Get up,' Leo is saying to him. He is holding the hammer by his side, the head loose in his fingers, as a child would hold a rag doll. 'You're not a very good host, are you? You should show your guests around.' Shane gets up slowly. He is surprised to be able to move and see and breathe. Janine smiles at him. His vision is inexact. He shuffles past them into the kitchen. Then something seems to rise up behind him, black and hawk-like, and it strikes.

The West Central Estate is dark. The last of the lamps guttered weeks ago. The wrecked cars are gone and the skip is empty. It has been dragged to the side and in the central space four white lines are scored in a square, where Gavin and Victor usually tussle and play. The ground in one part of the courtyard is blackened. Since the burning, all the unsleeping eyes which monitored the estate have been sewn up. The dobbers have slunk away.

Rex finally has his audience. At his home have congregated the chosen: the gutter-walkers, the child-stealers. The most talented in their field, with their crushing handshakes. The rooms throng with mobsters and their molls. Rex is no longer afraid of these people. They take an interest in him. It pleases them that he is carrying on a great tradition. The opening of the doors of the King of England has blasted the locks off the catacombs, and out have crawled the undead. Rex is at once the new father and the new son – fresh meat to be corrupted, patron, publican. Boss man.

Janine and Leo stand at the gate. They have journeyed back from Shane's place tired and silent. It was a difficult kill. Shane's body was lined with layers of pumped-up muscle, dense as lagging. He had a strong heart and lungs under there. They had to make it look like it was the work of a burglar – someone none too bright. There was no room for creative licence. The claw of the hammer only dented the thick white skin of Shane's back, gouging off curled shavings of flesh that resembled whalemeat. And he didn't want to go. He had a coward's fear of death. He kept breathing, and not just moaning but shouting, his voice clear and loud. After every blow, which landed him face-down on the kitchen floor, he pushed himself back up again. He would turn a quarter circle before, with the predictability of a Punch and Judy show, the side of the hammer cuffed him in the face and sent him sprawling on the lino once more. Eventually they had to go for the head. It was the only part of him where bone and veins lay immediately under the skin. So they inflicted some brain damage. They opened up the back of his skull and dragged his brains out, like a housewife emptying clothes from a washing machine. At the last moment, Janine hauled him up, looked straight into his eyes and spat in his face. Then they stubbed him out.

'Rex is having a party,' Janine says, 'because he's such a business tycoon. Lots of guys want to shoot the shit with him.' Her voice is hard. The patch of red paint at Lukas' door is scuffed and dull. There is ice in the air. Come tomorrow morning the railings and skip-edge will be frosted white. The estate has a way of playing tricks on the sight. Between one blink and the next, it seems to change position by just a degree. In the dark it produces the effect of seething movement on the periphery of the courtyard: shapeshifters in the wings.

Janine is looking forward to this. Their dealings with Shane jolted her with an almost electrical force. The episode has lent to her for one night alone a strength and fervent energy. She feels the desire for cruelty sting her into action. It will be nice to be reunited with Rex, to feel herself so strong and unbreakable, and him so flimsy. His is a mentality that half-begs to be shattered or shorn. Yet even as she thinks this, Janine recalls the realisation she'd had, in Shane's house, of the rapidity with which she had lowered herself to the level of secondary assassin. She had considered herself to be above reciprocative violence. She was a thinker, not a doer. A commander rather than a foot-soldier. The act itself was a blast of simple, rare physical pleasure – all the more sweet because it was uncharacteristic. But the circumstances were sordid and ugly, and nothing could convince her refined beauty-seeking eye otherwise. 'Our moment of glory was pretty brief, wasn't it?' she continues.

Leo takes her arm as they walk towards Rex's place. 'How d'you mean?' She notices that he has a cut across the back of his hand, a weal, fine and deep. The skin is puffy around the wound. They can hear music and voices. It is not in Rex's nature to give parties.

Janine sighs, resigned. 'The launch. That was our night.' They knock on Rex's door but are not heard. She rummages in the bottom of her bag for a hair pin or paper-clip.

As she fiddles with the lock, Leo watches her and says, 'What makes you think there isn't tons of glory to come? The launch was only a couple of nights ago.' Janine straightens up and hammers at the door. After catching and rattling a few times, the lock gives and it swings open.

'You're so naive, Leo. There's no glory. There never was. I thought we'd basically run a bar. It shouldn't have mattered that I was using dealers and you were calling in your ex-colleagues to get the project off the ground. To me, that's normal. It's crime lite. It's what you do to survive. But the way I see what happened, we threw a party and slime started oozing through the floorboards. All these men who Marlon used to know resurfaced. You know, old men with love and hate tattooed on their knuckles. People who don't know how to read. It was never in my gameplan to bludgeon a policeman to death, no matter what he did to Mark. I'm not saying I didn't enjoy it because I did, I really did. But if we hadn't got him, eventually he would have got us. That's what it's come to. We used to have a choice about what side of the line we walked on. Now there's no choice. So Rex wins. We've become like him. Reluctant or enthusiastic, it doesn't matter. He's not part of our life, we're part of his. Actually, he isn't the problem. He's like us. It's the others, fuck-ups like Neela and delinquents like Victor and Gavin. We've absorbed their values. We're thinking the way they think. We've started second-guessing them, which makes us just like them.' They go into Rex's house and reel at the sudden noise and heat. She pushes him forward. 'When I was shopping it was so nice. I was just a girl in a store, trying on clothes. I could have been anyone. Then I noticed Shane waiting on the other side of the street, watching me.' They separate in the hallway.

Rex pours champagne for Terence Blackheath. They are sitting at the kitchen table, talking about Janine's death. Terence smokes. 'I must admit,' he says in his lisping voice, 'I really am rather proud of myself – and eternally grateful to your good self, of course, for giving me the opportunity. It was covered in some of the newspapers, you know. With some beautiful photographs. The doorway with scorch marks reaching right across the ceiling, that's one I liked. And a lovely shot of the window frames.' Rex has spent a lot of money on Terence. In return for the burning pyre, a shower of coins. For the golden girl, a golden gift. It was a fair exchange. For the first time, he realised how sweet money could be. It looked sweet, in its bound blocks of pristine fifties. It even smelled sweet. And it has made his life into one long wish list. Rex has been spending with evangelical fervour. Money gives him courage where he had none, attitude where before was only fat boy's dyslexic bafflement.

Rex says he's going to get some fresh air. He leaves Terence rolling yet another cigarette. At the end of the kitchen is a door which opens onto the 'terrace' – a walled slot of air two bricks wide. Rex wedges himself in. His ears are ringing. Music and entertaining are not his scene. He didn't invite anybody around, but at seven that evening the bell had rung and there was Terence Blackheath on the Welcome mat, his eyes fishy and expectant. Next came all the felons, young men and old. They brought with them cigars and wine, all paid for by him, though authorised by Janine. They brought beautiful women. Now his flat is full of friends who are really strangers. The place looks tiny, the ceiling too low, the lighting dim. To Rex, it is the kind of party only a fake would throw. A bogus playboy with second-rate ambitions. A wannabe. Even the labels on the champagne bottles look phoney. Leo's lot are like a troupe of dancers, movement-loving and intense. Then Janine's posse, three dozen loners with mobile phones who never settle in one place. They circulate, their catch-all eyes ferocious and degenerate. Then there is the old school, Marlon's cohorts, watching over the proceedings like ancient widows at a baptism. Rex himself has contributed nothing, neither word nor deed. He feels like a dullard, nice but dim, amongst these people. It is good to press his face against the wall, cold and slightly damp. It makes his mind still. He wants to turn his mouth to its porous surface and suck out the rain. At the orphanage they had lain flat on the ground, limbs outstretched. Beneath them they would eventually sense the earth turning. *Can you feel it?* they would ask each other. *Shhh. I'm feeling it now. It turns fast.* That was many years ago.

The door from the kitchen opens, then coming towards him along the balcony – the ledge so narrow and dark – is Janine, wearing white as usual. She is tall and solid like him. Her hair is loose and full of static. It throws out sparks. Neither of them makes a sound. Rex's eyes grow huge. His nerves stand on point. She has him now. One side of her face is shadowed, then as she comes closer he realises it's a purple, soggy-looking bruise. It draws her out of beauty into coarseness and monstrosity, the eye all askew. Now he sees her, he could not imagine her burning. She would repel fire. Fire's flames would lick her once then fall away like unwound bandages.

'Rex,' she says, and her voice is caressing and soft. 'Rex, I don't know how this happened.' Above them the sky is choked with stars. She says, 'I was going to put the chills on you. I was planning it all out in my mind. I'd spring out in the night. I'd take that beautiful silver gun of yours and hold it to your temple. And I'd give a little speech. Something cool and butch, like "Once you fuck with Janine, you fuck with destiny", or "Twenty-four hours, pal, that's all you've got left. Better say your goodbyes. By this time tomorrow you'll be tucked up tight. In a body bag". Then I would pretend to reconsider, and do some kind of deal with you. I'd make a truce. And at the last minute I'd turn in the doorway and shoot you dead anyway. I

145

was going to do something artistic with the body. Skin you or scalp you or garrotte you. I thought about leaving pieces all over your flat. One bollock by the TV, another on the draining board.'

Janine stops short. At Rex's eyes are thick, scared tears. They do not drop but cluster on his lashes. 'I'm sorry,' he says like a child, 'I'm sorry, I'm sorry.' He wipes the tears away. 'I didn't have a choice. It was how she talked to me. I didn't know what I was doing. I was very tired. Please. I'm so sorry.'

She shakes her head and looks at him for a long time. Her expression has changed. 'You're pretty pathetic, you know that? Pretty and pathetic both.' She reaches out and flicks his lapel. 'I'm sorry, I'm sorry,' she mimics. She had thought they'd have a deep conversation out here, pressed together with the dogstar suspended low and bright on the horizon. They could talk contemplatively about free will and fate, like retired fraudsters in a New York diner. There'd be some kind of respect between them, the fastidious politesse of players contracted to destroy each other. Like bullfighter and bull. Equal strength in different forms. Instead, she gets this quivering, shivering wreck, snot running from his nose. That wide, wrinkled brow and bawling mouth. She was so idealistic when she stepped out to speak with him. She thought she would persuade him to break free from Neela's whispered words. They would shake on it – a pacifist pledge. They could do the right thing. Then what? Maybe go on a cruise somewhere hot. Maybe fly to Havana and open a little shop.

But she herself is different too. Janine has acquired a taste for blood. She turns away from Rex and opens the kitchen door. 'Forget it,' she says, 'Forget I spoke to you. I was going to say, whatever you do to me, there'll be no comeback. I was going to say, consider me out of the league – I'm not going to play he-said she-said. But maybe you don't deserve that. Maybe we could just keep firing and see who's standing at the end. Nobody's going to give me extra points for being the noble one. I'm not going to get despatched to heaven for it, am I? We both know that it doesn't exist.' She steps into the kitchen and leans out to him before closing the door. 'Today I took apart someone's cranium piece by piece. He was alive for a long time afterwards, but eventually we got him. You should have seen it. There's no heaven or hell after that.'

She walks back to the party. It is not a salubrious affair. It is a back-door fiesta for back-door people. An assembly of pick-pockets. Some of them sharply dressed, the majority dowdy. They do not mingle but huddle, and instead of trading clever aphorisms they swap X-rated nuggets of graphic news, like snuff-movie synopses. In one corner of the living room, Leo, Lukas and Victor are talking. They form a strange composition of physical types: Victor, a pubescent knot of knuckles and malformed joints; Lukas' broad, flaring, foxy whiteness; and Leo, tight and ready to spring. The entire room seems to move for and with him. He is a brightness against the wall, drawn with clarity where everyone else is a smudge. The cool boy in the class. Nobody would hurt Leo. He could kill his own mother and they would probably give him a trophy for it.

Lukas comes up to her. He picks up a champagne bottle. His long black hair hangs loose about his face. The eyes are two brush-strokes above a glittering smile. 'Janine,' he says, holding the bottle out to her, 'I owe you an apology.' She smiles at him. He is simple: a good-friend-bad-enemy type. A vast heart with an extreme thunderous beat. He would make a good lover; he'd incinerate you with his love. And if he turned against you, he'd hunt you till you were down. He doesn't possess the intelligence of a rebel. 'Leo clued me up on a few of the details about that incident at the restaurant. So I'm sorry for giving you that lecture. Sometimes I open my mouth and the voice of Al Pacino comes out. Forgive me. I prostrate myself before you. I place my neck beneath your foot. I grovel –' Janine laughs and takes the bottle. She touches his hand for a moment. His face turns serious. 'I'd never hurt Leo, and I'd never hurt a friend of Leo. OK? The same goes for Victor. Remember that. We're not the same as Neela and Gavin. I know you think of us in the same way, but there's a difference. Neela and Gavin are death people. They weren't born, they sprang out of the centre of the earth covered in ashes. They're pain people. That's their level. They hate themselves and they hate everything that isn't like them. They're looking for disciples. They're like fairground magicians, pulling stunts to draw you in. You see that. So do I. Rex doesn't, so we try to stay close to him. Before, it didn't matter if he listened to them. But now there's money and real power involved. I'm telling you this because I can see that you're good – well, my version of good. That killing at the restaurant, fair enough, I say. It went wrong, OK, but it was done in the right spirit. You have to do whatever it takes to stick by your friends. And you got him today, didn't you? You extracted the price of Mark's death. Congratulations for that. I mean it. You can't let these things go unpunished. There's no one up there in the sky, rooting for you and making sure people get what they deserve. You have to sentence and condemn where you see fit. It's the only way.'

Janine is tired. Her entire body throbs, the bruise most of all. Lukas continues talking to her but she pushes past him, collapsing into a chair. She is not superstitious. When your own father is killed by a tree, you cease being scared of ladders and lone magpies. But it's too late for Lukas' advice. It is not she but Rex who has let the death people in. The pain people, leaving a

148

trail of ashes. Her future is tied up in his, now her contacts have become his followers. Now she is living on Leo's charity, she has let herself into the ring. She glances up and realises Neela is staring at her from the other end of the room.

Neela drinks her water and watches, camera in hand. She is not really here, she is in the room but not 'at' the party. None of these people have spoken to her, and she wouldn't want them to. They don't like their photos taken, and without photos nothing is real. When something has happened and she has photographed it, she lays the shots on her bed in sequence. Then she makes up lies about them. She relives the scene but pushes herself forward in her own mind. Into the light. Groups scare her. It doesn't matter what tribe they are, she will never find her way into any of them. Crooks or preachermen, sign-painters or saints. None has a place for her. She is a dog, crawling between their knees, grateful for scraps. They reduce her to a strip of gristle, voiceless and cringing. There is Janine, her face an opera mask of swollen flesh. Janine – alive and groomed and plump as ever. Terence Blackheath should have been more vigilant, with his spark and his lighter fuel. He has pressed her even deeper into their lives. It must be nice, Neela thinks, to have been born with Janine's high, refined, witty nature. Maybe years ago they could have been friends. Like ten years ago, when Neela was nine. Then, she was not mad. She was lonely in the way children sometimes are – moody and blackly funny. And she had that quick, delighted, childish eye for what was beautiful and fragile. She would collect things – pebbles, postcards, scraps of cloth, only because they were pretty. Now the dog in her is strong. Her only triumph is knowing Janine fears her. To be feared is at least to be noticed. When Janine fears her, she makes her visible. It lifts the corner of some kind of near-sexual pleasure she has worked rigorously to bury. But it rises nonetheless. She can sense herself giving in to that blatant animal jealousy, the dog in her so fierce tonight.

Janine realises that she has been dozing. She forces herself to get up and go through to Rex's bedroom. At least there she can get some rest. Something stops her from simply going to Leo's and sleeping. She wants to maintain her presence amongst the false friends and errant collaborators she courted so diligently, not scurry home, cowed. In Rex's bedroom there are people sitting on the floor, all wearing cocaine's strained smile. All trying to laugh at cocaine's unfunny joke. There are broken champagne glasses in the middle of the room. Occasionally, someone will hurl and smash another listlessly. It must sound good, in that state: metallic and intense. A sheer, almost choral noise. Janine lies down on Rex's single bed – his hermit's bunk. Her limbs feel as though they're being absorbed into the white duvet. She closes her eyes. Slowly the other people run out of glasses. Someone reaches up and switches the light off.

In the living room, Lukas is holding Leo's wrist. 'Don't go,' he urges. 'She'll be fine. She's just sleeping.'

'I just want to have a quick word with her,' Leo says. He turns his arm to break Lukas' grip but the taller boy steps into his path.

'OK then, I'll go with you.'

'No,' replies Leo a little too quickly, 'I'll only be a second. I'll be back before you know it.' He checks nobody is looking, then goes and knocks on Rex's bedroom door. He opens it slightly. A thin white beam slices through Janine's sleep. She raises her head, then rises and goes to the door. The floor rolls under her feet. 'Are you OK?' Leo asks. In her dream state he looks like a satyr. 'I think I'm asleep,' she mumbles. She reaches out her hand. His skin is so smooth. She slides her fingers over his and he winces as she brushes the glass cut he suffered earlier. He radiates heat. Sleep keeps drawing a curtain over her thoughts. They are embracing. 'Oh, you smell so nice,' she says, resting her head on his shoulder. He comes in and closes the door behind him. They walk towards the bed, arms interlinked. As soon as she is back on the duvet she lets fatigue bear her away. She kisses Leo's forehead and turns away from him. He rests his face along her back. Then they wade together into sleep's sublime, inky pool.

In a bloodless dawn, Rex's place is a scrawl of fag ends and sleeping bodies. The air is stale. Janine lies on the bed. The pain of not having slept enough has set a headache into place. Usually she goes under for ten hours a night. Her tiredness has a hallucinogenic quality. Light hits the walls and glass with harsh precision. She cannot merely see the points of the smashed champagne flutes, she feels them carve the jelly of her eyeballs. Her hand rests on Leo's waist as they lie next to each other. But his skin is ice cold. She is aware of being monitored. She turns and there is Neela lying in Leo's place.

Neela smiles at Janine. Today will be a good day. She had gone to her own flat but at six something struck her into wakefulness. Her werewolf instinct, with its nose for blood. Rex's door was open, with Janine's trademark hairpin still in the lock. In the bedroom there lay sleeping beauty, the bruise bulbous. On the downy white sheets, fine slashes of blood. And on the floor, a miniature glass city. She almost respected Janine for a moment – fucking one of Rex's guests in his own bed. Trying to win back favour by lifting her hem. Neela can appreciate the beauty in that. 'Morning, lover,' she whispers, 'I just thought I'd lay me down for a little rest. Hope you don't mind.' It is exciting to lie next to Janine. Her body is so unlike Neela's, each bone so well wadded in perfect coppery skin. It invites teeth. It makes you want to bite deep. And all that hair, springing and dry where Neela's is a short greasy cap. Janine is all woman. 'You like a bit of rough, don't you?' Neela asks. 'You like to be handled.' She sits up and lays her legs over Janine's thighs, leaning her back against the wall. 'If you ever want a bit of pain you should come to me, girlfriend. I can do pain. We could come to some sort of arrangement.'

Neela's flesh is distinctly cold – colder than the room – even through her trousers. That must be what gives the girl her bleached appearance. Too little blood. But other than that it is strange to be touched by her. Her legs are heavy with strength. They press Janine into the bed. It is like a game of kiss-chase at school – like being shoved against a wall by a boy, a sleek muscular lad all smiling and sure of himself. But there is no deal here. If she offered herself up it wouldn't eradicate Neela's malice. She would be made weak then slain anyway. 'It's a pretty cheap thing to do,' Neela is saying, staring at the arcs of Leo's blood on the duvet, 'opening your legs for your lost business associates. Going behind Rex's back like that. You have his money now. All you need is to re-establish your loyalty base. And cunt is your strategy. Oh well, it's been going on for years I suppose. But it surprises me. I thought you had some politics. Maybe you're one of those who wears their principles only on their sleeve. Maybe by the time you get down to your knickers you've lost your social conscience.' She laughs abruptly. 'I've met plenty of people like that. So, who was it? It must have been one of the people in this room. Someone who broke the glasses. We'll have to do a check, like Cinderella. See who got cut last night and compare wounds. Maybe it was everyone. I could picture that. I've seen you eat. You're a woman of large appetites.'

Neela gets up but Janine stays lying down. She is sick with

tiredness. She closes her eyes but they snap wide open immediately because Neela is kissing her. It is so forceful it seems to snake down her throat and nip at her gut. There is no affection in it. It is a threat made flesh. A sign that Neela doesn't observe the boundaries other people do. Strangely, the girl's full lips are burning hot. They press themselves against Janine's mouth, then release. 'You leave it to me,' says Neela, straightening up. 'You just lie there and get some rest. I'm very lucky. I'll seek you out no matter how carefully you conceal your tracks. We don't have to do it just yet. I can bide my time. But I don't like that you're tricking Rex. I need to serve his interests. You're betraying him. He's my best friend, for God's sake! You can't expect me to sit back and do nothing!' She laughs loudly. Janine turns her face to the wall and hears her go. She closes her eyes again.

Outside, Neela walks down the steps from Rex's front door and crosses the courtyard. She has a paranoid, just-try-me walk, heavy on the heel. She plans to go into Soho and pace its streets until one of the cafes opens. She will take her drink and her morning meal onto a bench in the Square, eating with both hands, concentrating on her food like the dog she is. She will kick the pigeons away. Soon will come the Christmas shoppers. It will be the kind of day she likes to spend alone, in the cold.

6

Poker was the game to go for. A table piled with chips: the metaphorical battlefield of combatants everywhere. Lukas, Neela, Victor and Gavin sit in Rex's rooms at the King of England in the lethargic half-life of the late January afternoon. The bar will open tonight but for now the lights are dim, the cards are stacked and the whisky flows sweet and dark. The formality of the scene and their unfamiliarity with the game has made them awkward and polite.

'Didn't see you much over Christmas,' says Lukas to Neela.

She shrugs, her eyes on her cards. 'I was around. I went to all the parties we hosted here. You didn't see me because you were too busy slamming coke up your nose, gyrating with your top off and having tequila licked off your chest by some bimbo. But I was here. Strangely enough, I'm not the tits-out type.' Lukas knocks back his whisky and then pours more for himself and the others. Neela is sticking to water. 'That's one of the things I love about not drinking,' she continues. 'It's like being behind a two-way mirror next to a room full of apes. You watch the mating rituals, the territorial battles. You get to see all the fuck-ups fucking up. You become a witness.'

'Oh really,' Lukas teases. 'And what have you seen?' Victor shoots a look at his brother. The tips of his Dracula teeth rest on his lower lip. Neela slowly lays down a card. The light sculpts shadows into her face, steep in the socketbones. Then she looks up at him. 'Nothing,' she says, sounding surprised. 'I just mean, when you're sober and everyone else is drunk, you remember all their misdemeanours. I'm not saying anyone lets you in on some great secret about human nature.' She and Lukas watch each other.

'I fold. None of us knows how to play this piece-of-shit game anyway.' Gavin suddenly throws his cards on the table and begins dividing his matchsticks between the other three. No matter what the weather he's always in a T-shirt, his elbows raw. At least the cold has calmed his acne. Now it is only a dry terrain of scars. He accidentally knocks his whisky tumbler over. It seems to fall in slow motion, the heavy glass base leaving the table reluctantly before giving itself up to gravity, and the liquid falls across their cards in a continual silky sheet. Everyone draws their hands away. The atmosphere has broken and they are back to their petty bickering. Lukas pulls Gavin closer to the table-top and starts mopping up the spilt drink with his T-shirt. There is something offensive and gloating in the puny boy's total lack of grace that makes Lukas want to beat him and break his bones.

'Your mess, your problem. Since you like playing with whisky so much, you can smell of it for the rest of the day.'

Gavin bends out of Lukas' grasp and takes off his T-shirt. Underneath, his concave torso is a hairless rack with tiny red nipples like zits. He sits back down again, crossing his arms. 'I'll tell you something, Lukas. I see things too. It's not just Neela. I have eyes as well.' He usually never speaks, except to insult someone or complain.

'Oh, what d'you want to tell me?' asks Lukas, irritated. Gavin looks like a labour camp victim. It is possible to count every single one of the bones in his upper body. He reaches over and takes Lukas' glass and drinks from it. Then he takes a packet of cigarettes and a book of matches out of Lukas' shirt pocket. He curls his whole body into lighting up. All his movements have a flirtatious, flippant air.

Lukas grabs his cigarettes back. Neela gets up, goes over to a mini fridge at the end of the room and gets another bottle of whisky. Leo didn't have any say over this zone. Rex bought the stuff for it. The place is decked out like the crash-pad of a stylistically impoverished bachelor: the stark designer chairs, the wooden flooring, the low wraparound leather sofa and onyx-topped coffee table. The windows are all blinded. There are the security monitors, the fridge, a computer, the sound and video system all against one wall. Neela thinks of it as Rex's 'bank of technology', a teenage fantasy gleaned from too many space-exploration movies where perspiring US generals sit in front of two dozen winking neon info screens. She comes back to the table. Victor's grinning at her, his side-teeth exposed. He isn't scared of her. That's what his smile says: he thinks she's scum. Neela used to be a little bit good. Not all, but a little bit. No matter what Lukas says, Victor was never good. He was born a killer, his knife-hand ready.

Gavin takes the whisky bottle from Neela and drinks straight from it. He has a hardened drunk's capacity for liquor. Then he sets the bottle down in front of Lukas. 'You're fine, I'm fine. But Janine and Rex, they're the finest of all. Our very own Miss Piggy keeps company in her sty these nights.'

Lukas shrugs: 'So what? Nothing wrong in giving a fuck to a friend.'

Gavin interrupts him. 'Look, Janine's a top-of-the-range rip-off artist. I mean, we're not naive, we know how this place runs. It's the only venue where you can get your fix by asking a bartender. You go to the bogs for an innocent shit and you can't get the cubicle door open for the powder. Turn on the main lights and it's like Return Of The Living Dead. Rex takes away his support and his money – she takes away the drugs. And Leo's the same. Where d'you think the bouncers and staff came from? Who d'you think made the bar to serve the drinks on? Rex didn't organise any of it. He couldn't put his own dick back into his pants after a piss. Take away Janine, Rex would have nothing. But the main point is, Janine would have – does have – everything. And that whore's relying on you for protection. She knows all about me. That's no fucking mystery, is it? She knows I'd have her raped in broad daylight if I could. The bitch gets my deal. But you're a big nice good guy who'd never let a little creep like me sway his thinking.'

Lukas has been listening. He frowns slightly. Before he can say anything, Gavin continues: 'I just say we should tell Rex. Open his eyes. We have to put the snake in his brain. We have to start the rot. He's scared of Janine now anyway. Ever since the Terence Blackheath deal bombed she makes him want to vomit with fear. He thinks the flat was burning and she just walked out of the flames.' He keeps his scarred face lowered, knowing Lukas' simple brain is processing the status of the game. Trying to see who's operating on greatest risk. He begins to toy with the book of matches, striking one then putting it out between his fingertips. 'We need to be Rex's strength where he has no strength. He won't act, so we have to act for him. We have to propel him, drive him, operate him. Janine's robbing us of what we deserve. We should hold her and strip her and sell her clothes. Rip those studs out of her ears. We've known Rex all his life. He owes us. It's time for us to stake our claim.'

Suddenly Lukas rises and starts to flip the window-blinds up. Stripes of hard, bleak light slam down along the room. Gavin shrinks away from it, shielding his eyes. Neela and Victor are slumped in their chairs. Lukas stays away from the poker table, which is now sticky with spilt whisky. His natural environment involves the sun. It heats his white skin without burning it. It has a way of warming and sorting his thoughts when the boy's shadowy match-play has yanked his sense aside. That strong solar energy fuses with his nerves. To win this round, he has to think like Gavin thinks. He can't defend Leo and Janine in the name of friendship, because to Gavin that's no reason at all. He has to remake his personality, invert it, reverse it so that good becomes bad. Instead of flowering towards the light he has to thrust his nature downwards, curling it tight around itself and relishing its obscure, clammy niche. 'Gavin, you've got it wrong. We're not losing, we're winning. Janine and Leo may be winning more, but who cares? You said it yourself – without them, we wouldn't be here at all. There'd be no bar to argue about. The estate wanted us dead before Leo came along to deal with Max Stein and the fat man. He's the kind of person you need on your side. Don't forget they're in a bind too, him and Janine. They've handed over all their power to Rex. They could leave but the pushers and pimps and bouncers wouldn't go with them. They've got money but they've paid another kind of price. We're the ones who're free. The other three are all dependent on each other. We need to gain from their trauma. See, you're smiling, I knew you'd like this. We have to make ourselves strong where they're weak. We're going to introduce ourselves to the action. Stick with Leo, paste ourselves to him. Anything he does, we have to press into the situation. But we need him to think we're his friends.' He goes over to Rex's desk and pulls open a drawer. Inside is a box of cigars, the fancy porno-mogul kind, and a pure silver Asprey & Garrard cutter. Lukas becomes absorbed in the ritual for a few moments and finally gazes up again, the lit cigar clamped between his jaws.

Neela looks over to him and laughs. 'From here you look like you're smoking a big turd. No, don't take it out, it suits you. You've always been a shit-eater.' Her deep elegant voice carries across the room to Lukas' ear. She is amused by his bluff. His attempt at a double-blind, a hustle – it tickles her. 'Since you like him so much,' she says to Lukas, 'we'll spare Leo. But I'm having Janine.' Before he can reply, she gets up and shrugs on her jacket. Gavin springs up as well. 'Rex is due in now,' Neela says. 'I'm going to go down and bother him. But don't worry,' she calls over her shoulder, 'I'll keep you out of my sordid affairs.'

Rex doesn't feel comfortable downstairs in the King of England. It is not the kind of place they would ever let him into, were he in his normal clothes – his ripped parka and fray-cuffed jeans. And even with its interior walls knocked down, it is just a map of executions and conflicts, duels of the tongue and hand. Here his mother stood, there his father. He saw, one day some months ago when they were building this place up, that many of the floorboards were stained with blood. His nerves are beginning to give way, thread by thread. Maybe he should turn this place into a comedy club, inject a bit of mirth into the situation. That would be a nice touch. He could bring the whole gang round and they could sit around a red-shaded table by the stage, laughing and slapping each other on the back, tears of joy rolling down their cheeks. Then they could keep each other amused for the rest of the night: *hey, bozo, didja hear the one about ...*

Rex lets himself into the King and uses the private staircase at the back of the first-floor bar. He isn't quick on his feet. Neela comes down the stairs, her head lowered. Gavin is close behind her. She has a long stride and throws herself down the steps three at a time. She accidentally jumps onto Rex, full-frontal.

Then she springs back and laughs. 'Just the man I wanted to see. Leaping out at you is my only pleasure in life, I swear, it really is.' She has a small mouth full of brilliant white teeth. She puts her hands square on his chest and begins to push him back down towards the bar. 'I don't know what's happening to me. Lately, whenever I get near you I become quite hysterical.'

Gavin is grinning too. The boy has no charisma. He smiles the smile of a Woolworth's shoplifter. 'Neela's on the hunt,' he tells Rex. The two of them are like possessed children in a horror movie – their eyes huge and glistening, their faces pale. They don't seem to walk forward so much as appear a couple of feet closer every time Rex looks. Then Gavin darts away and there is only him and Neela. They hear the staff door of the King slam shut. Neela has not stopped smiling. The blood has risen strong in her face, making it glow. She would make a good pop-art painting – yellow skin, green eyes, white teeth.

They sit, once again, on the couches in the main bar. 'I'm giving you a second chance,' says Neela. That low voice of hers lays itself against him. She watches Rex intently. She is relying on his fear of her being greater than his fear of Janine. Calling on the old voodoo force to aid her powers of persuasion. He fears Janine rationally enough. She seems to be bullet-proof and fire-resistant; the one victim in Terence Blackheath's case history that got away. But he fears Neela in the way that a child fears the dark. The fear is already in his blood. He was born with the fear. 'I've been nice to you for too long. You think I haven't noticed you running away from me. You're wrong. My flat's two down from yours and I can still feel you at night, cringing in your bed because you think I'm going to come knocking. Well, here I am. And I want Janine.' She talks like she walks, with a hard rhythmic strut. A pimp jive. She can lay two phrases side by side together so both resonate like chimes. 'I want her, and you're going to get her for me. I want that hair hacked off at the root. I'll sell it to a doll-maker. I want those beautiful clothes she wears – which you bought, by the way. I want her fat buttery body disarticulated. You've got all you need from her. You've wrung her out. Her people are your people now. You're a success. Now give me my kill.' Rex lies down suddenly on his couch, face down, his forehead resting on his forearms. He looks like a kid playing dead lions. Neela picks up a plastic ashtray from the coffee table and throws it at him. 'You're hiding because you want to do it. I know you. You want her face down, floating in the bath. I can give you a reason, if you like. If all you need is a motive: they're going to rip you off. Every time they meet, they plan it a little further. It's a coup, sweet thing. They take your money and they put it in their name. They don't spend it. Even Janine doesn't get through cream cakes and caviar that fast. Then they buy you out, you beautiful, bankrupt buffoon.' She goes over to him, kneels by his couch and croons in his ear. 'Get her. Frame her. Humiliate her. It'll be so sweet. When she falls, Leo falls. She's the brains behind it, not him. He just does what she tells him to. You can do this.'

Rex stares into the darkness inside his eyelids. He already knows – she already knows – that Neela has won. Because he can see Janine in that bath, her mouth silent-screaming. He can see her, hairless, those crinkly gold locks being glued to naked staring dolls' heads. To him, those images are as sweet as a wedding photograph would be to someone else. But he wants to hide his keenness. To raise his head and look at Neela would be to see himself. She's already inside his DNA. She's the fear. He became her when he dialled Terence's number. 'You're like a bitch in heat,' he says to her, his voice muffled. It feel so good to insult her, like uttering something profane in a church or shitting on consecrated ground.

162

But then she grasps his shoulder and hisses, 'Yes! That's exactly what I'm like. I'm a fucking dog.' She leans against the coffee table and laughs. She looks like someone on a bad trip, her head back, and that laugh which finds no pleasure in the world. 'I'm a fucking dog and I want my bones. OK? I like my bones fresh and big, and I eat my meat tender.'

At midnight that evening, Neela takes to the dancefloor. Janine isn't around. She set the club up and did her greeting-the-fans routine but left an hour ago. Leo is upstairs in Rex's quarters. The King of England is throwing a party for a fashion company and the rooms are packed with intense, vacant people wearing interesting clothes. A DJ takes a record from his box and lays it on one deck, ear bent to his headphone-piece. The lighting is solid red. Usually, Neela would be scowling in a corner but the occasion calls for a jubilant unhinged village-dance, eyes closed, arms in the air, an offering to the skies.

Around her, couples and groups of friends are jiving, their bodies mirroring one another. Their faces are slashes of smiling teeth. Neela is not immune to music. Occasionally a snatch of opera heard from a passing car will set her soul alight. She could bury herself in the earthy vibrato of a soul singer's lament and feels her senses thicken with adrenaline when that deep electronic bass rises out of the ground. She has an athlete's adoration of strength combined with controlled motion – for limbs corded with muscle. She begins to move.

There is still a grain of conscience inside her. It is literally a grain, a speck, truly tiny, but it is there nonetheless. It reveals to her in sudden unwanted bursts, like flashes of electricity on night-time train-tracks, sinister and sudden, that she and Janine are similar. Occasionally her intuition is acute and relays to her these recognitions. Leo and Janine are not fucking, that she is certain of. Janine is too autonomous to let herself get into a knickers-and-toothbrushes situation. Money is what she loves really. The beautiful things money can buy. Money is her marriage-mate. Anyway, it is too easy to find a willing, fit body to screw – even Neela could do that if she scoured the sewers for long enough. But an actual friend who speaks and moves and thinks of you, a real one who exists outside of your imagination? That is an achievement.

The music climbs up her spinal cord bone by bone. It sinks itself into her fibres. Oh, but the dog in her is dancing too. The dog can talk. It talks with the pain of a thousand years. It forces her hand. It makes her say the unspeakable – *get me my kill*. Janine, Janine, homecoming Queen. Neela is tempted to try the bed trick just once more, simply for another close-range look at her lush, biteable skin. It would be the only instance that she could get near a person like that. Mostly she has spent her time huddled in a corner watching the beautiful people. Beauty could make her senses churn with pleasure. She used to pray for it but it never came to her. It doesn't matter any more, though. She will have her day.

Janine lies in the bedroom at Leo's place, watching TV. In the few months that she's been staying here it has begun to feel like a family home, complete with the rituals of family life: coffee and croissants in the morning, the evenings spent sprawled loose-limbed on the sofa. He is her son, her father, her brother. Occasionally, presents will appear here or at her office in the King of England: books, cards. Once, a notebook made of thick slats of handmade cream paper bound in soft tan leather. Another time, a silk bias-cut dress from the Thirties, all hung with minute crystal beads. She has done things for him in return, in her indolent unhurried way. She sometimes cuts his hair, laying an old towel on his shoulders and angling a lamp to stroke its beam across the back of his neck. Then she takes up the scissors and loosely grasps locks of his thick brown hair, his scalp warm against her fingers. Puffs of trimmed hair float down and dust his face. He bows his head, obedient and silent, his eyes shut, while she gradually moves around from one side to the other. She directs the blades close to the nape of his neck and ears. Sometimes the sheer sight of those long dark eyelashes against his olive skin, their points all upcurled, his patient choirboy expression, make her want to scream and moan with tenderness. And yet they do not want each other. They lie together in the bed but their pelvises are apart. Their lives have knocked lust out of them – at least that is so for Janine. She does not ask Leo his reason.

At one-thirty, Janine prepares for sleep. She is wearing one of Leo's T-shirts – red with WHITE TRASH written on it in lime green. She goes into the bathroom and slowly begins to remove all her makeup. Running the hot water tap hard, she sings to herself as steam starts to rise. The tiles begin to film over. She takes off the T-shirt, then dunks her face into the scalding water. It is so nice to be naked in a warm room, feeling her flesh spread and quiver in the humidity. Her skin has a deep, expensive, well-loved sheen to it. She snaps her head back, shuddering, and starts scrubbing her skin with a flannel. She yanks out the plug and runs the flannel under the cold tap before reapplying it to her face. Next, she gets into the bath and pulls the plastic curtain across. The shower-head coughs into life and sends out bolts of hot water to dull the golden down on her spine. It pummels the backs of her thighs and her full broad bottom.

On the other side of the door Neela prepares for her entrance. She hears water striking skin and Janine's trained contralto. Getting in was easier than she expected: Leo had left

165

his keys in the cloakroom of the King of England. She'd been anticipating a brisk climb up the pipes and through a back window. In her waistband is Rex's gun. She is not usually a fan of firearms. Bullets simplify the conflict. They circumvent the mental and physical challenges of confrontation. It should be a contest of personalities, not gun types. Neela would like to fight like antelopes locking horns in the woods, with clashing, painful, hoarse cries. She likes to wear down her opponent, outpace them, tire them, spook them. Damage them. A bullet gives people no time for contemplation of their own situation. No time to plead or bleed.

She silently goes into the bathroom and stands just on the other side of the shower curtain. Janine is bent over, running a soapy flannel over her foot. It has a high ballet-school arch and long toes. The nails are painted gold. There is a thin gold chain around the ankle. Neela would like to scale that form, licking, nuzzling, roaming its contour-map curves: hip to knee, shoulder-blade to haunch, throat to stomach. The room is full of steam, choking hot. When Neela takes a shower it's in cold water. She walks in January with her jacket open. Heat dulls her. It mires her thoughts and blunts her movements. She takes a breath, then grasps the side of the shower curtain and pulls it back. The metal rings screech along the pole. She steps into the bath fully clothed.

Janine's head shoots up. Her jaw widens and lets loose an open bellow of utter shock. Her entire body jerks backward. She's like an animal struck by lights in the dark – frozen, hunched, all staring eyes and moist mouth. Neela comes to stand under the jets of water. Her shoes are streaming mud. 'Not so cool now, are you?' she asks Janine. She takes Rex's gun from her waistband and both of them stare at it for a few moments under the water. 'I know you like beautiful things. I

thought, if I was going to come after you I should do it in style.'
She reaches out and draws the end of the gun across the tips of
Janine's breasts. It is a movement so cold and obscene, so sexu-
ally threatening that she can find no reaction for it. It's like a
stranger on the pavement suddenly ducking and running their
fingers between her legs. Janine looks at Neela, trembling. The
smaller girl's hair is plastered against her skull so now she is all
bone, her eyes just emerald slits in a jaundiced drum-skin face.
There is something almost pornographic about her being
clothed in the shower. Neela is panting slightly, her powerful
athlete's lungs trying to drain the steamy air of what little
oxygen there is. 'You don't like the cold, do you?' she says
between shallow breaths. 'You like to protect that luxury pelt of
yours.' She steps a bit closer and presses the side of the gun
along Janine's throat. Jealousy sprays the inside of her brain.
The gun looks like jewellery on Janine, like an elaborate avant-
garde choker. A baroque theatre prop. It actually suits her.
Neela's vision is becoming gauzy and atonal. White leaks in
through the edges of the picture. She wishes she could get some
air. 'Marlon gave Rex this gun to protect him from people like
you. So think of me as one of Rex's foot-soldiers. Bearer of his
will. The trumpeter of his divine tune.' She flicks her wrist and
flips the gun back, pulling its trigger sharply. The sound echoes
like a burst of fierce mocking laughter. Behind her the small
bathroom window bucks but holds and through the bullet hole
slides dark icy January. January, all smoky-smelling and crisp,
delicious in her throat.

Only when her body heat plummets does Neela regain full
consciousness. She closes her eyes for a second, but into the darkness plunges a very fine pain so intense it's gorgeous – a
soprano-wail of pain, a scrape under her eye. Janine is there, her
skin dull and reptilian with goosebumps. In her hand is a women's

double-blade razor, lilac plastic with a pink logo, and with that feeble pastel toy she's slashed open the skin across Neela's cheekbone. There is a silence which is almost comical. It is either carry on fighting or start laughing. Neela is now totally soaked. The blood washes off her cheek even as it springs up but the wounds are long and deep, two perfect narrow parallel incisions across the bone. 'Oh, you'll have to do more than that,' she says, coming forward again with the gun pointing at Janine's stomach. 'I wasn't made delicate. I don't smother myself in creams and lotions and makeup. I like pain.' She holds out her wrist: 'Come on, cut me once more. I want you to. I'm begging you.'

Janine starts shivering. She stares at Neela. It is not just the cold that makes her bones quake but the total gracelessness of the scene, the unstaged ridiculous vision of this thin-faced demented girl so deft with Rex's gun, and herself naked and fat, all nipples and pubes. She knows from Leo that Neela believes herself to be ugly, but in truth she looks very beautiful now, and the face-wound makes her even more so, like a pirate or a thief, tough and damaged and passionate. The two of them stare at one another, the gun high in one hand, the razor – for a faster, smoother shave – in the other.

Janine eventually breaks the silence. She turns and there is Gavin drooling by the side of the bath, smelling of cigarettes and beer. His fingertips are grubby. He reaches out and turns the shower off, staring at Janine's body the whole time. His eyes gobble at her tits and thighs. The steam has evaporated and now there is only Janine, freezing and naked in a bath, Neela in her wet clothes, and the boy, the juvenile, the bag-snatcher with his bad skin. These are people Janine will never understand: the death people, the dog people, devoid of hope.

Neela does not like Gavin's slackened, lustful stare. The way he seems to hang over Janine, his tongue loose in his mouth. It

168

makes him a man, not the deformed changeling child she usually thinks of him as. Since the first despicable worm of desire in her belly – a worm since ignored, reviled, shunned – she has known it is not men she craves. Or would crave, if she let herself. She shudders to see their groping dirty fingers and the outline of that curled nestling creature in their groin, blind, ugly and comical. She would rather kiss a goat's anus. And in any case, Janine is *her* woman. She wanted to scare her, hurt her privately, not place her at the mercy of Gavin and his dick-led looks. She will show Janine that she too has some style. That lone remaining particle of nobility will do this one thing for her.

Without a word, Neela gets out of the bath and tucks the gun back into her waistband. She selects the largest, lushest towel from the rack and hands it to Janine to wrap around her body. Then she takes another towel, unfolds it and places it on Janine's head, bundling her hair up. Janine is darting astonished looks at her but she won't meet her eyes. Instead, she helps her fold and tuck the smaller towel into a turban. Neela's touch is sure and strong and Janine feels those few seconds of rare deliberate grace resonating deep in her rib-cage. There is nothing but the two of them gathering handfuls of dripping ringleted hair, pressing the water out and then tucking the locks under the towel's edge.

The next thing Neela knows, the air in the room has turned very hot, and something has drawn back and grabbed her neck, then slammed her forehead-first against the side of the bath. She hears Leo's unmistakable laugh before she blacks out. By the time she opens her eyes again it feels as though someone has lifted a plate of bone from the top of her skull and meddled at her brain with a garden fork. She lies there on the floor still dazed, her mouth open against the carpet, her tongue lolling out picking up fluff. She enjoys and can stand being cut, scored,

169

scratched. But this kind of pain, coming from right inside her head, it grips her eyeballs and every one of her teeth. It plays a solo on her eardrums and rings her nostrils. It hurts so much the slice under her eye stops bleeding with the shock. She is aware of things being very still in the bathroom, but there are voices coming from outside. Then movement closer to her. It is Leo. Rex's gun is prised out of her waistband. Then a great thunderclap strikes her head and sends her hurtling back into the dark.

When she comes to she is outside. Her face is tight with dried blood. Someone has placed her in the centre of the courtyard, her head towards the gate and pillars. The ground smells of petrol. It is two-thirty in the morning and the estate is a circle of jutting brick angles and broken street-lamps, all leaning inwards and over her in fish-eye distortion. And there is a crude white bulge way up to one side. For a moment Neela thinks it is a trick of her eyes, a slant of light thrown into her cornea from her splintered bone, a bruised optical membrane pulsing awry. She turns her head slowly to look at it. Any quick movements and she will dislodge agony from its precarious holding. A slow craven cackle emanates from her dry throat, for there is Gavin hanging by his own belt from the window of Leo's bedroom. His tongue protrudes, his eyes are agog. It is the perfect murder – humorous yet poignant, sensational yet effective. It confers upon Gavin a poise and grandeur that he did not possess in life. A certain gravitas – literally – yet also a kind of charming whimsy. A hanged body does not dangle loose-limbed like a craft-stall mobile in the breeze; it is more a wire sculpture hoisted aloft, the neck frozen in its acute jerk, the feet apart, doing a groundless jig. It takes a nasty, comic sensibility to hang a boy with his own belt.

Neela gets onto all fours, then slowly sits back on her heels. Her hands are numb from the cold. She wrestles Rex's gun from her waistband and realises there is blood on the butt. Then she touches her fingertips to her face and runs them lightly across her skull. Leo must have noticed Gavin leaving the party on the security monitors, then followed. She has been butt-whipped across the back of the head, and her brow smashed against the bath. In both areas lumps have risen up and split open, and the basic pain they generate could set car alarms wailing. She crawls over to a puddle and looks at her reflection. At first she thinks the water is bending her features but in fact it is she who is bent and broken – the eyebrows bulging, the slit cheek puffy. She lowers her face and begins to wash. This is where she belongs, her eyelids grazing the silt at the bottom of a puddle, on her hands and knees in the middle of the night with a fractured skull. She sets herself upright and begins to walk.

Outside the King of England, the party-goers are dispersing, disturbing the air with their cries and exclamations. They watch Neela approach curiously and part as she walks through them. They eyeball her misshapen face. The dog is so close to the surface now that other people can almost see it – the dog-fur under her hair, the canine-teeth behind her own. Madness marks her out. Neela has become like one of those pavement-walking crazy ladies who notices things which aren't there and has arguments with people who don't exist. A deviant.

Upstairs, Lukas and Rex are drinking vodka shots and messing about with playing cards as staff clear up after the party. Victor is asleep on the sofa, curled up, hugging a pillow. They shuffle and cut, shuffle and cut in the light of just one table lamp. They practise flexing the deck in one hand and sending a ribbon of curved cards flying in an arc between hands. Rex somehow knows that Neela is outside. Whenever she is around there is a change of current in the air. They should issue a series of health guidelines with her, like an earthquake warning or thunderstorm alert: when Neela's coming, get under a table and stay away from trees. Lock up your animals. Keep your children calm.

The door to Rex's room swings open and there she is, shaking and battered. Her forehead is a cloven ridge of reddened flesh and the wound on her cheek has split open. Crazy-girl speaks: 'Do you know how cold it is outside, Rex?' She holds up her hands, which are shrivelled and purple, as though she is begging. There is something strange about her voice – she seems to be talking through a thickened, inactive tongue, chewing the words before they dribble from her mouth. She moves forward and slumps on the table, ignoring Lukas. 'Do you know how dark it is? I almost lost my way. I've done this route a thousand times but tonight the streets look different. I think my eyes may be damaged. I can see you here' – she reaches her arm out and stretches the thumb and index finger into an L – 'but also here' – she moves her arm a few inches to one side. She grabs his shot glass and knocks back the vodka in one go. 'Stoli, Stoli, makes me so very jolly,' she sings, then coughs as it burns her throat. Rex and Lukas are staring at her. This is not Neela's style. She favours the bare bulb and controlled, calibrated menace of the inquisition room to the unhinged after-hours solo performance of a drunken night-club singer. But composure and self-regulation have been struck from her thoughts. Leo had to hit her, during her moment of charity. As she was handling those maize yellow curls, he sent her down. Leo blasted agony into her skull willy-nilly. He broke her. 'It's time to stick up for your friends, Rex, old buddy, old pal. You've got to show your love. No time left for prevarication. He did this' – she points to the back of her head – 'with your gun.' She takes it from her waistband and puts it on the table. It lies there in its own pocket of light. They don't really look at it; it seems to look at them, inviting flattery, requiring appeasement. It is a strange, solid machine. Rex cannot imagine Marlon buying it from a dealer or organising for it to be assembled from scattered, disparate pieces. Instead, he would not be surprised if it had been somehow mined, exhumed, discovered, brought up from the deep earth already in its finished glistening state, complete.

Neela says, 'I didn't realise it until just now, but you know why Leo didn't take the gun for himself? Because it's yours. That's friendship for you. Despite all the reciprocal damage you could do to him using it, he still returns it.' She nods. 'That's nice. I appreciate that. But it didn't stop him hurting me. He'd already knocked me out once, but he wanted to do something more. Something for me to remember him by. He stood over me when I was already half-gone' – she gets up, leaning on the back of the chair for support – 'twisted his gun hand' – she takes up the gun and lifts her palm away from it slightly, angling her wrist, raises her pinkie delicately and bares one corner of the butt – 'then without any prior notice, without an if-you-please, he brought it down on me.' She reaches over and with a sharp jerk, her forearm muscles taut, she cuffs Rex across the face with the butt of the gun. Her swipe is so hard and swift he has no time to feel it. His head snaps to the side and then back to centre. His lower lip opens up and fresh bright blood pumps out. He automatically raises his hand to catch it but it runs between his knuckles and down his wrist.

Lukas leaps to his feet, knocking his chair over. 'You're sick,' he spits at Neela, but she ignores him.

'It hurts, doesn't it,' she says to Rex, 'being hit by a gun? And you know what else? He took my dear, gentle Gavin and –' she mimes the hanging so accurately as to leave no doubt about what happened.

Lukas interjects: 'So what? That was too good a fate. That was a divine blessing. Gavin deserved to be roasted alive on a spit.'

'What more proof do you need of their guilt?' Neela yells at him, and he yells back, 'You goaded Janine. You deliberately went over there. You were begging for it because you get off on it. And you knew Leo would follow.' He spins towards Rex. 'Don't listen to her.' His hands go up and grab his silky black hair. 'I can't stand this. She's nuts. She's lying. Please.' But Rex isn't looking at him. Lukas turns on his heel and marches to the other end of the room, out of the light, slumping next to Victor's prone body. He groans and lies down as well, his hands covering his face.

'Looks like it's just you and me. As usual.' Neela sits back down heavily. Rex watches her. She does not need to win him over, to pitch her case. He is won. The crime of Leo and Janine is small and common, and there are options he could take, involving balding men in grey suits and lowly court-rooms, with their Formica-table canteens and beige lino. He could send them any number of letters, all in neat white envelopes. He could have them for embezzlement, fraud, even trafficking. Vice would be good. A vice-crime stamped onto the records would suit that pair. But those are not Neela's methods. She is the type who always packs a slim dagger inside her boot. To her, battles in the present day are echoes of other, ancient fights which occurred millennia before she was born but are still part of her, part of the fabric of rage from which she was fashioned. It is exhilarating to be caught in Neela's world, to feel that white-knuckle sensation of having given oneself up totally. There are only her eyes, narrowed with pain, inhuman pale green, and her voice, saying to him, 'You're with me on this, aren't you? I'm

174

wearing their crime all over my face. The more I bleed, the deeper is their culpability. It's time for them to atone. They have to confess their sins. You need to show your face, establish your rule. I'm your friend. Only me. Leo's fucking with you, giving your gun back. He's trying to come between us. Trying to play us off against each other. Don't let yourself be taken in. I want you to defend me, love me, serve me. You're part of me now.'

Rex nods, sucking the cut on his lip. It has a hot, tart, pleasing taste. His shirt cuff is soaked burgundy with blood. Neela has the same talent that Marlon did, for eliminating Rex's ability to make choices. She impels the action forward through sheer force of will. There is no longer any question of who did what to whom. Rex emits a sigh of relief, for things are so far out of his hands. Fat boy belongs! Finally. Fat boy has arrived.

They rouse Victor and Lukas and together the four of them walk back to the estate, the brothers lagging behind. Neela's cocky paranoid gait has been dismantled. She drags her feet. The night is a dank yellow accented by pink neon: GIRLS GIRLS GIRLS and POPPERS. Bars spew out their last few drinkers. Soon the trash will be wiped from the gutters but for now the small silent group wades through footprinted newspapers and trampled cigarette butts, ignoring cab-drivers and tired-looking civilians. They have bypassed normal life altogether. All the other men, women and children populating the city – talking, travelling, working, shopping – are like pixels on a screen, pulsing with Technicolor coherence for a nanosecond before tumbling apart. The alleys and pavements of Soho fade to a scrawl of nameless anonymous streets. There only remains the estate and the King of England.

Suddenly, Lukas swerves away. 'You go on. I want to be alone for a bit. I'm going to find a place that's still open.' His shoulders are hunched in the cold and his breath comes out in white clouds.

Victor looks at him curiously. 'Are you ill? Can I come?'

Lukas shakes his head. Victor persists and his brother throws him off with one hand. 'No. Go to bed, you're already half asleep. I just want to think.'

Neela laughs and all the buildings around them seem to laugh too, with a haughty two-tone echo. 'Think all you like. Put a nice spin on things. But before you do that, just look at me for a second. See my face? That's how good a guy Leo is. And look out for Gavin when you get home. Then do a bit more thinking.' She turns her back on him, Rex close behind. Victor hesitates, then follows them.

The estate is waiting for them. Its iron entrance gates stand wide, the latch flung open. The three stop by the pillars. Inside the courtyard Neela notices something new: a black car, a BMW, its body shiny and buffed. It reflects the porch light by Lukas' door along its side. The car waits in the shadows. 'Oh God,' Rex exclaims, the bile rising in his throat, 'look at that. Look at him.' He is staring at the white body hanging stark against Leo's wall. Where Neela was relieved at the death – it seemed like sweet, swift karma for that underfed titty-ogling runt 'sidekick' of hers – Rex didn't know Gavin well enough. He just sees a poor dumb kid, his face all bloated and puffy, his skinny stiffened body a bundle of sticks thrown randomly together.

Strong, sweeping yellow light spreads itself across the ground and halfway up the flats, the confident beam denuding the estate of its grainy urban menace. The BMW edges forward. Victor, Rex and Neela watch as it approaches them. Its lights rake their faces, picking them out, pinning their pupils. The car seems to hold itself back for a second. Then it jerks, a tight thrust towards them, propelled forward by its back wheels, leaping in the dark – black, immense, a brute in the night. It reconnects with the ground then seems to pounce once more, heavy and intent and inexorable, before the air around it gathers and sharpens and it speeds through the gates, silent, and is gone. And right at the foot of that wrought-iron entrance Victor lies, a tangle of dislocated limbs. Victor, usually so cheeky and bright, caught during a rare moment of drowsiness, his reflexes slowed, his muscles unwilling. He wears his bloodsucker smile. There is no gore except for a dark ribbon escaping from the side of his mouth, and one from his ear. But other than that he is pristine, the obtuse facial angles of pubescence perfectly retained. But what a tragedy – Victor demolished, Victor abolished. Neela and Rex emerge from behind one of the pillars. She looks up at Gavin, then back down to Victor. She remarks, 'Two down. Two more to go.' She touches Victor's cheek with the toe of her boot and then says, her voice mock-tender, 'It's what he would have wanted.'

7

From the windows of the cafe at Benwick Lodging House Janine and Leo can watch the sea hurling itself listlessly against the brown pebbles. There is a sodden, crumbling pier from which people attempting suicide take running jumps in the night, their pockets weighted with stones. A row of empty wooden stands lines the pier, their kitsch painted signs chipped: Hot Dogs, Larry's Burgers. Real Cream Milkshakes. Seagulls cruise on a hard salty wind, their unmoving wings wide and flat. An opaque sky presses itself low against the town. Janine stares down at the table: its white linen cloth, the silver tiers crammed with minia-ture pastries and cakes, the sugar tongs, the paper doilies and heavy-handled silverware. The two cups and two saucers, each with a painted ring of roses at the rim. She looks at Leo, who's sitting opposite her. 'What. The fuck. Are we doing here?' Leo grins and pours her some more tea, handling the pot delicately. Then he pushes a silver sugar bowl over to her.

'Listen. We had a clear ideological choice. We could do our low-down dirty old gangster shit, or we could have ourselves a lovely weekend break in a coastal town with its delicious health-giving sea air. If we'd taken the first route we wouldn't be here enjoying a nice civilised cup of char, we'd be hiding out in a closed-down night-club or a freezing car park or a dodgy ware-house making deals with blokes called One-Eyed Jack or Black 'n' Decker Eric or something. And that's what Neela would have done, isn't it? She'd sleep on the streets if she had to. I thought we should divorce ourselves from the scum a little. We've acquired a dinky little car, we've got a splendid view of the beach from our room. If anything blows up, Lukas knows where we are. Otherwise, who's going to think of coming here? Now, have another cake.'

She watches him dubiously for a second, then picks a raspberry tart from the stand. The other people in the cafe are watching her from the corners of their eyes. Maybe they're wondering if she's going to try and pocket the sugar tongs. This is not the kind of scenario she is used to. Her childhood haunts were the chandeliered venues of international politics; formal dinners with witty, learned guests, where she was babied and indulged. Later it was the blistering, glamorous thousand-faces scuzz of city nights. But this place, with its twee net curtains, powder-blue paintwork, and genteel behatted OAPs with their coral nail polish, it unsettles her. It is too white. Usually in this country she has not felt conspicuous. On London tube carriages it always pleased her to see that white people were generally outnumbered by their tanned brethren. In places where she was the sole heathen, it didn't matter because she was invariably the most beautiful person in the room. And even if that wasn't true, at least she was elegant. Now she feels like someone who's clambered out of the trees: so dark only her eyes and teeth are visible, her hair trailing twigs and moss, her beautiful white clothes rent and smeared with faeces. She glances over at Leo as she cuts into the tart with the side of her fork. 'I used to come down here when I was much younger,' he is saying, breaking her thoughts. 'I'd run away from my parents and me and some friends would come out to play for the night. There was a kind of fairground and circus further along the beach. The horror-film kind, with broken rides and crystal ball-gazers, and a big top with rickety trapeze swings and a torn safety net. You could get toffee apples and home-made cookies, none of that pink-tinted candyfloss crap. To be honest, we didn't really go for the fair itself. We used to pickpocket the other visitors.'

Janine doesn't smile. For the first time since she met him, it strikes her that Leo is to be feared. That the greatness people perceive in him, the quality he possesses of flaming and iridescent beauty, is the alternative side of an unhinged or unrealistic craziness. He functions on another plane, one which ridicules repression and limitation while gleefully and almost childishly exalting physicality above all else. But he has no consciousness. Nothing checks his movements. Leo is in perpetual motion towards combat. Janine freezes, her tea-cup halfway up to her mouth, as she realises that they have not escaped to Benwick at all. It holds no real attraction for him as the location of his boyhood escapades. He has *brought* her here for some other purpose. It has been planned in advance, either way. She knows that his mind operates, in certain respects, as hers does: he has a keen instinct and an inherent yearning for what is pleasing to the eye and the senses. Leo is a dramatist. He is waiting for something. He wishes for the last conflicts to take place here, not lost in the noise of a capital city but stark and booming amidst the silence. The seething malady of the King of England will be transplanted to Benwick – indeed, not transplanted but even summoned, Janine thinks. Leo has upped the ante by this move. He aims to tantalise Rex and Lukas and Neela, to draw them out, to make them come to him. He wishes to arch his will over them, to enclose their desires within the greater victory of having made them the questors and himself the destination. A life-protecting impulse makes her want to cry out against this latest development. Benwick is strange to her. It is not her element. The buildings in the town seem to have been constructed from rice-paper and icing. The bland beach and pier fringe a thick, ravenous sea. She realises that Leo is grinning at her and forces herself to grin back. 'Just relax,' he says. 'Not long now.'

It wasn't too hard getting Gavin down. Rex didn't want to touch him, so Neela let herself into Leo's flat, went through to the bedroom and unjammed the belt from the window. Gavin fell about ten or fifteen feet. When the sun began to rise and they figured Leo and Janine weren't coming back, Neela pulled him by his noose all the way up the stairs, dumping him on Leo's couch. Victor she dragged face down by the feet, across the courtyard and up to the flat, to settle beside Gavin in front of the telly. She mopped the blood off them but there was nothing she could do about the skin they'd lost on the bumpy journey across the gravel and up the rough stairs. She found a Nike baseball cap in Leo's wardrobe and set it on Victor's head. Then she found a heavy gold tube of lipstick in the bathroom cabinet and applied it to Gavin's mean blue mouth, laughing hysterically to herself while she did it. They looked so absurd, the two of them under-developed and bony, stiff on the couch in the dawn's light.

Now she is in Rex's kitchen making coffee: turning the kettle on, spooning granules into two mugs. It is late in the afternoon but she has just got up. In her narrow bed she fell asleep instantly. When at last Neela awoke she looked in the mirror: the bashed, enlarged forehead was almost black and untouchably painful, the cheekbone drawn out wide and skinless, those double-dealt slices leaking clear fluid. But the mouth was smiling. Country singers warble about life being a journey: sometimes a thrilling ride, sometimes a grey, lonely highway. But until recently Neela's existence had been like repeatedly navigating the same suburban roundabout. It wasn't a journey as such, more like one long, bad camping trip. Now, something has electrified their lives, its serpentine knots mysterious and mythic as a Celtic amulet – snakes' heads swallowing other snakes' tails.

So often during this time her conscience has perturbed her in the night with its dubious acid-trip memories, so distant and dreamlike, of when she had actually been good. When she had shown promise as a human being. This is probably going back to when she was five, or maybe ten, and her hair was long and silky down her back. She was very pretty then. Before her face thinned out over the bone it was a fleshy oval with red cheeks and feline eyes. She learned to read and write early, and her work made its way onto the much-coveted star-pupil section of wall beside the blackboard. She wrote quirky stories about her life, all lies, but they earned her friends. She also loved to paint, turning the long hairs of the brush in palettes of pure watered blue and applying it to the paper with the precision of a Chinese calligrapher.

She pours out the boiling water, then knocks on Rex's bedroom door before going to sit down with her own coffee at the kitchen table. It looks like a gloomy day outside, a sullen English waterlogged wind. Neela takes a sip. Something went wrong at age eleven, twelve. It wasn't just to do with her colour, there were other non-white people in the school and the orphanage. At puberty her voice became deep and she developed a way of speaking that made people think she was laughing at them. Out of her puppy fat rose a tough body and a handsome face with high bones and long, arrogant eyes. People began to shy away from her. And she wasn't a flirt. She never got crushes. Anything to do with the body – with fingers and lips and touching and fucking – repulsed her.

Rex comes out of his bedroom, still wearing the same clothes from last night. He makes straight for the coffee, his eyes shrunken apertures, puffy with fatigue. His hands look pathetic wrapped around the mug – the strong, masculine fingers all grey and shivering. Neela watches him for a few moments, then leans back and puts her feet up on the table. 'Excited?' she says nastily.

He comes to sit opposite her at the table. 'You actually slept, didn't you? Two bodies within the space of a few hours, and you were out like a light. You're really having fun. This has just been a game to you.' He holds his face poised over the steam from his coffee.

Neela doesn't say anything for a while. Eventually she sighs and shuts her eyes. 'Well, you know, I've got what I call the dog theory. There's normal life: shopping, going out with friends, wearing nice clothes, having a good time, doing some decent work. That's the prototype. That's what you grow up thinking you're going to have. And you think it's worth it. The trade-off is what you give to the world – your energy and your talent – because in return you get certain things: money, status, some-times even fame. Right? I mean, you've followed the basic model yourself, sort of.' She takes her feet off the table and swings herself forward again, resting on her elbows. 'Then there's the dog. You can't ignore the dog. The dog spent its whole fucking life, day after day, being kicked, beaten, tricked, ignored. It's never met any other dogs so it doesn't know how to behave. It just knows what it's seen. Sometimes the dog gets a hold of you and it won't let go. You try to be good to it. You access all the grace and humility and charity you can find in yourself.' Reaching across the table, she begins to pat Rex on the head. 'Nice doggy.' She takes her hand away. 'But it doesn't give a shit. You try and be decent. You try to live with it. Close it off in some part of your basement. But every time you open your eyes in the night there it is, sitting on your bed. So you decide to fight.' She gets up and starts rummaging in Rex's fridge for

184

food. She finds a large hunk of expensive walnut bread and tears some off, then straightens up. 'What can I tell you? The dog's winning.'

Rex bends forward and lays his face on his crossed forearms. He closes his eyes. He's so tired that it's keeping him awake; all he can think about is how exhausted he is – it makes his brain race. He hears Neela cross behind his chair and go through to the living room, then turn the TV on. Somehow, her ruined features suit her. They fit with her personality. It's the face she always deserved to have, the ogress behind that impassive taut-skinned mask. He forcibly stops his train of thought. He has begun to see things the way she does, rubbing his hands together and gloating over other people's suffering. He was never a malicious child. On the first day of school, he puked his lunchtime milk over the height-chart on the wall, and things went downhill from there. Years of bullying knocked out of him any fascination with hurting people. He was the pasty kid in the corner. Dough boy, his face smeared with icing-sugar and chocolate spread.

If he opens his eyes just a fraction he can see Neela on the sofa. Every so often she will raise her hands and slowly, lightly pass them over her brow and temples and mouth. She isn't really watching the television; her irises wear that veiled look of recent, barely-tolerated physical damage. Nobody had ever told her that she was actually attractive, in her own way. He certainly hadn't. It was a hostile, pared-down sort of look that didn't invite compliments. Now there's no need.

The doorbell goes and Neela gets up to answer it. Everything she does seems to be enclosed in a brace of high-gauge pain which doesn't come so much from the fracture in her skull as rise from the core of the earth and surge into her body through the soles of her feet. This is what they've been waiting for, her

185

and Rex. The fallout. On the steps sits Lukas, his back and shoulders tense, staring out across the courtyard. His hands are tightly clasped. Every so often he pushes a lock of greasy long hair behind his ear. Neela goes to sit next to him. By now they have reached such a level of animosity – they know and spurn each other's natures so intently – that they are able to talk to each other like old friends. He's got that streety look about him, the chilled rained-upon demeanour of someone who's been walking for hours, face turned down to the pavement. On the landing is a scruffy, tightly packed travel bag. 'You don't look good,' says Neela, checking out the black lines under his eyes. 'You didn't get home until recently, did you?'

He shakes his head. 'I had myself a coffee and took an old newspaper with me. But I was daydreaming. The next thing I knew there was a row of empty coffee cups on my table, the waiters were looking at me funny and my jaw was so tight I could have used it as a car-jack. I had breakfast in another place. After that I just wandered around. I went into all the shops, down all the streets. I got in maybe an hour ago.' Lukas wearily searches his pockets and locates his cigarettes. He tears the filter off one and lights it, then indicates Leo's flat with a jerk of his thumb. 'They've taken off, haven't they? I thought they might.' He shakes his head. 'I admire you. You're so fantastically disgusting, so pathetic and snide, such a liar, that you actually drove them away. And you don't care. Or you find it funny. I wish I was like you sometimes.'

Neela lies right down across the steps and looks at the sky. 'Oh, flattery will get you nowhere,' she says, 'I've just got a very low give-a-shit threshold.' The estate has a dull in-limbo atmosphere to it, the feel of sullen teenagers' bedrooms, of Sunday-closing and bank holidays. What looks like an incipient storm has layered the air with silvery lunar light.

Lukas takes a last drag on his cigarette before tossing it down into the courtyard. Being with Neela is like having your head held under water. You can struggle and thrash against your fate. You can be docile and submit. But either way, you drown. That is all they know, Neela and her death tribe. Away from them, Lukas could reprise his loving wolfhound ways, maybe free up the gruff, boundless affection the death people attempted to shackle. He puts his arm around his bag and looks earnestly at her. 'People always say you should fight fire with fire. I never saw the sense in that. Surely you just wind up with more fucking fire? The thing is, people like you fall in love with the fire itself. You like to see stuff burn. You want the fire to spread from thing to thing to thing. The argument doesn't matter any more.' He gets up and hoists his bag onto his shoulder. Neela sits up, a strange expectant grin on her face. He goes on, 'I'm not like you, thank God. I was never in this to be some dude on the scene, I just wanted to see my friend do well. But you've got him now and that's cool too. Well done. Whatever jerk-off game you're playing, you've won, OK? I'm not going to fight with you. You'll get yours, I truly believe that. Whatever you've done to people it'll come back ten times as hard. In fact, judging by that beef stroganoff you call a face, payback time's already started. I'm just going to pick Victor up and we'll be off. I take it he crashed at yours or Rex's? I forgot to give him the keys.'

Neela lets her smile open out fully. 'Oh no,' she says. 'We got in and Leo's place was empty so I said he could go there. He wanted to wait up for you.'

If at any point in her dotage Neela was asked to elect her life's top ten moments, this would surely be one of them. Lukas goes over to Leo's flat, bangs on the front door and then steps back, startled, as it swings back already unlocked. The house is ice cold and all the curtains have been drawn. He leaves his bag in the doorway and makes his way down the hall. He gently pushes open the door to the bedroom, thinking Victor may still be asleep. But the bed is empty, though it has been used. A foolish brotherly grin begins to stretch Lukas' face: the boy is probably scoffing his breakfast at the table. He pads back down the hallway and ducks in through the kitchen, but the work-surfaces are clean and bare, the sink empty, the packets of food in the fridge untouched. No crumbs anywhere. The kitchen leads into the lounge and the television is on with the sound turned low. It is the only source of light in the room. Lukas frowns and goes towards it. He plans to join Leo and Janine in Benwick by tonight. The four of them could have a meal together, cosied up with their glasses of red wine, the muted heavy movements of the sea churning just yards away.

Lukas enters the dim living room just as Neela comes into the house. She slams the front door behind her, and he turns and there are Gavin and Victor outlined on the sofa, their faces dark. Images from the TV screen play over the floor. Neela comes and leans in the doorway, watching. It is wonderful to see Lukas' large, strong form befuddled in the shaded room. He is one of those who can't tolerate the dark; it creeps him out – especially curtains drawn against daylight. It snaps his senses off. His instinct is to go towards the TV, like a moth. He has to force himself to approach the figures on the sofa. 'Hi there,' he says quizzically. 'Vic? Why've you got the sound down?' He takes another step.

Neela, unable to bear it any longer, yells, 'Hey, look!' then slaps her hand over the light switch, and the sudden blaze of a hundred-watt bulb dislocates his vision. 'Spook-out!' Light is pouring from the bulb. It makes everything in the room change colour. Objects appear harsh and one-dimensional, abrasively grained after the silky liquid blue of the darkness. The boys are sitting on the couch with direct, lively expressions. Gavin still has his belt around his neck and his face is a tight cricket-ball red. Victor looks a bit better, apart from the side of his face without any skin on it. 'They're playing a game,' says Neela, 'called "At home with the Unluckies". Victor's playing Mr Unlucky, see his cap, and Gavin insisted upon wearing lipstick for his starring role as the lovely Mrs Unlucky. I think they were made for their parts. It's like they were always meant to be Unlucky. They're just Unlucky all over.'

Lukas is so horrified he starts to smile. Then the blood drains from his face and he faints. Neela watches. She has seen women faint before – their knees weakening, their centre of gravity throwing them out to the side, the arms and shoulders loose. But men faint as though something has kicked them in the small of the back. Like they've been baseball-batted down. Bam! They fall fast and heavy.

He's out for quite a while, maybe two or three minutes. Neela looks from him to the boys, and every time she sees Gavin with his lipstick it makes her laugh. Eventually she goes and kneels by Lukas, turning him onto his back with difficulty. There is a string of spit hanging from his lips. Neela draws her hand back and administers a stiff, ringing slap across his face, liking the way the room sends back a crisp four-fold echo from each of its walls. She does it again, the other way, flipping his face back. He opens his eyes and then rears up. The movement is so instinctive and sudden that he puts his hand square on her chest and pushes her back without realising. Stumbling towards the kitchen sink he begins to vomit before he even gets there. He holds his hands up to his face and it fills his palms, then he leans across the draining board and empties his guts over the plughole in a series of tight heaves.

Neela has followed Lukas into the kitchen and hoists herself up onto the work-top. The non-dog part of her is rapidly diminishing, so high and delirious is she on the sight and smell of pain. That rank human agony, so grounding and extreme. It's something to be worshipped. *What can I say? The dog's winning.* Never has she – or could she – feel that level of love for someone, though for so long she wanted to. It's a cellular, physical love, elemental as carbon. She rips a square of kitchen paper off the roll and sits there with it. When he's done, she taps him on the shoulder and offers it to him but he raises his hand, palm towards her, and starts to back off warily. His eyes are pink and watery. 'No. Stay away from me.' She opens her mouth to say something but he cuts her off. 'No. Whatever it is, just no. Please, Neela. I can't think of anything to say to you. I don't even want to look at you.' He turns away from her and takes a couple of steps. Then a bolt of grief – she can almost see it, translucent, high-voltage, ripping through floor and ceiling and spearing him – makes him spin around again. He keens like a wounded animal, raises his hand in a claw and brings it to his face, then quite deliberately scores himself, his white cheeks and lips, dragging the nails deep and slow all the way from one ear to the other.

Neela stares. Something in Lukas' gesture mesmerises her, the primitive desire to harm himself. A pain and a movement so eloquent she is almost jealous of its grace. She wishes he would lunge and try to annihilate her, tussle and tear and rend her limbs from their sockets. That he would discard his nobility and become like her. He points, not accusingly but as though he has chosen or elected her, and his voice is very quiet. 'You're very clever. I see that. You did the one thing in the world that could make me a participant in your game. The one thing.' He reaches forward and closes his hand over her face, pressing her cheeks in against her teeth. She can feel the effort he's making to not simply give in and crush her jawbones together. He gives her

190

face a little shake, his fingertips pressing cold and hard against her slit cheekbone. Pain bleaches out her eyesight for a moment. His breath smells of vomit. 'If I walk away from you, you win because you have my brother. If I fight you, you win because I've turned into you.' He lets go and runs the cold water tap. He washes his hands, then grips the side of the sink. 'There's no real choice.' His cheeks turn pink and he begins to cry, choking man-sobs breaking his voice. 'I can show you. I can be abhorrent too. I can make myself as hideous as you.'

Neela leans very close to him and says into his ear, 'Here's some front-page news. I didn't kill your sadistic bat-mutant of a brother. OK? I'm glad he's dead but it wasn't me who offed him.' She hops off the counter. 'It was your friend Leo, and his friend Janine. Big shock, no? Everything you thought about them was wrong. They came racing out of the courtyard in a stolen BMW and they caught him at the gates. He was just standing there. They'd hit the accelerator so hard he slithered up the bonnet all spread out. He shot up the windscreen and then he went for the big one. It must have been ten feet in the air he rose, or maybe twenty. But after that he lost momentum and gravity pulled him right down. He smacked into the ground almost like it was rising up to meet him at the same time. I think he even bounced. And they didn't even pause. Last thing we saw of them was the light hitting their rear bumper as they made their getaway. Did you get that? They didn't give a shit. If they looked in their mirror they probably saw him laid out on the gravel, legs this-a-way, arms that-a-way. They probably laughed and high-fived each other.' She claps him on the back. 'So I guess we're all on the same side now, matey.'

An hour later, the three of them are driving out of London in a bottle green Jag they found parked by a mews house just a short walk from the estate. It slices through the road so quickly that worms of rain hit the windscreen and then dart straight off again. The storm is breaking at the end of the motorway – a sheet of sodden black cloud illuminated strangely from behind, and they are flying into its heart. Neela lounges on the back seat watching Lukas' white hands on the steering wheel. Every so often he will mutter inaudibly to himself.

'So,' she says, 'who taught you how to jump-start cars?'

His jaw tightens: 'Leo did.'

Neela laughs: 'I know. I just wanted to hear you say it.' For the trip she has brought nothing with her except her camera. Two rolls of film will be all she needs to convince herself that these things are happening: the boys' heads in front of her, nodding with tiredness; the squall and torrent waiting to greet them on the pebble-beach when they alight; the golden boy and the golden girl – melted down, incinerated. She doesn't ask herself what she will do then. There's plenty of options: open up a hot-dog stall in the street. Hustle people in pool-halls. Become a shoe-maker.

Rex stares out of the window. They are overtaking everyone, though it doesn't feel like it. The car barely makes a noise. It just feels like an extension of the tarmac, an upraised ripple like a cartoon cat racing under the carpet. Space-buggies loaded with multicoloured kids' ephemera and roof racks bearing his 'n' hers mountain bikes stay level with them for a few seconds. then fall back. The crash barriers blur. The oncoming storm has varnished the horizon a metallic empty grey. They speed towards the vacuum. He turns and checks on Neela, who's lying on her back staring up through the window with a visionary, almost ecstatic expression on her face. He reaches over and lifts her camera out of her hands, then takes a shot of her. 'I always said I wanted to see where he'd hung out as a boy. I hadn't thought it'd pan out quite like this. I imagined I'd pack a thermos, some boiled sweets and a picnic blanket. Instead, I've got here a bereaved sibling, a psycho with a broken face, and bullets rolling around in the glove compartment.' He lays the camera back on her stomach. Her eyes unroll from the sky and fix themselves on him. She doesn't say anything, and she doesn't smile. Slowly, the malevolence gathers in her look. It's like watching mercury beads drawing together. A few seconds ago, she was a girl daydreaming in the back of a car. A strange girl, an ugly forgotten girl, but harmless. Then the whimsical face fades and it is the Neela they know and hate.

The sun has gone down on Benwick. There are no safety lamps along the pier, no bars or shops. The walkways and beachfront are empty. There is only a thrashing sea and, right above it, the alien electric glow of the storm. After a thick brief silence, as though the town is holding its breath, the rains start. Blinding, solid rain which aims to obliterate anything it hits. Ripping over the pebbles, scattering the stones. Drops the size of fists reach down from the sky to punch the air out of Benwick.

Janine watches Leo standing on their balcony. Like the rest of the quaint place it is faded, the light blue wooden slats nicked and chipped with time. There are pretty touches, though: white pots of flowers, a row of polished stones, the low lovers' bench. Leo's head is back, his arms held a little way out from his body. He sticks his tongue out to drink the rain, his long, mobile pink tongue. He draws it back in and swallows. Janine is lying down, dropping in and out of sleep, only one lamp illuminating the room. When they got here this morning they saw that they'd been given two iron-framed single beds, each one covered in its own floral embroidered cloth, and nailed to the floor. There are two of everything: two sinks, two old-fashioned gaudy porcelain washing bowls and jugs, two brush-and-comb sets backed with mother-of-pearl, two hinged vanity mirrors, a small oak trunk at the foot of each bed.

Leo is singing and laughing to himself in the rain, windmilling his arms and then shadowboxing against the powerful wind. Janine hugs her pillow. Mayhem is not in her blood. She is too lazy for a life of excitement. At the end of the day she would rather spoon ice-cream into her mouth and stroke a Persian cat before a vigorous red fire than venture onto the streets to pursue a foe. Fingering the beadwork on an evening dress would always be preferable to trying to pick brain out of it. Let the foes of this world do what they like. They can never really touch her. The stunt with Shane Chisholm was a blast, dizzying and bold as a tequila shot. And she is not above the occasional midnight threat, the slow pleasurable shredding of a feeble though intelligent psyche such as Rex's. Those are sweet triumphs. But she would never have broken someone's face like he did to Neela's.

She is ashamed to find herself beginning to hate and pity Leo. He is just like a child. Simple. She peers at his leaping, writhing shape on the balcony. So simple. But there it is, nonetheless. He is starting to repel her because he has no limits, no refinement. She watched his face as he drove the BMW, the long eyes and tight skin just like – well, just like Neela's. His knee had jerked on the floor of the car, so impatient, pressing that accelerator down because he was that keen. He hasn't said anything about it, but they are only here because he wanted the others to chase them. He desires a final battle on the wet and slippery stones of Benwick, the seagulls circling down low. Death beneath the pier, and blood running between the pebbles.

Some people find God. They discover the noble elderly hand calmly guiding and protecting, the benevolent wisdom presiding over their every act. Well, Janine was always far luckier than that. She finds hard cash. Whatever she sets her mind to always comes to her eventually, postage paid, in a jewel-encrusted envelope. She thinks of it sentimentally as the spirit of her father – and there was a man who understood the value of gold – taking care of her in this, her earthly existence. Their scam has worked, and Neela was absolutely right: she and Leo have the King of England's money divided up in their own names. She could resurface in another part of London or another city altogether, rebirthed and modestly, untaxably wealthy, and step into a new life like she stepped into Rex's. They could so easily go their separate ways, making themselves bland and anonymous for a time.

But it is not anonymity that Leo wants. He is like a child born poor, the last of a great litter, who will caper and bite and kick until every eye in the room is fastened upon him. If he cannot captivate his friends with good deeds, he will captivate his enemies with acts of violence. He will show them, is what he thinks. Everything for effect.

The handle of their locked door is moving, Janine notices. Very softly and slowly, the dainty painted glass knob with its scalloped, gilded detailing is making a cautious quarter turn. So she gets up silently and plays the oldest trick in the slapstick comedy book, the most tired, predictable gag: she stands in the corner behind the door. Suddenly, a shot makes the delicate handle spring apart in starburst segments. The brass lock mechanism also leaps out, leaving a perfect splintery wooden circle in the door. In the ensuing silence, Neela and Lukas edge into the room. Leo is all they have eyes for and he is right opposite them, now shirtless and rain-polished on the balcony. Janine has to fight the urge to laugh. It is too easy: she simply walks out.

Neela's eyes run over Leo's hard, toned torso. Even his body looks like hers, a series of unforgiving angles snagging the eye, at once beautiful and somehow austere. She wonders if Janine has run her lips over that golden skin, licked shower-water from between his shoulder blades, kissed the narrow sinewy throat. She can feel it too: a mouth on hers, pliant and hot. Their faces are no longer alike though, he saw to that. His is intact, hers flawed. His grinning now, a beacon of blazing white teeth; her own mouth so dry, bitter both in taste and sentiment. She would claw his eyeballs out if she could, if pain didn't cling to her quite so tenaciously. She would rip his skin away from the bone and eat it, were it not for the weakness which makes even a pen too heavy to hold. Right now, if it were a choice between leaping on Leo and leaping into that bed beside her – a bed so soft-looking, the pretty cover a sumptuously decorated white poplin, and such fat pillows tucked underneath – she would take the shut-eye option. But the show must go on.

Outside Benwick Lodging House, Janine turns once and looks up at their room. It is the only stable illuminated scene in the gloom, and even that is made surreal by the slanting rain. There is movement on or around the balcony, the clumsy unchoreo-graphed lunges of a proletarian scuffle. Neela must be pretty weak. She lost a lot of blood in their bathroom at the estate, pints of it, enough to scare even Leo for a moment. That was why they laid her in the courtyard afterwards – so she didn't see the mat and the carpet made so marshy and dark. Janine walks away from the house and alongside the beach towards the pier. The rain has sharpened to a sleety, frozen onslaught, like nails raking her back. For once it feels good to be in a storm, to feel so minuscule and powerless, to leave other humans to their clumsy fisticuffs and make herself bare before the hail. The night has reduced everything to the one-dimen-sional difference of textures: the glossy spread pebbles, the wide strip of glistening sea, and the pier, a black ribbon pinning it all together.

There is a tall man by the pier. Something about him, maybe the strength in the shoulders or the long legs, marks him out as attractive. Janine sees him dimly. It is hard to breathe in the wind. Instead of inhaling, the storm seems to sock air into her lungs like a baseballer practising hits. The man is wearing a long black coat and looks out, away from Benwick. Janine draws towards him and he glances at her. 'Rex,' she says, astonished, and he smiles. His handsome face is translucent, the wide silvery eyes at home in the bizarre ultraviolet light that crackles on the horizon. He knows what she and Leo have done, his smile so full of complicity. And he is no longer scared of her, just exhausted. She is also tiring of this game. She feels a trill of fear. There is so much violence he could unleash upon her. She is not strong, and the sea is deep and cold. A sea like that would savour her. It would enjoy bashing her against the pebbles, caught on the prickly little points of its waves.

Instead, they stand together like fishermen watching their lines, side by side and silent for a moment. Rex looks at her, then indicates the lodging house with a jerk of his head. 'I'm sitting this one out. I'm not really the breaking-and-entering sort. Lukas has my gun.' He grins. 'That old thing seems to be passed around like an unwanted child these days.' For the first time, Janine feels awkward around him. It is not like her to be caught in the night, her clothes pasted wet to her body, her mind a mute stone bereft of punchlines. Alone, out here, Rex is the stronger. He feeds off the pitching water and the bone-numbing icy wind. She opens her mouth to speak but he claps a hand on her shoulder. His touch is warm and confident. 'It's OK, what you did. It was clever.' He sighs. 'People like you get somewhere in life. You'd do better with that money than I ever could. It never felt like any of that was meant to be mine anyway. It was just the way things fell.' He plucks a pair of gloves from his pocket and offers them to her. She stares down at them stupidly for a second, then takes them. He continues, 'I was always the slow type. Lazy too – God, fatally lazy. You know, it never occurred to me that I could do things, like actually instigate a series of events for myself. Marlon came along, then you came along, then Neela added her unique seasoning to the recipe. And it's nice to just do what people say, like a servant. It absolves you of blame.' He shakes his head sharply as though to make himself forget something. 'It's like starting up a car before tipping it over a cliff. You've got your hand on the key, and you deliberately turn it. You hear the car starting and you feel it rumble then sort of sit up. It starts going and at first you're faster than it is. Then you're running with it. Eventually it's so fast you have to let go or you'll fall. It goes over the edge and it spins out then drops, I don't know, seventy or eighty feet, and let's say you watch it go down. It bounces once, it bounces another time, and by the time it reaches the bottom it's a metal pancake with a number plate. It's nothing like the car whose ignition you turned on.' He watches her put the gloves on, then turns back to look at the sea. 'If you go now you'll be back in London by dawn. Be careful on the roads.'

The first finger of lightning flicks the end of the pier. Janine is shivering violently. She plucks at Rex's sleeve. 'Why don't you come with me? We can leave the three of them to it.' But he shakes his head and pushes her gently away from him, down the beach. In the distance are lights, modern electric lights, not the enchanted lunar mist of the storm. She looks towards them then back at him. Janine has that talent for tripping freely in and out of other people's stories, always gaining. Everyone else has to accept their fate, *it's just the way things fall*. Ordinary, unlucky, minor people like him and Neela and Lukas, with ugly souls. They are stuck with just one story, its tired circumlocutions and inevitable, bathetic conclusion: 'No, I can't. I have to see to things here.'

Benwick Lodging House is silent and seemingly empty. The other guests and staff are nowhere to be found. All that is left of the flapper-girl receptionist is a gold cigarette case by the telephone. In the cafe, only the faintest whiff of too-sweet perfume remains of the lady diners. The piano is lidded and covered, the staircases – each step painted with curling vines and creepers, with roses and lilies – undisturbed by the passage of doddery though elegantly shod feet. Without, a raging storm and thunderous white light arcing out of the clouds, the sea trying to escape itself – rising, rocking, reaching up. Within, smudged sherry glasses and sheet music on the lobby table, the lodging-house cat asleep on the chaise longue.

In Leo's room the gun drags light to it. It is brighter than the lamp, brighter than the pulsing sky, quivering in Lukas' hands. There is Leo, with his back to the wall, his fingers spread. He wears the idiotic, daredevil smile that Janine has grown to despise. There is Lukas, aiming the gun, tears rolling down his face. And there lies Neela on one of the beds, her face white with pain, talking tiredly through a bone-dry throat: 'Pull the trigger, Lukas. Then we can all go home. I need you to do this for me ...' At times she cannot hear her own voice and her vision blacks out, or she perceives non-existent things in the corners of the room – darting, snatching folds of light. She carries on talking, not knowing if Lukas can hear her or not. Sometimes it seems like she is only thinking the words, not saying them aloud. Pain has got her in its fist and is holding her up to the light. It clasps her and begins to squeeze tighter and tighter. It presses everything else out of her body. Suddenly, she breaks.

Leo and Lukas stare as Neela's body jerks on the bed. Her eyes roll into her head and her limbs stiffen. Her fingers spread and her jaw clenches. The muscles in her thighs flex. One arm goes out and knocks the lamp off the bedside stand. Her spine arches right back. She utters a gurgling, strangled cry and then falls flimsily back onto the mattress.

They are in near darkness now. Neither of them goes to help Neela. Individually, they choke back the jubilant laughter that surges into their mouths: an unphotogenic demise for an unphotogenic girl. Lukas becomes oafish without light. He swings his hands out, scared to make a step. His harsh breathing turns to a whimper, high in the lungs. Leo leans against the wall and watches him. He is not Lukas' friend, he never was. He does not like those lolloping types, with their dogged all-for-one sort of love. He takes a quick side-step then shimmies along the wall so that he is behind him. 'Lu-kas,' he calls teasingly, his voice merry, and the tall, strong boy whips around and trips over his own feet, falling onto his knees as if to propose. Leo laughs down at him. The darkness makes him quick-eyed and agile. 'Lukas, if you take the gun and just lift it a little, here I am. I'm next to one of the vanity mirrors.' He reaches out and bats the mirror off the dresser. The three silver panels rock for a second and then fall quickly, springing out of their cheap frames and showering the floor with tinsel-like splinters. Lukas yelps with fear. Leo continues, his voice smooth as a Twenties cocktail-party host: 'See. Right here. I'm waving. Can you see my arm?' He gives Lukas the finger. 'D'you see me now? Shoot me if you like. Keep your finger on the trigger and one of the bullets is bound to hit. I killed your brother after all. It was an accident, but I still did it. And you've got me now. So what're you waiting for? I deserve it.'

On the floor, Lukas moans and repeats the motion Neela found so fascinating: he raises his hand and scratches his own face. Then he scores his own chest. Outside, the rain and wind hammer the balcony. It is very cold in the room. 'No,' he says, his voice a disembodied, shaky whine of sadness. 'No, Leo, I would never hurt you.' He puts the gun into his jacket pocket, stands up very slowly and reaches around him, fingers spread. 'I don't harm my friends.' He gropes around, stumbling against the end of one of the beds. Trying to keep his balance, he accidentally grips Neela's thigh, then utters a disgusted cry and snatches his hand away. He straightens up again. 'I see what you're like now, so I won't say anything more. I didn't realise until I heard your voice just then. You don't care. But it doesn't matter. This is my victory over you.' There is no reply. Lukas truly hates and fears the dark. It seems solid, with a caustic, mocking personality of its own. He bumps into a wall and slides along it and finally, thank God, he finds the main light switch. He flicks it and the room burns against his retina, suddenly coloured, and he sees – of course – that Leo has gone. There is only the villain girl passed out on the bed, the rain-washed boards of the balcony dampening the rug, the demolished mirror in its myriad winking, sparkling pieces. Perhaps Leo's wily laugh echoes down the corridor, but nothing more.

8

The tempest ceases as suddenly as it began. Benwick has withstood many such squalls – the elements beating themselves against its boards, salt harsh in the air, grating down the painted signs like sandpaper. Now the distant spectral light deepens then cracks to reveal a molten sun heaving itself out of the water, the waves turning blood red.

Janine lies huddled in the back seat of the BMW a few hundred yards from the beach. She has only had a few hours' rest but the sunrise is so fierce she has no choice but to wake up. It doesn't prompt her out of sleep so much as forcibly cram her irises with coruscating crimson beams. After leaving Rex at the pier she had tried to drive towards home but the windscreen had shuddered under the sleet and the wheels slid about. Gravel flew out of nowhere to strike the wing mirrors. The headlights hardly seemed to split the gloom. Benwick was determined not to let her out; the place seemed to be turning itself about every time she inched around a corner. Always the same row of shops to one side: the ladies' hairdressers with its pink net frontage; the tiny glass panes of the newsagent's; the hand-written menus posted up in the tea-room windows. She finally lost her wits when a prong of perfect lightning seemed to stab the road right in front of her, its neon blue wire bent into jagged steps.

She raises her head and peers out towards the horizon. Never before in her life has she felt so wretched, here in this two-bit town, this hamlet, this shack begging to be mown down and made into a motorway or theme park. Her skin papery with saltwater, her hair a ragged bush of wind-flogged strands. She struggles to sit up, licking her dry lips which taste like the ocean. The sky is blazing now, the sea and beach scarlet-daubed slivers in the distance, the pier rising up, not black but red too, charred-looking. Janine gets out of the car and walks parallel with the coast line. Occasionally she turns and scans the burning horizon. Her joints are stiff. The lion in her wants to stretch and bask in the light, to open its amber eyes to be heated. The BMW made a cold, narrow resting-place. When she was a girl, at age thirteen or so, she had a white four-poster bed stacked with duck-feather pillows. She slept naked under creamy linen.

She comes to the lodging house. The hanging wooden sign is still set upon its bracket, the window-boxes perhaps a little awry but no real damage. The glass in the windows though is scarred by grit, and silt from the sea-bed collects in the corners of the frames. Janine pushes the door open and walks up to the reception but nobody is there. The lobby has the appearance of a discarded stage-set, a collection of dubious period details awaiting actors with cigarette-holders and ostrich-feather hats to bring it alive. There is a black rotary telephone on the desk, and an open visitors' book with a tasselled tapestry bookmark resting on it. Everything is basted with sunlight. Janine rings the brass Attention bell but by the way the sound pierces the building she can tell the place is empty. Even the cat has disappeared. Ordinarily, she would just reach over, pull the phone book off the shelf – if there is a phone book for this no-man shit-hole – and call herself a cab. But there is probably no cab service here, only donkeys to rent by the hour, or an old man willing to pedal you home on the back of his bicycle.

She mounts the stairs to their room. The ragged hole in the door where the lock used to be forces from her a snort of cynical laughter. It embodies every single difference that could possibly be thrust into the gulf between herself and Rex's clan. Where she would crouch and tease with a hairpin, they would send steel charging into the grain. Where she would scrub from herself every trace of scum no matter how stubbornly it clung, and enter the next chapter of her life renewed and remade, they would embrace death with mindless stupidity, as though it were the only option. She knows her own nature well enough. Ultimately, no magic or coincidence could submerge it in the twisted conventions of primitive superstition. She will never be one of those who runs screaming from fire believing it to be the first chapter of the apocalypse. Nonetheless, she has unwittingly absorbed some of the ritualism of the King of England and its acolytes, and been humbled by the unlikeliest of people: Rex, Neela.

The balcony doors are open, the sunrise red upon glossy red. There is no blood anywhere, only the broken lamp and mirror – a cheap mirror, Janine spots that immediately. Someone has lain and writhed in her bed, for the covers have been rucked in the shape of two digging heels and two grabbing fists. There is nothing portentous or grand about the scene. Conflict doesn't hang in the air. It is just one more wrecked, dishevelled room in a seaside flophouse. Janine's desire to make a final bold state-ment dies right there. She had thought perhaps to shear all her hair off and don some dark robes to signal her departure from the arena. Maybe she could even walk back to London like a penitent, bare-footed, her pockets empty, wailing, throwing ashes along the path. But she goes into their tiny bathroom and sees in the savage carmine light that she isn't as haggard as she feels: her yellow eyes intense, her hair in crisp curls. Tiredness has laid a flattering paleness just below her skin. Perhaps she will take a shower before leaving, and pack all her clothes up neatly.

Or go down and see if there are any more raspberry tartlets in the cafe. She notices a wooden rack fastened to the wall, bearing pink-ribboned vials of bubble-bath and other unguents. Uncorking one she releases its synthetic sweetness and thinks, since the night was so uncomfortable, that actually a hot bath is what her cramped muscles need.

The last thing Neela knew, Leo was smiling and Lukas had hefted the gun. A sizzling white light broke over her and the bed started shaking. When she opened her eyes again the rain was still batting the lodging-house walls but the room was empty and dark. A hot pain slid into her neck, a pain so intense and localised it was almost solid, a real object she would have liked to clutch and draw from her throat. She rolled herself onto the floor but she had not known about the broken mirror and it pierced her many times over. Then came the tears. She bowed her head and silently cried. This was all so ugly, the room, herself, the sprinkles of bric-a-brac mirror embedded in her palms. They were all like goblins or dwarves, she and Leo especially, living on the edges of human society but untouched by it. Scavenging in the human world, causing mischief in human lives, but always returning to their cave of chicken-bones and cinders. She was monstrous, dying, bleeding inside her brain. So hideous and shameful to see. Yet out of the boiling tears she shed there rose a sudden realisation. She could feel a difference. She had been emancipated. The dog and its blood-lust had drowned in the storm. That cowardly pup, that neurotic mutt – real, genuine pain had sent it whining home.

The pain made it impossible to sleep and she needed to feel ice and water cold against her skin. She found her camera under the bed and slung it around her neck. There were only a few frames left; she would have to judge well. In a corner of the room was a length of polished wood with a tight hook at one end for drawing the curtains across, and she used that as a walking-stick. Slowly she made her way downstairs, then released herself into the night.

The sun has risen and she is still walking. One step can take her as long as five minutes, but she is not rushing herself. This day seems like a luxury, a gift. She has so much time to think and watch, if she could only stay awake. There is the blue sea, happily rolling back on itself. There the pebbles, all shades of brown, knocking against each other with a blunt clacking noise. She wants to hold a mass for the dog. She wants to spread the word. All hail! The dog is dead. Except nobody is around, it is only six in the morning. The ice-cream parlour and the barber shop are closed. The fortune-teller's stall is bare. But it is going to be a fine, church-going Sunday. Neela is very sleepy but there are still things she has to see. People to meet, places to go. If she lets herself rest now, her eyes will never open again.

At the end of the beach she finds something which rewards her long trek. There is the fairground Leo mentioned to Janine, not the same sinister collection of faded tents he remembers, but a set of rides belonging to a newer company. Neela smiles and shakily shades her eyes. The sun is so bright it makes shapes swim into one another. There is a merry-go-round, a riot of laughing horse-mouths and stiff wooden hair. A set of coconuts on posts. Any number of miscellaneous try-your-luck tasks – shooting, fishing, throwing. There is a test-your-strength machine formed like a giant barometer, with a wooden comic-book hammer and MAN OF STEEL!!! painted at the very top. A serious shooting range where the ducks are beaten tin outlines rather than bath accessories. Neela draws close and leans upon the counter of the range. Nobody has manned this fairground in a while. Everything is coated in grime and the levers – she attempts to start the ducks on their procession – are stiff. Or maybe she is too weak. She would love to swing one of those guns high on her shoulder and level that long bear-hunting barrel, discharging its thunderous shot. She could make believe she was in the mountains, up high where the air runs thin, tracking deer. Perhaps in another life she will find herself there: a Thermos of strong black coffee in her knapsack, along with a well-used map folded in segments.

At the back of the fairground, closest to the sea, is a handsome dodgems track. Its cars glisten as though newly painted: orange, a dusty Fifties blue, searing red, white. They are shiny and perfect, like pool balls. Neela never liked the dodgems. It did not seem to be much of a laughing matter, to be jostled and jogged with such ferocity. But still and silent are these, with the sun shining full upon them, lush as fruit. She mounts the track and goes to sit upon the 'hood' of one of the cars. This morning she has been filled with a childlike delight at the look and feel of things. She is experiencing the world as it should be experienced, drinking in the optimistic yellow of her car, stretching her legs over its smooth curve. She yawns. Today was the first time she ever watched a proper sunrise. There's so much she's missed out on.

Neela looks over at the other cars. In one of them someone has left an old bag stuffed to overflowing with rubbish and newspaper. She blinks and the bag becomes a dark padded coat. Then it turns into Lukas; he is sitting in the blue car and watching her with an inscrutable expression. He has probably killed Leo by now. She tries to give him a wave, but it is difficult to raise her hand. The sun seems to flash and then Neela finds herself splay-legged on the floor of the track. The walking stick has tumbled over the other side of her car, but it doesn't matter. Crawling is easier. She begins to make her way over to him.

Something bright and soft falls onto her fingers as she goes, and it is her own drool. She laughs when she sees it. She has become like a very old woman. Her camera drags on the ground. She hauls herself up so that she is kneeling with her arms along the side of Lukas' seat. She stretches her hand out and lightly buffets him upon the chest. She draws her hand back and there is a dark spot on it – her eyesight must be playing up again. The spot shrinks and expands.

Then, miraculously, some instinct strikes a little sense into her brain for a few minutes. She stares at the mark on her fingers and it becomes a neat round of dark blood. Confused, she thinks Leo or Rex must be lurking nearby and that she has somehow been set up, until her eye falls on the gun in Lukas' hand and the clean square of paper beside him. His face bears an enigmatic smile as he looks out at the fairground. He is at peace with himself. He did the right thing: he shot himself in the heart. Neela takes a photograph. Then she picks up the note, which is timed and dated. It says only: I AM SO SORRY, but pain has made her raw and intuitive and she realises it was meant as a sign for her. The time and the date so carefully set down, like a record. Then she gets it: he never had any intention of killing Leo. This was always his plan. He wrote the note after he discovered Victor and before they left for Benwick. Neela laughs without any humour. This is his triumph over her and the dear departed dog. He shot himself in the heart. She feels like singing: The boy! He shot himself! In the heart! It feels so right. They are all erasing themselves, the orphans: Gavin, Victor, Lukas. Herself soon, she hopes. Wipe-out.

She takes Rex's gun from Lukas, laboriously uncurling each finger from the butt. Once she has it, it seems to be magnetically attracted to the floor, because that is where she winds up again, this time sprawled on her belly with her camera digging into her ribs. The machine skitters out of her hand. The metal base of the dodgems track is so refreshing and cold. She snuggles her cheek against it and feels her eyelids becoming heavy. The next thing she knows, something grips her shoulder and she isn't looking to the side but up into the light, yet it is not light – it is like a broad white sail. Neela smiles. Janine is here, descended from the skies, impeccable Janine clad all in white, so healthy and beautiful. She drags her camera over her face and presses the shutter without looking.

Janine helps Neela sit up, her back against Lukas' car. She had been driving parallel to the coast, about to turn off and make her way back to London, when the jagged outline of the rides caught her eye. She slowed and peered and there, sure enough, was a fairground, and in the distance the sun bouncing off a garish cluster of dodgem cars. She had been wanting to see Neela, and in reality had been crawling along, scanning both town and beach, reluctant to take that final exit which would deliver her to the city. She had not expected to find her like this, though. At times the girl is barely focusing and her mouth hangs open. It seems wrong that her body, so used to its fluid powerful stride, should be so humiliated by pain. That her rights over language should be annulled. Then, suddenly, a light will flick on and self-awareness will gather in her face. The eyes will become exact and the mind hose itself down with clarity.

Janine reaches into her bag and takes from it a bottle of Evian, which she gives to Neela. 'I can get some food if you want.' Her voice comes out so gently she shocks herself. Neela shakes her head. The cold, clean water seems to sink directly into the stultified channels of her brain and shock them into life.

She says, 'Do you have a mirror?' Janine looks at her for a moment, wondering whether to lie. Eventually she sighs, opens her antique compact and holds it in front of Neela's face. Neela grins bitterly. Her mouth is her only untouched feature, though it is not a particularly nice one. Smiling means peeling her lips back to reveal all of those keen, strong teeth. It disrupts the rest of her face. She pushes the mirror away. 'I look like a hammerhead shark. And those cuts you made in my cheek look like gills.' She is finding it hard to speak. The words present themselves to her tongue as though pressed in from outside, not from her own throat, unwieldy and chafing as a horse's bit. Janine can't look her in the eye. She remembers the night she was accosted in the shower, the sincere terror she had felt when Neela's shoes began to muddy the water and it ran past her own toes, the girl's face all hungry, and her exciting bestial way of moving. The animal grace of muscles. Neela seems to have followed what she was thinking. She claps a hand on Janine's knee. 'I wasn't going to let Gavin touch you, you know, that night. I didn't like the way he was looking at you. It wasn't right.' That was when everything between them had changed – when Neela turned and tucked the gun away, then lifted the biggest towel from the rack and let its folded squares fall open, blocking Gavin's view. The white of the towel seemed to blank out everything that had passed between them before. Neela lays her head on Janine's shoulder: 'It was nice in the shower, just you and me.' Her voice hardens. 'Before everyone else crowded in.' She takes another long, grateful pull of water. 'But he punished me good, Leo. You forgot that he's been trained. He can kill slow, he can kill fast. He's very strong. When you see him, tell him it worked. He got me.'

Janine moans and puts her hand over her eyes. 'For God's sake, Neela, why are you lying here like this? You should have called someone. There must be some kind of hospital nearby.'

Neela emits her wicked-stepsister cackle. 'No, there isn't. There's nothing. You think maybe I should go somewhere

211

private. I could have a nice room and the water for my flowers changed daily, maybe get the in-house manicurist to drop by and fix my nails. But I would never do that. That's what you'd do, in your world. You'd have your brain transplant then whip off the oxygen mask, sit up in the surgical theatre and share a champagne toast with all the doctors. I just want to lie on a rock and have crows peck my eyes out.' She leans against Janine once more, this time using her whole torso. In her mind she is a bow-backed crone imparting messages from the spirit world. A soothsayer. Her voice is the voice of ages and her heart a misshapen wishing-stone. She exploits her link with the underworld and spins from it fairy stories and folktales, and Janine is straining to listen to her like a very young child willing to be instructed. 'You'll be glad when this is over. I know you. It'll feel like you've finally woken up after a bad dream.' Her eyes close of their own accord. 'In the beginning, your people shunned my people. You went into the sunlight and your hair grew long and lustrous, but we stayed huddled behind rocks. You explored the earth and laid down sticks to mark where you'd been, but we scurried through the undergrowth, never looking around us. You formed friendships and families and the years went by as you held glorious feasts and celebrations. But we had no such things. We fought over crusts of bread and we developed strange secret codes. We tried to divine the future and cast spells to trick you and fell you. We grew accustomed to the dark and you can still identify us by our night-vision. It was always so. Your people and my people, they were never friends.'

Weakly, she holds her camera out at arm's length and aims it at the two of them. 'Not even an earthquake can shake me out of my nature.' Her thumb presses the shutter release button and light stamps itself on the film: Janine, her hair filling the entire background of the shot, her eyes enormous amber bulbs made

212

iridescent in the sun, the mouth soft and formless with crying, her head inclined protectively over Neela. And Neela, herself with tears on her cheeks, the pale face one tight pinch of pain, the green eyes dark and desperate. There is a click and the camera automatically begins to rewind the film. They've reached the end of the second roll. Neela fumbles to get a blue plastic envelope out of her jacket pocket. It is the kind for processing photos on budget deals. She lets it fall into Janine's lap along with the first roll, then wrestles the back of the camera open and extracts the most recent film. 'Post all of that and get them sent to wherever you are. I don't have anything else to give you, really, though you can take the camera too. I want you to have something of mine. There are other photographs in boxes under my bed, if you want to see. Hundreds of them. Of Rex and the King of England, Lukas and Leo, Gavin and Victor. Those fireworks we let off in the courtyard. The fog. A few from the party at Rex's flat. Some beautiful ones of you.' Neela looks over to where Lukas is sitting, that contented smile on his face. 'But now there's just one more thing I have to do. You need to take me to see Rex. I want to return his gun.' She scrambles onto her knees but feels herself tipping forward, until Janine lays a hand upon her haunch to steady her. She laughs weakly. 'Not now, darling, I've got a headache.' But nonetheless the touch went straight to her groin.

Eventually they are up, Janine's arm around Neela, the gun in Neela's waistband. The air is totally clear, the sea a dash of benign blue. A glorious, crisp winter morning. They slowly turn and take in their surroundings: the dodgem cars, solid white, pea green, orange. Lukas monochrome in his lonely seat: black coat, white face, black hair. Red, red heart. 'Are you looking?' Janine is cooing, as if to a baby. 'It's so gorgeous out. Look at the horses on the carousel.' They are making their way towards it now. 'I like that black one with the roses in its hair. This was always my favourite ride in a fair. Some carousels I've seen, the grander kind, the horses have nylon hair plaited and threaded with glass beads. But those kind of give me the creeps.' Janine keeps talking because if she stops she will throw back her head and scream. A scream so shrill and loud it'll transmute into pure atomic energy and set the bell atop the MAN OF STEEL barometer clanging. She should summon some paramedics to run over and help, their stethoscopes bouncing on their chests. Or race back to the cafe and stand amidst the fondant fancies, yelling, Is there a doctor in the house? while the ladies of Benwick drop their teacups in astonishment. She will never comprehend whatever corrupted sense of justice makes Neela prefer to have ravens feeding on her face. What a waste. Earth could do with that acerbic tongue.

Neela's eyes are open though she is not really blinking, and her steps are heavy and stumbling. But she is glad to be at the fairground. It feels like a special treat, a half-day off school. The ducks are in their shooting range, painted smiles on their faces. The cuddly toys for game-winners are hanging on iron hooks: Pink Panther, Mickey Mouse. All is right with the world. She is just about to say something to that effect when a hole bursts open under her feet and she drops into it.

Janine is nearly yanked to the ground as Neela's muscles give up and her spine becomes liquid. It is amazing how swiftly breathing, moving bodies can be reduced to a rubble of limbs. Janine doesn't utter any cry, only lays her down then picks her up again properly, one arm around her back and the other under her knees. There is no time for histrionics. She begins to carry her over the beach towards the BMW. Her hair flies about, wild gold curls loose, and tendrils of it fall forward across Neela's face. Behind them is the satiny water wrinkling then smoothing

214

out, the high silvery sun, the rides and stalls becoming merely darkened outlines. Janine frowns and labours on, clutching Neela's heavy compact body against her. Occasionally she stumbles. They are both growing cold. Neela groans, an unconscious underwater sound so deep that it seems to come not from her mouth but from her solar plexus, and it makes her whole body vibrate. Janine sobs just once, for pity and shame, and tightens her hold. The beach seems very long now as she toils up it, and so bare and hostile, the pebbles slippery under her feet. It feels as though she is not getting any nearer to the walkway but boring downwards like a drill, displacing the slimy stones.

Finally, panting, she reaches the car and lays Neela in the passenger seat, then tries to jump-start the engine, frantically touching the exposed wire-ends together. Eventually the BMW jerks into life. Instead of turning it around, though, Janine simply puts it into reverse and backs straight along the coast-line towards the dark jut of the pier. Benwick goes by: the pastel-painted buildings with their rickety balconies, the tea room, the lodging house and its yellowed, frothy drapes.

Neela finally crawls out of the hole and opens her eyes. Death has a strange knack of unfolding new dimensions in this life. Like time-tunnels in space: the real world let her through and she was falling faster and faster, she hit the bottom with a bump, opened her eyes – and she was in the real world again. At least she has left pain behind, on her last trip. Somehow when she was falling pain became tiny, then slipped off her, spinning away. She sits up straight and tries to memorise everything that she sees, although the car is reversing fast and things are snatched out of view: a red flower in a blue pot, a calligraphied sign in the teashop saying 'Do NOT Take Your Own Cakes – Ask For Service', an empty bubble-gum dispenser and a twine-tied stack of fresh papers outside the newsagent's. The BMW stops with a jolt. Neela looks around and notices that the sea-gulls have come out. They circle the pier, perhaps a dozen or two dozen of them slanting in the air and coming down low. Their cries are coarse and mean.

She can feel Janine trembling next to her. Poor little rich-girl. Thrust into a nightmare; a swift and graceless descent into this beach-side denouement. She knows Janine is thinking it is her own fault. Greedy Janine! Overfondness for luxury items and clothing a tragedy must make. Her sentence – guilt itself, a life-time's worth. But it is not so. Neela is older than Janine, and she knows more. Right now, Neela calculates she must be, oh, several thousands of years old at least. She can see the entire map of history spread in front of her. She leans forward and taps Janine gently on the shoulder. 'I'm so glad to have known you, Janine,' she says. 'You brought some colour to my world. Because before there wasn't anything, only the days and the nights all following each other, and they all seemed the same to me. I used to dream about meeting someone like you, someone all bold and confident and unafraid. That was what I was like as well, in my head. Popular. Dynamic. So full of curiosity about things. But in truth everything frightened me. Then you came and acted with such spirit and I was jealous.' She takes a crinkle of Janine's hair and rubs its soft, newly-washed strands between her fingertips. 'I always felt dirty. You know, on the inside. I thought if anyone stood too close to me they could see the dirt and they'd know I wasn't like other people.' She sighs and looks away. 'The world just seemed like such a frightening place. Always waiting to trip you up. And you were so easy in it. Laughing, joking, smiling. Wearing those clothes of yours. You expected it to treat you well, and it did. But it wasn't the same for me. I used to walk the streets on a Saturday night and watch all the party people. Always alone. Like a rat. Like people would turn and notice me and scream because I was so disgusting to them. Because I'd crawled from the garbage and the drains into their lives. Because I'd shown my face and it made them sick.' There are more seagulls by the pier now, turning sharply. The stones and the water both glitter in the sun. Neela continues, 'Just don't forget me. OK? Janine? Go to as many countries as you like, make as many friends as you want. Get out there. See the sights. You know that's why I love you. Because you're not afraid to show your face. You grab life. But occasionally, you know, in between all your dinner engagements and your appointments, think about me.'

Neela waits for a reaction but there isn't one; Janine is still hugging the steering-wheel and staring out across the sea. She is very beautiful, the sandy eyes and skin and hair. Neela spies herself in the wing-mirror. It is good that she is not vain: her top-heavy slab of a head is crooked, inclined towards her shoulder. The eyes are an unnaturally bright, bloodless emerald. The mouth hangs open somewhat, and dried white spit collects in its corners. Her skin has renewed its allegiance to the yellow spectrum. It is not the face of a living, thinking person. It is a face that someone discovers washed up in a river or uncovered from the earth. A tomb-face, a demonic doll. A zombie-mask for a Halloween ball. 'Hey, Janine,' Neela says, but in the mirror she sees her lips don't form the words and her throat remains dry. She hasn't said anything, just now, only lain there in the seat. Her entire soliloquy – it never even happened, her words just a rogue electrical pulse, joyriding in the ruptured tubes of her brain. She is like those patients who wake up during their own operations, their reflexes deadened with anaesthetic. Neela blinks, puzzled. She has yet more to say. More words of tenderness she has stored up for a long time – twenty years. Many sweet phrases she never spoke to anybody, except in her own mind. Tears throng her eyes, salty, clinging, full. Heavy tears they are, plentiful and lush; she is crying hard but quiet, and so too is Janine. Outside the car it is a fine, brisk day. Neela sees herself, disabled, a vegetable. A non-person. She needs just one last burst of motion to get herself near to the water beneath the pier, in the rot and the slime, away from the sun. She wishes to be returned to her natural habitat so she can regroup with the rest of her species – the beetles or the worms. She can't wait to feel the tide closing around her neck, the water rolling so smooth and seamless against her collarbone. Though she doesn't want to wind up on the sea floor for ever, her hands and feet lodged in mud, with stingrays flapping around her and a starfish pasted square across her face. It would be nice instead to come ashore somewhere remote and cold, too cold for humans, and have her features slowly covered in layers of hard, protective ice.

With great effort she collects air into her lungs and hardens it to form an audible phrase: 'Let me out now.' Her voice trembles. Janine's golden hand caresses her cheek for a moment, then reaches across and opens the door.

Rex sits beneath the pier, wrapped in his – Marlon's – coat. After he saw Janine in the night he stood looking out at the water for what must have been hours. Thinking hard. For the first time in his life he felt truly at home. The darkness always seemed malevolent to him, yet day offered no comfort. But when lightning began making its abrupt incisions in the sky and the horizon struck up its unnatural, humming blue, that opalescent glow, he felt his cells dissolve or wish to dissolve straight into the night. Rex could make himself into the man on the moon: he shared its silvery features and deep, tidal habits. It almost emitted a sound – he could imagine that it really did so, if you got closer to it –

218

like sirens' songs. One high operatic chord. A little step off the last soggy board and he would rebond with whatever made the moon and the ghost-lights in the distance. He would be gathered back into the chain of chemical life. Or perhaps crushed to grain against some sharp rocks. Even that would be welcome. The sea kneaded itself against the pebbles and seemed to invite him in, down into its beating heart. He believed it would not freeze his muscles but enfold them, comfort them. It would warm him up. From his slow, large body came an entirely new response never felt before: every sense pricked up like a sprinter at the starting block. He had to cling tight to the railings, otherwise he would have thrown himself in. He flung his arms wide and bayed, his voice drowned out, and he liked it that way. Repeatedly the urge came over him and he wanted to be tumbling into the waves, feeling them clutch and tug him gladly like a long-denied lover. The storm was so vast and himself so small in comparison – but he shared some of its insanity.

He had left the estate wanting to kill. Neela did it, it was her fault, she manipulated him through her spell-casting and her hypnotism. He yearned to sink his fingers hard into Leo and Janine's still-beating hearts. That terrible twosome – those remorseless thieves – they took his money! They made him into a fool! He was a pauper who could have been a king. So brutally deceived! How could he not be enraged? Neela would not take her claws out of his soul. She was like a cat in the tall grasses of the jungle, mauling him for her amusement. Whenever he tried to protest, there was Neela, her eyes that unholy flaming green. She had infected him. Whenever she spoke into his ear, he became ready for blood.

He had his epiphany when they neared Benwick. Neela was asleep in the back seat, Lukas was silent. There was the town – bare, squat, dull. A short stack of buildings and a drab beach.

Two bikes chained to a post and a selection of deckchairs leaning against the railings. The whole sorry vista in the colour scheme of a faded postcard. Benwick didn't look like their destination – it looked like something another driver had thrown by the road-side. It looked like trash. And there they were, in a Jag. It was ludicrous and somehow all the more tragic because of it. Neela and Lukas' wrath was going to play itself out against a backdrop of too-sweet pastries and signs saying: Deckchair's For Whole Family's.

It is only below the pier that Rex has found signs of normal life in Benwick – condoms and broken glass, syringes, bottles, hubcaps and unidentifiable metal debris. All are embedded amidst the muddy pebbles. It is hard to see anything in much detail. The sun is straight above him now and shadow-lines cut smart as razors on either side of him. Beyond the shadows the beach is tame. Yet within them there is only bizarre junk in slime and stony bog. Boxes, shoes, old suitcases. Umbrella-skeletons. Everything is there. The division between land and water has been erased. Walk out ten yards and you find yourself waist-deep.

Rex has been here all night. He hasn't slept. Instead, he sits in a muddied armchair, staring into the water as if daring it to come and claim him. He would quite like to be borne away to foreign lands, perfectly upright in his little throne. The storm prompted some feral, instinctive understanding of himself. Where Neela favoured ice and Janine the dripping bronze sun – and indeed they embodied those elements physically – this he realised was to be his domain. He was made of the storm. He saw his life not as a series of humiliating accidents but somehow the direct descendant of the torrent and the gale; his life had been written into mountain-sides years before he was born. Neela had been asleep in the back seat of the car when the sky blackened and the storm-child in him awoke. It was that child who told her No when they were about to raid Leo's room. It was that child who let Janine go.

But the child is a demon – Rex sees that now. Sent by the sleet and the clamorous thunder to trick his hysterical, nervous nature. Sent to bring him low. As he contemplated the tempest and later the violent red sunrise, the child taught him certain things. In the light of the storm it pointed out where the real fault lay – the original sin. It was not with Leo and Janine, nor Neela, nor even Marlon. It was his dead mother and his dead father: Alun and Isobel. Both were monsters in their way, so Rex too is full-bred monster. When he had stared in awful silence at the silver gun in his hand, that afternoon at the strange diamond-dealers' bar, he was not being pulled into a deviation of his intended fate, he was beginning his true life. Serving his heredity. It was all the years he had spent before, in the orphanage, in schools and parks and street-corners – all those years he was so misguided. Lost. Marlon arrived to return him to his true self. When they tore the boards off the King of England, the end was already in sight and events unfurled themselves on tracks laid down for them aeons before.

As dawn came and the crimson sun blasted the beach, he had laughed full and loud with horror at himself. He saw it all so vividly: Leo and Janine were simply criminals, no more, no less; Neela was damaged. Their foibles were the first-generation flaws of circumstantial hardship. Poor things – they had had bad childhoods. They weren't loved enough. They fell on tough times. But he himself – he was a direct product of violence and revenge. As Marlon told him right at the very beginning, terrorism and thuggery lay close beneath his surface. He may not have acted it just then but he certainly attracted it. He is his father's son, to be sure. Before, he had thought of himself as the victim of other people's diseased interests. He had let himself be terrified, cajoled, intimidated. He had quivered at a few threatening words. But he was so naive. Rex finally comprehends Neela's dog theory – except he is worse, because he was born with dog blood, animal blood. And his dog never grew, it was already within him, fully developed. It had been primed for years. It was his own closeted, totally unwanted savagery that unconsciously drew other savages to him. For all along, he was the fiend, the devil. And the Dragon was his genesis.

It does not make him proud, nor bold. He is cursed. The longer he continues, the more villains he will collect. He will be ringmaster of a circus of rascals, all pressing their teeth into each other's necks. And he would rather die than bequeath upon the next generation such a history of depravity and insolence. During the killing of Max Stein he was terrified by the naked, gloating exultation which overtook his senses. It was his one self-willed act. Nobody had goaded him into it. As he pumped that man's face with bullets, the full dose of his parents' anarchic choler suffused his nerves and wrestled from him any direct responsibility. It was Alun holding the gun – or Isobel – or Marlon, even. Your father's son! Your mother's son! That's what his nerves screamed.

Rex waits in his armchair and looks at the waves coming towards him. The black, pleated water so lulling to watch, striking the broad support-poles ferociously. Rex sees everything now. His life has only been trauma and blood. Even the love he had was the sick, lonely type. The passion of Godless, loveless people.

Something brushes his neck, then Neela appears before him, crouched and shaking. One minute only garbage and water were there, now, the sallow girl. Rex laughs a little wildly. He had forgotten her ability to advance unimpeded through the dark, to make herself as one with the mud and the swamp. He reaches forward but cannot bring himself to touch her. She seems strangely and wrongly enlivened, a collection of vile dead features animated by sorcery. For the taut-skinned eyes have lost their icy light, the mouth its licentious sneer. She is ready for the earth, that is obvious. Ready to feel silt and grit closing in over her face. Rex lets his hands drop back onto the arm of the chair. He still fears her. But he fears himself more, for her wickedness was enclosed by his, was prompted by it. The dog in her secretly worshipped the beast in him.

With a jerk, Neela throws herself forward into Rex's lap. Rex wants to vomit on contact. Neela is not human any more, she is like a botched operation. Something you'd pick out of the off-cuts bin in a surgery. His spine stiffens and he grips the chair. Dirt oozes from the damp cushions, squeezing between his fingers.

Her face pressed against his thighs, Neela is smiling to herself. What does he think? That hand-in-hand they will brave the opaque waters and let its insistent currents slowly rub away their differences? She must have at least a little more fun before she goes to commune with the scallops. It makes her giggle to feel him squirm under her. Eventually she draws away and takes his gun from her waistband, bearing it up like a sacrifice. It is now a besmeared, leaden thing giving off a weak waxy light.

It means nothing to Rex now, that shabby lump of metal. Marlon made it into a thing of beauty so that he would be seduced. It was created to tempt him, to awaken his bloodlust. But he is no longer so easily beguiled. He takes it out of Neela's hands, and with it comes a crumpled note – Lukas' final missive. He stares at it for a moment. The words merge and separate nonsensically on the page. At first he thinks Neela wrote it, then the handwriting makes itself recognisable. The storm-child utters a great howl: *Mea culpa*! It bares its chest and beats its breast, faces the heavens and screams: don't take him, take me. Rex wrings his hands together silently, his head bowed and shaking slow: no. One big no. All wrong. Lukas dead by his own hand. Lukas who was innocent. His only crime: that he was good. Rex turns the note to damp shreds between his palms.

He raises his head and observes Neela. There is no humility or tenderness in her answering look. She wants to spit in his perfect face, to laugh at him, sat there in his grimy chair. She wants to pull him by the hair and slap his cheeks at the sight of his eyes wide with fear, his mouth a slack duh of stupidity. He is a coward and always will be. A responsibility-shirker, a good-for-nothing. Like a village madman made superstitious by bad luck and bitterness – always in the grip of some occult obsession. Never to blame for anything, directly, for one minute it will be: The Gods are punishing me!, another time: The devils are upon me!, and another: It is a curse! Fool! There is no curse. No historic monster waiting to be unleashed. Nothing he could not himself deny, curb, deter. He let Janine go not through nobility but cowardice. Janine believes otherwise but Neela knows the truth. She growls and Rex shrinks back. Honour will always elude him. He should be struck against one of these pillars, his skeleton shattering as though of no more consequence than a mouse's. Swept in amongst the other miscellaneous detritus of human existence. No marker for his grave. Neela has brought the gun out of respect for Lukas, who would have wanted it to be returned – Lukas the brave, who could put a bullet into his own body on such a splendid day.

It becomes very bright, underneath the pier. Neela straightens up as best she can. Sunlight seems to come down between the boards. She opens her mouth and exhales hard, but no sound comes out. It is very cold, the extreme heartless cold that she adores – like ice burning and sticking to her skin. She tries again and starts, 'I –' but as she does so one hand rises up of its own accord and she clutches her own throat. Rex fades out of sight and in his place is the image Neela always conjures up when she can't sleep: a snow-float of boundless parameters beckoning for her to lay her footprints upon its untouched white surface. The other hand presents itself palm up. Rex stares at her. She can almost feel the snowflakes falling onto her lips and melting there as she marks out the blizzard with her long stride. Her eyes widen and her spine stiffens. Amidst the snow and the ice is where she can finally find a home. It will be a towering, crystalline palace and her only company will be polar bears and Arctic foxes. She will need no mirror, only the polished surface of a frozen pool, and her face will be as cold and distant as it ever was on earth. Yet in her chilly kingdom they will call it beauty. She says 'I –' once more, takes a sharp, snatched breath, then slumps forward against Rex.

Blindly, Rex pushes her off him. She falls heavily into the mud and in his fever he treads upon her face. Stumbling, he treads on her again, his boot-heel against her stomach. He falls and screams – it feels like she is flinging herself all over him: her arms, her legs, her head rolling. Eventually he grasps and throws her from him. This is what he deserves – a grapple with a dead girl. He screams again until his lungs are empty and aching. He snatches up his gun and holds it to his temple, then pulls the trigger, but it's not loaded. He shouts with laughter. It is so funny, such an epic comedy. Plenty of bullets for everyone else – none for him. Plenty of death to hand out, but when the basket comes round to him – empty. His father killed Jon Duke. Cancer killed his father. He killed his own mother. A stranger killed Marlon. He killed Max Stein. Leo killed the fat man and Gavin and Neela. Janine and Leo both killed Shane Chisholm

225

and Victor. Lukas killed himself. When could he have stopped it? It was a furious waltz events led him on. His mind, for so long hanging in place by only a few fraying threads, finally topples, and he walks forwards, his glistening eyes rapturous and reflective.

The water is gripping his ankles. It is as he thought: not cold at all but warm, almost hot. A strong, hearty, persuasive sea. Above him the dark pier, and above that an indifferent sun. Rex steps in further. He will let the water enfold him and crown him with pink coral. He is waist-deep now, firmly clasped. It feels as though he is wearing the sea like a set of great billowing skirts. He smiles. They will be his triumphal robes, for he has abolished the legacy of his blighted ancestors. History will no longer pass through him. He will sleep for years, awakening only when a tornado whisks the water. At that time, he will perform a jubilant dance. It will be a dance celebrating not life but death. He will boogie, and shake his booty. The waves kiss at his neck. He raises the gun with difficulty and holds it up. It has been cleaned and restored by its brief immersion. Rex gasps as though he is seeing it for the first time. Such heavy silver. Long, smooth silver. Cold, hard silver. It is a ravishing object. As the waves seal themselves with an infinitely gentle rocking motion over his staring eyes, his mouth open in wonderment, he holds it aloft for as long as he can. Marlon finally claimed him when he accepted the gun. Rex became his when he felts its barrel against his fingers and squeezed its gleaming trigger into life. But how could he not accept it? He begins to weep underwater. It wasn't his fault. It was deliberately designed to relight a fuse that had been laid deep inside him eighteen years before. Rex takes a deep breath and salty polluted water fills his lungs. It wasn't his fault! He was the son of Alun the Dragon and Isobel Aurora Paine. From them came the fury. And the fury spread. Neela

226

caught it. Leo caught it. His body wants to float but he wishes to stride onwards, to be utterly held, massaged, laid on the ocean bed. When the storm-child reawakens in the night, his whitened bones will frolic. He looks up one last time. Such a handsome machine.

The sun shines, the sea shines, the pebbles shine. Yellow, blue, brown. A simple picture. Everything looks clean. Benwick is a sleepy coastal town of few inhabitants. It is a place where old people come to die in peace. A place where children are taken for outings. In Benwick, Sunday is and always has been a sacred day. The shops remain closed, the walkways deserted. On this Sunday, however, there is a great babble of voices by the pier. They are the voices of birds – seagulls – such excited, inquisitive animals. The birds swivel in the air urging each other onwards, downwards. Nobody comes to shoo them away. There is a mighty host of them, a blur of dirty grey and white, and they seem competitive, jostling each other. The scrape of stiff feathers makes a dry, rustling sound. Together, the seagulls go from the brightness into the dark. Beneath the pier they eventually fall silent. Their eyes blink and dart. Occasionally the group will disrupt itself, ill-footed in the mud, and a flurry of wings will rise up. The birds surround Neela's body and look at her curiously. They eye her long neck and the palms of her hands. Her abdomen, her eyes – especially her eyes, those glittering emerald slits. They shuffle closer. They land on her shoulder, along her thigh. They perch on her boots. Claws grip her hair. Then, as one, they begin to eat.

EPILOGUE

Even though it is a pleasant spring morning, the West Central Estate carries inside it the unmistakable stench of rank disease, of inescapable and abominable squalor. The whiff of death clings to the black gates, the stone pillars, the round of flats. Because of this, it has acquired an improbable, enigmatic glamour. It fascinates people with its now-infamous history.

After the bodies of Victor and Gavin were discovered – by the postman, a comely chap, innocently slotting letters into the box of an open front door – the coppers moved in. They made merry with their HAZARD gaffer tape and began to hear stories of barbarous, rancorous feuds. Prossies, junkies, hustlers all materialised, and when they opened their mouths the coppers were transfixed. These were members of a community not generally expected to be articulate. Not poor, but somehow worse than poor: illegal and criminal. Yet this rabble did not have the innocence or the humility of the underfed. They were quick and canny. They wanted to make deals. They spoke with a syntax peculiar to the night people, an unflinching visceral way of arranging words which made scenes spring to life. It was a specific vocabulary they drew from, one which comprehended the texture of skin and blood, the harshness of an unheated winter, the particular weight of a roll of money. They told what they thought could be the truth, for no one really knew. A medley of glorious inventions and expedient lies, seasoned with

reality. They told of the fog and the fire. Of the spiteful androgynous thing with her tight face, the pale Russian-looking boy
and his long black hair. The young golden man so popular, and
the golden girl, well dressed, like a doll, but cold underneath –
anyone could see that – a frigid, unfeeling, ambitious one, her.
So perfect on the outside, no doubt deceptive and hard within.
All nowhere to be found. The detectives eventually prised open
the secrets of the estate, of Max Stein and his mortal foe Alun
the Dragon, and of the youngster, the strange silent Rex, with
his coronet of platinum hair and his oh-cut-me cheekbones.
Also mysteriously disappeared. And on the boys, those poor,
innocent children, they could find no marks. For their slayer, he
was a true professional.

It was over. Rex was officially bankrupt, he had not a penny to
his name. The party was going on, but nobody could foot the
bill. Dead gangsters stalked the news pages. Marlon and Alun
hounded the newshounds. The presses shuddered and spat,
shuddered and spat, inscribing the latest onto tablets of white
paper. The tablets were halved, then halved again. The story
came out, in corrupted, halved-then-halved-again form. Mostly
falsehoods engineered by streetside stirrers – spurious friends
and neighbours of the deceased – but enough to suggest that
beneath civilisation lay the kingdom of the beasts. Humankind
had not appeased its animal half. The Minotaur in men was
wont to buck and rebel, and here was the proof. For a few hours
that morning the death people met the life people. Mothers and
fathers, siblings and lovers, all cast their eyes over the fresh ink
and marvelled. For to them it was unthinkable that existence,
with its daily rites and easy loving friendships, could be so easily
dismantled. The papers brought them into uneasy touch with
another world entirely, a world cultish and extreme, which ran

parallel to their own but which they rarely glimpsed. In this world, wine flowed like water, and blood like wine. The life people wondered: who were these characters – these imbeciles – these monsters?

Across a couple of bars at the gates is a grubby rosette of Police tape, though that is the only remnant of the investigation. On this day of rare warmth and sun comes Janine. She is a tall, strong-looking figure, and on both hands she wears real diamonds. They are hands a mugger would covet – heavy with jewels. The amber eyes are wise and nonchalant, the hair an explosion of ringlets. She shivers as she enters the estate. How did she ever live here? Eat her daily meals within its clammy, oppressive parameters? The place could turn the tenderest veal to stone.

She goes straight to Leo's flat and notices the locks have been changed. No matter. There is always a hairpin or some other implement secreted in her makeup bag. Taking a quick glance around she huddles and sets to work, but someone loosens the latch from the inside and the door swings open. Leo stands in the hallway, grinning. His eyes remain cold. 'Hey, girl. Looking fabulous as ever.' Janine feels her insides contract. She had forgotten how much Leo looks like the girl, the dreadful vulnerable creature, Neela. Born from the slime, returned to the slime. That name burns in her brain. He looks like the girl; but he slew the girl. It was a killing he executed for his own fun. Not necessary at all – they had it all in hand, there was nothing going on. But he liked to strike from behind. And he laughed while he did it. Her phantom friend, her soul-sister. But that is a lie. If Neela had lived, they would never have been pals. Janine is under no illusions about that. She cannot imagine what they would have done together. Maybe gone to the movies or painted each other's nails.

She shrugs the thoughts off. Janine is neither sentimental nor whimsical. What's gone is gone. The past is like a wardrobe of outmoded clothes – ugly to the eye and mind and fingers. An embarrassment, to be bundled away in an attic somewhere and never again uncovered. She grins back: 'Hey, you. Long time no nothing.' He steps aside to let her in.

It is maybe two or three months since she last saw him. Then, he was stripped to the waist on the balcony of Benwick Lodging House, the rain making his muscles look silky. He was valiant as a prince, a Pan, glossy-bodied. Now as he potters and chatters in the kitchen she watches him, fascinated. His every move is designed to inflict damage. He holds the kettle-handle as though to strangle it, and does not so much lift as wrestle the mugs from their hooks. He extracts a tea-bag from its box as though riffling through a stranger's wallet. He repulses her but she knows now why she was so intrigued by him. It was the same thing that drew her to Neela: a trip-wire physicality and raw strength that was sexual even though it didn't intend to be. She herself was always of a more lazy type, like those Romans, with their betoga'd bellies and their bunches of grapes.

But her mind is so obstinate. She wishes she could reach across and grasp Leo by the ear, twist it and scold him and question him. But she would extract no answers, he would only give her jokes and word-play. He doesn't care. He sets a mug of coffee in front of her and they go to sit at the kitchen table. 'So,' he says, all smiles, 'we're rich. All to your credit, of course. I myself would never have come up with such a devious plan. Though I do take the credit for our nifty pig-defying getaway. If ever you need to eradicate yourself from a scene, call on me. Fingerprints, hairs, I'm an expert with all of them. I can make you untraceable. But you've shown me the light in other ways.' His voice fills with glee and he points upwards, like a politician making a pledge. 'Violence isn't the only answer. There are other ways of harming people too.' Janine stares at him. Such a charmless thing, he is. At least she dresses her greed up in fine manners, wears a patina of civility. 'So where've you been staying?' he asks, getting out his cigarettes and offering her one.

'Hotel, sweetie,' she says indifferently. They smoke together like old friends.

What can she do? Tear her hair out and scream and stamp? She would never part with that money. The girl can stay dead. Leo goes into the lounge for a second and returns with a package – the photographs Neela took in Benwick. Janine puts them into her bag without looking at them, and she will not be hunting out the other grubby candids stored under the girl's bed either. The very idea makes her contort with displeasure. All those years, five at least, of dogged documentation. It's pathetic. Neela had her shot at life and she blew it. Janine is not going to depress herself as she sorts and piles the relics of another person's lonely, marginalised existence. It is a cruel thing to have asked her to do.

She has bought herself three plane tickets: to Marrakech, to the South of France, to Florence. In her hotel room later today she will close her eyes and reach for one. As the summer comes she shall coat herself in oil and bask on a roof-top terrace, letting her skin become burnished and ruddy. Flowers will bloom and tree-leaves will shine a thick, healthy green. She will spread her hair out and wait while the strands turn nearly white. Slices of pink meat, nearly translucent, and freshly-baked bread can serve as her breakfast. There will be red wine and white. She need not find adventure, it always seeks her out. Within two days of being in a new place she will find handsome men and beautiful women collected around her table, she is certain. And the last year, as Neela said, will seem just like a dream.

'What are you going to do?' she asks Leo. He stubs his cigarette out and grabs their empty mugs. As he is washing them by the sink, he says, 'I don't know. Probably go back to the clubs. Something in that line, anyway. I might rent a flat somewhere, or I may just stay here. One idea I had was to see if I could buy the King of England back. It doesn't belong to anyone now. It's all boarded up in the same way the pub was when we first got here. I could make it mine.' He comes back and leads her through to the living room: 'But really I wasn't the best business partner for you. I'm no good at spending money. I wasn't brought up handling it like you were. I'll just stick it somewhere and leave it at that. I'm not ambitious.' His tone is hard.

Leo has gathered up the last of Janine's things and left them on the sofa. They no longer have anything to say to each other. The room is shady and warm but it smells stale. Suddenly he jumps upon her, grabs her arm and hisses, 'I see you, you know, the way you look at me. You think I'm one kind of person and you're another kind of person, but you're wrong. We're identical.' He gives her a little shake. 'Did you get that? Our methods may be different but our minds, they work the same way. A little bit of carnage shouldn't make you think otherwise. Rex is dead, Neela's dead. We never gave a damn about them anyway, fair enough. But Lukas and Victor were meant to be our friends and I didn't see you shed any tears over them. I certainly didn't. Maggots could chew on their eyeballs, for all we care.' He grabs her with his other hand as well. 'What makes me hurt people is what makes you cheat and lie and steal from them. And you don't get nightmares, do you? Nothing keeps you awake at night. So don't pull the morality trick on me. Now,' he lets her go, 'I just wanted to tell you that. I wanted to imprint it on your brain. If ever you find yourself getting delusions about how good you are, how clean, how righteous, remember this time we've spent together. Remember how close we were, that afternoon at Shane Chisholm's house. And that at times it wasn't me holding the hammer but you – and you liked it.'

Janine steps back and stares at him wide-eyed. If she cuffs him round the face he will not think twice about deleting her. He would kill her the way she fears most – by drowning. It will be a most unglamorous demise.

She shrugs and stalks past him, then goes into the bathroom. He is a low, creeping thing. One day she may return and crush him like a beetle. Or send someone. He will probably go to his death unrepentant, but it doesn't matter. Nobody will remember his name. Janine is to lead her life across five continents while Leo remains in this hovel, carrying out his sordid deeds of fist and foot. Notoriety and fame will be hers, censure and sorrow his.

In the bathroom cabinet she finds one thing that Leo overlooked. It is the lipstick Neela dabbed upon Gavin's mouth. Janine falls upon it with a little cry: she had been missing this, a lush, lickable red encased in heavy real gold. She cannot decide what she loves most – the shade, the intense hue of a poisoned Disney apple, or the tube, which is engraved all over with squares within squares and other Art Deco fancies. Janine starts to apply it from cupid's-bow to corner. She is thankful for the small luxuries life yields: a bite of bitter chocolate, a single gold band on her wrist, and lipstick like this – creamy, moist, deep true crimson. Janine has an aptitude for gentility and beauty that is entirely wasted upon these people and their grovelling, misery-corroded lives. Already this bathroom means nothing to her, nor the apartment beyond it. It could be a motel, an airport rest-room. As she comes into the hall she sees the front door slam shut, and she laughs. Petulant boy. She would rather be alone anyway.

She takes up her bags, leaves the flat and stands for a moment on the top step, looking out across the estate. She will not be sorry to extricate herself from the dementia of these damned people. It was weak of her to be so drawn into their mania in the first place, to scramble upon a pebble beach, to stare into a churning scarlet sunrise. Those were the actions of a woman infected – a woman beguiled and crazed, caught up in the dance. She closes her eyes to block out the images: whey-faced Lukas and his last inscrutable smile; Neela hauling herself across the dodgems track by her fingertips; Rex so strangely calm on the pier as the sea bucked beneath their feet. It was a hellish night. The wanton mesmerising electricity of the storm had come down to taunt and madden the death people. It was sent to exacerbate their malady and drive them towards psychopathy and decay. There, in so ignominious a setting as Benwick, a place almost designed to strip them of their dignity and make them figures of fun and farce, they writhed with their affliction. Yet she had not shared in their agony. The storm had not abused her as it abused them.

Yes, Janine thinks, as she exits the gates and feels the sun's rays tumble upon her cheeks, it will be good to leave. She walks down the pavement, her back to the flats. She did not and could never understand the estate-dwellers and their morbid lunacy. With a sudden, paralysing pang she recalls Neela's words: *Your people and my people, they were never friends.* Janine can almost hear and feel that voice, so unexpectedly low and gracious, its elegant vibrato humming inside her cells. *In the beginning, your people shunned my people. It was always so.*